P9-CKF-044

APR 26 2022

Magnolia Library

Praise for *The Chase*

"A heart-pounding, seemingly never-ending (in a good way) chase to the conclusion of the novel. The anticipation builds until readers crash into the novel's finale."

Life Is Story

"This whirlwind, fast-paced chase will please fans of Terri Blackstock."

Publishers Weekly

"The second book in the US Marshals series picks up right where the first left off with all the action, drama, suspense, and romance a book lover could ask for! . . . The US Marshals books are by far my favorites by Lisa Harris."

Write-Read-Life

NO LONGER PROPERTY OF SEATTLE PUBLIC LIBRARY

Praise for *The Escape*

"An excellent thriller with well-drawn characters and the suspenseful start to Harris's new US Marshals series."

Booklist

"There are so many unexpected twists and turns that I was engaged from beginning until end. I can't wait for the next book in the series."

Relz Reviewz

"This story gripped me from the very beginning and didn't let go. Of all the Lisa Harris books I have read, I would easily say this is my favorite and one I recommend to readers who like a high-thrill ride with characters they can relate to and a story that will keep them on the edge of their seat late into the night."

Write-Read-Life

Praise for *The Traitor's Pawn*

"Harris presents a fast-paced adventure that balances intriguing clues, complex suspects, light romance, and messages of forgiveness to create an excellent, entertaining read."

Booklist

"Lisa Harris never fails to bring an action-packed, adrenaline-filled romantic suspense to her readers."

Interviews & Reviews

Praise for *Deadly Intentions*

"A story of corruption and greed, but also a story of romance and healing."

Compass Book Ratings

"Lisa Harris never fails to amaze me with her high-intensity, adrenaline-fueled, action-packed plots and beautifully crafted characters racing against time and enemies to find the solution to a looming threat."

Interviews & Reviews

THE CATCH

Books by Lisa Harris

A Secret to Die For

Deadly Intentions

The Traitor's Pawn

Southern Crimes

Dangerous Passage

Fatal Exchange

Hidden Agenda

Nikki Boyd Files

Vendetta

Missing

Pursued

Vanishing Point

US Marshals

The Escape

The Chase

The Catch

US MARSHALS · 3

THE CATCH

LISA HARRIS

Revell
a division of Baker Publishing Group
Grand Rapids, Michigan

© 2022 by Lisa Harris

Published by Revell
a division of Baker Publishing Group
PO Box 6287, Grand Rapids, MI 49516-6287
www.revellbooks.com

Printed in the United States of America

All rights reserved. No part of this publication may be reproduced, stored in a retrieval system, or transmitted in any form or by any means—for example, electronic, photocopy, recording—without the prior written permission of the publisher. The only exception is brief quotations in printed reviews.

Library of Congress Cataloging-in-Publication Data
Names: Harris, Lisa, 1969– author.
Title: The catch / Lisa Harris.
Description: Grand Rapids, MI : Revell, a division of Baker Publishing Group, [2022] | Series: US Marshals ; 3
Identifiers: LCCN 2021023641 | ISBN 9780800737320 | ISBN 9780800741075 (casebound) | ISBN 9781493434176 (ebook)
Subjects: GSAFD: Christian fiction. | Suspense fiction. | LCGFT: Christian fiction. | Thrillers (Fiction)
Classification: LCC PS3608.A78315 C37 2022 | DDC 813/.6—dc23
LC record available at https://lccn.loc.gov/2021023641

This book is a work of fiction. Names, characters, places, and incidents are the product of the author's imagination or are used fictitiously. Any resemblance to actual events, locales, or persons, living or dead, is coincidental

The author is represented by Hartline Literary Agency, LLC.

Baker Publishing Group publications use paper produced from sustainable forestry practices and post-consumer waste whenever possible.

22 23 24 25 26 27 28 7 6 5 4 3 2 1

ONE

He'd lied to her again.

It was her fault for believing him in the first place. For trusting the slew of promises he never kept. He told her he loved her. Told her he'd leave his wife for her so they could be together. Becca played the fool and believed him. She knew now that he never intended to stay with her, and as far as she was concerned, he wasn't capable of being faithful. Today was no different, and yet he called and she came running.

She sat in her car, watching the gated house where he lived with *her*, trying to gather her frayed nerves. While she'd never been inside the five-thousand-square-foot house, she knew it included a chef's kitchen, a vaulted back porch, and a three-car garage. The apartment she shared with their son was less than a thousand square feet. Robert paid for the majority of her expenses, but it was never quite enough, so she continued to work at the café and relied on his handouts and promises that he was going to leave his wife for her.

She gripped the steering wheel and frowned. The reality was that she didn't care about the big house. She wasn't even sure she loved him anymore. She cared only about their son.

Her son.

She drew in a deep breath as the gates swung open slowly. Then she parked, got out of the car, and headed to the front door. It was strange that he'd asked her to the house. He'd never done that before. The closest she'd gotten was when she'd driven by one time. She'd wanted to know where he lived and spent his time when he wasn't with her. She felt guilty about their arrangement since the beginning, but Robert had swept in and given her the feeling of family she'd never had. Saying no seemed impossible until she realized that it was nothing more than a fairy tale that could never have a happy ending.

Still, as much as she wanted to, she never found the courage to walk away.

Until now.

Today, all of that would change. No matter what he said, she was going to tell him that she was leaving him. She was tired of the tangled web she'd found herself in as the scorned mistress who could never show her face at his office or at one of his political fundraisers. She'd seen the coverage of him and Myra on the news last night, smiling into the camera as if they didn't have a care in the world. She had once believed that could be her standing next to him one day. His expression had told her otherwise. He would never give up his life for her.

Becca put her hand on the brass doorknob, then stopped. Was she supposed to walk in or knock?

She didn't have to answer the question because the door swung open.

Robert's wife, Myra, stood in the doorway, a smile plastered on her face. "Becca Lambert . . . It's nice to finally meet you in person, though I guess you weren't expecting me to be here."

"I don't understand." Becca studied the woman's pale blue

pencil skirt, button-up white blouse, and matching jacket that likely cost more than what she earned in a month. "How do you know me?"

"I'm not near as clueless as Robert thinks I am. I'm the one who sent you the message from his phone. Well, his . . . other phone, that is." She sneered. "I thought we could . . . talk."

Becca took a step backward, fighting every instinct in her body that told her to run. "I'm not sure that's a good idea."

"It won't take long. Just a few minutes. It's time you and I got to know each other."

She didn't want to talk to Robert's wife. Didn't want to be in the same room with the woman. "Where's Robert?"

"At work. Or so he says. He's always working, but you don't really think you're the only pretty girl who's caught his eye, do you?"

Becca blinked back tears as she tried to stuff down the guilt. She'd been working at an upscale restaurant when she met Robert. He was handsome and charismatic, and he paid attention to her. She'd grown up in foster care, and for the first time in her life, she felt loved. Special.

Then she found out she was pregnant.

There was nothing she could do to change their understanding. He promised to pay the bills as long as she promised to be quiet. His wife was never to find out. None of his associates could be confided in either. No one could know he was the father of her baby.

Becca shook her head. "I need to leave—"

"I wouldn't if I were you. I know everything about you and Robert, including the fact that you had his son."

Becca's mouth went dry. "Robert told you that?"

Myra motioned her inside. "It didn't take much detective

work to find out where he really spends his time away from me."

"I made mistakes," Becca said, stepping through the imposing entryway to a boldly decorated living room that was far too gaudy for her taste, though the red-and-coral theme seemed to fit Myra perfectly. "But you have to understand that I didn't know he was married when I first started seeing him." By the time she found out the truth about Robert's marital status, she'd already lost her heart.

Guilt pressed against her chest. How many times had she told herself she needed to walk away? How many times had she chastised herself for not taking her own advice?

Myra's smile disappeared as she turned around in the middle of the room. "Don't play innocent with me."

"I'm not," Becca started to argue, then stopped. She had no idea what this woman wanted from her, but clearly Myra wasn't interested in a string of apologies.

Myra narrowed her gaze. "You need to know that I have the ability to make your life extremely miserable, but . . . I'm going to offer you a onetime deal."

Becca's fingers clenched her purse strap. "What do you mean?"

"I will give you enough money to leave Seattle and start over. I don't care where or how, as long as it's far away from here."

Becca forced herself to relax her hands, but she couldn't absorb what she was hearing. "You want to pay me off?"

"You make it sound so . . . so illicit."

"Isn't it?"

Myra's glare seemed to pierce through her. "No more illicit than sleeping with someone else's husband."

Becca's gaze dropped to the expensive rug on the wooden

floor, then followed the dark-orange squiggly pattern along the edge. Nausea swept through her, making her feel like she would vomit. She should have known this day would come. Nothing good ever came from keeping secrets.

"You're going to walk away and never contact Robert again. And"—she tapped her manicured fingers together—"you will sign over parental rights of the baby to Robert."

Becca's head shot up. "I won't do that."

Myra's brows rose. "Then you don't understand how things work. Without money and power, you're nothing but a waitress working overtime for tips. If you try to fight me, you'll lose."

"No." Becca straightened her shoulders, determined to dig up enough courage to fight back. "You can't buy me off."

"Then you're more foolish than I thought," she said, her voice cold. "Robert doesn't love you, Becca. He never did. Not really. You've been nothing more than a temporary distraction."

"I'm not taking your money."

"Then I'll need to find something to persuade you."

"What do you mean?"

"I know you left your son with his sitter this morning," Myra said.

Becca's heart pounded in her chest. If Myra did anything to hurt her son, or Ava . . .

"What did you do?" Becca asked.

"It's not what I've done, it's what I will do if you don't cooperate. You will sign the papers I've had drawn up, giving Robert full custody of the child, and walk away with the money."

"No—"

"You seem to think you can fight this, but you can't. Robert will hire the best lawyers in the city, and in the end, you will still give up your rights to your son. Now it's just up to you to decide if you take the money or end up losing everything."

Becca stumbled backward. "No. I'll never give up my baby."

She grabbed her handgun out of her purse—ironically, the gun that Robert had bought her. There wasn't time to think through the consequences. All she knew was that she wasn't going to lose her son.

TWO

Falling was inevitable, but it was also a skill that worked against every instinct. Madison James held her right hand on the brake of the belay device and watched from the ground of the indoor climbing gym as her sister reached for the blue handhold above her.

"Just a couple more inches," Madison yelled up to her.

Danielle's foot slipped.

From the ground, Madison held tight to the safety rope to keep her sister from falling. "You good?"

Danielle blew out a puff of air. "For the moment."

"You're a natural," Madison said.

"That would explain the rope burn on my leg and the scrape on my arm."

"Go up a couple more feet, then we'll work on the fall."

"I don't know . . . I'm still not sold on the idea."

Climbing was as much mental as it was physical, and trust of your spotter was essential. Madison had already taught Danielle the basics of climbing, but taking it one step further meant pushing herself past her comfort zone. In her own life, climbing had helped her conquer fear, because the more prepared she was, the more she was able to handle whatever her job as a US Marshal threw at her.

"It seemed like a good idea when I was on the ground, but from up here—"

"You're doing fine, Danielle."

The muscles in Madison's arms twitched as her sister shifted some of the weight. All Danielle needed was a few more inches and she'd reach the top. Her mind ran through the suggestions she'd given Danielle. If done properly, her fall would go smoothly. If she ended up getting tangled in the rope, her leg could catch on it and flip her upside down, something neither of them wanted.

Madison took in a deep breath as Danielle got to the thirty-five-foot mark. She needed to be high enough that the rope was able to stretch. High enough that she wouldn't hit the ground while avoiding a route with any obstructions.

Danielle reached for the last handhold while Madison held the belay rope steady. "I can't get a grip."

"Yes, you can. It's just like a puzzle."

"You know I hate puzzles."

"Reach up and grab hold. Trust your instincts and stay focused. You're almost there."

Danielle pulled herself up and firmly grasped the handhold.

"When you're ready, I want you to fall," Madison said. "Trust me."

The word *trust* reverberated through Madison. She'd never been good at giving up control to someone else. Doing things right meant doing things herself. But climbing forced you to trust more than just your skills. You had to trust that your harness was secure and would hold you. That the belayer below was ready to catch you. That the bolts were secure and the anchors were set, and that the rope was strong enough to hold you if you fell.

Not an easy assignment for someone needing to be in control.

Danielle pulled her knees up level with her hips while Madison gave the rope some slack, keeping an eye on her sister. Madison was the counterbalance whose job was to ensure Danielle didn't swing down too fast and slam into the rock.

"Make sure you look where you're falling," Madison said. "Know where the rope is and aim to fall straight down."

"You make it sound so easy."

Danielle blew the air out of her lungs and then, seconds later, pushed off the wall. Madison waited for the right moment, then jumped as the rope pulled her up. She braced her feet against the wall. Another few seconds and they were both on the ground.

"You did good up there," Madison said.

"That was both terrifying and exhilarating at the same time." Danielle braced her hands against her thighs. "I think I know why you like to come here."

"So you're finally a believer?"

Danielle laughed. "I think I still prefer jogging, but this might be growing on me."

"Seriously, you're a natural."

"Ha. You're the natural adrenaline junkie."

"I'm thinking you're ready to try heading out to Darrington some weekend."

Danielle dropped the chalk bag she'd been using to keep her hands steady onto the ground, then bent over to stretch her calves. "Challenge accepted."

Madison knew her sister was ready, but indoor climbing

on the wall she'd just scaled was nothing like climbing a rock face. Here routes were marked by colors giving defined places to grab or step on to. Mapping out a clear path in the outdoors was more of a mental game.

Just like mapping out a clear path forward in life.

Madison frowned at the thought. She'd never expected to be a widow before she was thirty. Life had thrown the unexpected at her, but just like when climbing, she was determined not to give up.

"Madison?"

"Sorry." She turned back to her sister. "Do you want to go up again?"

Danielle started pulling off her climbing harness. "Yes, but I probably need to get home. Ethan's with the kids, but he needs to go in to work."

"That's okay." Madison glanced at her watch. "I've got a bunch of stuff to do today as well."

"On your next day off, I'll get Ethan to watch the kids and Daddy. We'll make a day of it and head out to Darrington."

Madison smiled as they headed to the locker rooms. "It's a date."

"Daddy loved going to the flight museum with you, by the way," Danielle said.

"Not as much as I did. Especially in the moments when I felt like he was there again with me."

"It might not be as often as it used to be, but he's still in there."

Their father's downward spiral had been hard on all of them, but while Alzheimer's might have stolen parts of him away, there were still those fleeting moments when they were able to see glimpses of the man he used to be.

Madison grabbed her stuff out of her locker and quickly changed back into her street clothes. So much about these past few years had been both unexpected and painful. Her husband's murder, Daddy's diagnosis with Alzheimer's, and her getting shot. But not everything had been bad.

Four months ago, she'd remet Jonas.

She squeezed her eyes shut for a moment. When they first started working together, she hadn't been looking for a relationship. There were too many loose ends surrounding Luke's death. She needed closure, and yet somehow, she'd found herself falling for Jonas. He'd made it clear that he wanted her in his life permanently, even if he had to wait for her.

"Hey." Danielle's fingers brushed her arm. "Are you okay?"

"Yeah. Sorry." She grabbed her jacket out of the locker. "I'm just a bit preoccupied, I guess."

"Does this have anything to do with Jonas?"

Madison frowned. Her sister could always read her, but Jonas wasn't the only thing that had her preoccupied today. She pulled on her jacket, knowing there were things she couldn't tell Danielle, like the eerie feeling she hadn't been able to shake that someone had been following her over the past few weeks. She'd tried to blame it on being overworked, but she knew she was going to have to talk to her boss at some point.

"Jonas got into town last night," she finally said.

"Have you talked to him?"

She sat down on the wooden bench to pull on her boots. "Just on the phone last night. He stopped to see his mother on his way home and was pretty tired. But I promised to cook him dinner tonight."

"Aww . . . that sounds romantic."

She hadn't been surprised when Jonas had told her he was

planning to interview with the Marshals' Special Operations Group. The monthlong training was vigorous. Those who passed were allowed to continue their full-time duties with the US Marshal Service, while remaining on call 24/7 for special missions that included apprehending fugitives, protecting dignitaries, and providing court security.

Danielle pulled her bag out of the locker. "What is your heart saying, Madison?"

"I'm still trying to figure that out."

"Maybe the real question is what's stopping you from figuring it out?" Danielle's question hit its mark. "It's obvious Jonas is crazy about you, and from everything you've told me, you feel the same way."

"It's complicated. You know that." Madison rubbed a hand over her face. "I'm not ready to make a commitment. Not until I know without a shadow of a doubt that I'm not putting his life in danger."

"Nothing can change what happened the day Luke died, but Jonas can take care of himself—he's a trained marshal, in case you forgot. You're not protecting Jonas by pushing him away. You're only hurting yourself. And him."

Madison's defenses rose. "I'm not pushing him away, Danielle—"

"Are you sure about that? Because your answer sounds more like an excuse."

She pressed her lips together, glad there was no one else in the locker room at the moment. "Whoever shot Luke—whoever shot me—is still out there. I can't just ignore that. I was the target, and until they're caught, Jonas is as well."

Danielle frowned. "So you're simply trying to protect him?"

Madison nodded, but her sister clearly wasn't buying her

response. Danielle might not understand but getting shot by an intruder in her own home had shaken Madison. Especially knowing that whoever had pulled the trigger had also shot and murdered her husband.

"All I know is that Jonas would risk his life for you," Danielle said, "and he's not afraid of whoever's still out there."

But I am.

The thought took her off guard. How was it that she could risk her life chasing down fugitives but not stop whoever had killed her husband and shot her?

"I'm sorry." Danielle squeezed her shoulder. "I know this isn't easy for you. I just want you to be happy. And I know it's easy for me to say, but nothing you do can change what happened to Luke. Don't start second-guessing the past. It never works."

Madison knew she was right, but that didn't make it any easier.

"Can I give you some advice?"

Madison finished tying the second boot, then planted her feet on the floor. "If I say no, you'll give it to me anyway."

"Funny. I just spent about an hour up on that wall, and to be honest, for most of it I was terrified. And yet nothing happened."

Madison stood. "What are you trying to say?"

"Let yourself be vulnerable by exposing yourself to the fear when it comes to your heart. As I fell, I realized that I could trust both you and the rope and harness holding me. I was also reminded that God is like our rope and harness. He didn't give us a spirit of fear. He calls us to trust him. And I'm not just talking about when climbing."

The analogy might be good, but emotions were more complicated than that. They were messy and sometimes ugly, and no matter how hard she tried, taking the plunge still seemed out of reach. She knew she couldn't expect Jonas to wait for her indefinitely. She was going to have to take that step forward at some point. She just wished the fear didn't seem so impossible to overcome.

She caught her sister's gaze. "I know you're right, it's just not always easy."

"Things worth fighting for never are."

Madison pulled her phone out of her locker, wishing she could control her emotions as tightly as her climbing moves. She checked her messages. Her boss, Chief Deputy Carl Michaels, had called three times.

"I've been trying to get ahold of you," he said as soon as her call went through.

"Sorry I missed your calls. I came early to the gym to do some rock climbing with my sister."

"I know you'd planned to take the day off, but I need you to come down to the courthouse."

"Okay. What's going on?"

"A threat was made against several judges and prosecutors, and we need to have additional security in place in case they decide to follow through."

"Who's behind the threats?" Madison asked.

"Maxim Cervantes's boys. His arraignment is scheduled for today."

Madison snatched her keys out of her locker, then glanced at her watch. "I can be there in twenty minutes."

"Is everything okay?" Danielle asked after Madison ended the call.

She put her phone in her pocket. "Just a security issue at the courthouse."

"Promise me you'll be careful."

"Always." She shot her sister a smile. "Don't worry."

"About your job as a marshal or your love life?"

Madison laughed. "Both."

"You know I can't help it. Are they calling in Jonas as well?"

"Michaels didn't say, but I wouldn't be surprised."

"Nothing like jumping back into work after a month of training."

Madison's heart fluttered at the thought of seeing him again, but this wasn't about her or Jonas. As a Deputy US Marshal, one of her jobs was to ensure the protection of judicial proceedings, which included protecting federal judges, jurors, and other court officials. And when it came to combating active threats, there was no margin for error.

THREE

The briefing Jonas Quinn received on the extensive rap sheet of Maxim Cervantes was enough to send chills through even a seasoned agent. And the company the man kept was just as disturbing. Cervantes was on the most wanted list for a dozen violent crimes—racketeering, kidnapping of a federal agent, three counts of felony murder. Deputy US Marshals had tracked him well—ending their chase twenty-five miles south of Seattle, outside a gas station where he'd grabbed one of the marshals on his trail and shot and killed one of the employees. Today, he was scheduled to go before the judge to find out if he would be bonded out or, much more likely, denied bail. If the district attorney got his way, Cervantes would never see the light of day again and be sentenced to a maximum-security prison for life.

But there were some individuals loyal to Cervantes who were determined to see he didn't serve time. The sitting judge in the case had been openly threatened, along with the DA. So, to beef up normal security, four marshals, all from the Special Operations Group, had been called in to provide additional backup at the courthouse. A counterassault team was currently on standby.

Jonas headed up the steps of the courthouse with another member of the SOG, Tucker Shaw. They had no idea who they were looking for, which made the job more complicated, but they were ready for anything.

Court security inspectors had evaluated both the equipment and security procedures. Screening stations with state-of-the-art detection software, designed to search for unauthorized weapons and explosives, had been set up at the entrances. A communications system was also in place so every agent was connected. But Cervantes had a large number of loyal followers who were willing to sacrifice their lives for him. The fear that they would try to attack the courthouse during the trial wasn't a stretch of the imagination.

"You think she's here?" Tucker said as they stepped into the lobby.

"I'm guessing you're not talking about Cervantes's mistress?"

"Funny. No. I'm talking about the woman you've tried to avoid talking about the past month."

Jonas frowned at the other deputy as they showed their credentials and made their way through security. While he respected the fellow deputy marshal and was pleased his old friend had been relocated to Seattle, the man had an annoying tendency to pry.

"She is a Deputy US Marshal," Tucker said.

"I don't remember giving any details."

"Not other than the fact that she's gorgeous, smart, and can shoot better than you or me."

"You sure are nosey."

Apparently Tucker wasn't finished. "Just observant. I thought if she was here, I could meet her. The boss did say all-hands-on-deck."

"It's very probable she is, but I wasn't told who will be here from the marshals' office today."

"You haven't spoken to her since you got back?"

"I called her when I got in last night. She's making me dinner tonight."

A fact he should have kept to himself.

He had missed Madison. Four weeks of intense training with the SOG had pushed him to his limits, and there hadn't been a lot of downtime to talk with the woman he'd fallen in love with. The last time he'd seen her before heading to the training facility, he told her he wanted to be in her life—now and forever. That no matter what happened with the events surrounding her husband's cold case investigation, they could face it together. He hadn't asked for a time frame forward for the two of them. He hadn't asked for anything, and she hadn't made any promises.

But while the last four weeks had pushed him harder physically than he'd been pushed in a long time, he never wavered from how he felt about Madison. He'd called her last night to let her know he'd gotten in safely, but it was late and they'd planned to see each other today. He hadn't even tried to hide the anticipation in his voice at seeing her again, and he was pretty sure he hadn't imagined the same reaction from her.

"We'll talk about my supposed love life later," Jonas said as they strode across the white marble flooring. "We've got a job to do."

Tucker grinned. "Oh, I'm counting on it."

Jonas forced himself to focus on the task at hand. The last

few weeks, training officers had led them through a grueling regimen to become part of an elite group who hunt the worst of the worst. Which was why they were here right now. A slip in focus could quickly spell disaster.

The high-rise courthouse with its multiple floors, steel structure, and brick façade gave them a lot of ground to cover, but the threats received pointed toward Maxim Cervantes's case and hopefully narrowed things down. Their job was to anticipate and deter all threats.

An older gentleman in a brown suit using a cane shuffled down the hallway ahead of them. A couple holding hands whispered intently about something, while three men, whom Jonas assumed were lawyers, carried briefcases, not even trying to muffle their loud voices.

Something clattered behind him and Jonas turned back. The older man had leaned his cane against the wall. He faced the security checkpoint as he reached into the bag he was carrying.

"Tucker . . ." Jonas reached for his weapon, as the man pulled out a handkerchief. Jonas's finger tapped on the grip of his gun. "Never mind. We're clear."

They kept walking, searching for anything that was out of place as they headed to the courtroom.

A gunshot fired behind them.

Jonas swung around, shoving his way past a couple reporters with badges. "Shots fired! Shots fired!" he yelled into his comm.

"How many shooters?" an agent responded.

"Stand by," Jonas said. He and Tucker ran toward the lobby where the chaos had erupted. People were screaming and running, while a guard lay on the ground, curled up in a ball. Three armed men in black had just charged through security.

One of them swiveled toward them, then rolled a flash-bang into the middle of the large lobby. Light burst from it. Jonas blinked. The muscles in his body froze as he fought the intense wave of dizziness.

Jonas leaned over and braced his hands against his thighs before speaking into his comm. "We've got an active shooter at security and need backup. I repeat, we need backup here and the building locked down. Now."

He glanced over to where Tucker had been standing next to him and found him slouched against the wall.

He could hear gunfire in the background, along with police vehicles and sirens. There was no sign of the shooter. Where was he?

"Tucker?"

Tucker groaned, then forced himself to his feet. "I'm okay. Where are the shooters?"

"I don't know, but we need to find out." Jonas ran over to the downed security guard who was holding his leg.

"I'll be okay," the guard said, "but there were at least five of them. I think they're headed upstairs."

Jonas spat out directions to the other security guards, then passed on the update through his comm. "We need to get to the courtroom via the judge's access."

Jonas ran with Tucker past the elevator to the staircase. The courtrooms themselves still retained the original woodwork, benches, and jury boxes from the early 1920s, but security measures had been significantly upgraded. Courtroom layout was crucial to allow separate entry points for the judge, jury, prisoner, and public. But that also meant four access doors into the courtroom.

Someone was shouting orders in the courtroom as they

approached. The counterassault team had been called in and had breached the other three accesses. Jonas quickly scanned the large room. Two shooters stood in the middle with half a dozen guns pointing back at them.

Jonas and Tucker found the judge behind a bulletproof glass shield. A woman wearing a US Marshals jacket was kneeling by his side.

Jonas crouched down beside them. "Madison?"

She turned toward him. "A bullet grazed his arm, but it's not life-threatening." The confusion in the courtroom muffled the sound of her voice. "We need to get him out of here."

The judge's glasses had shattered, and he was holding them in his hand as if he didn't know what to do with them.

"Are you hurt anywhere else?" Jonas asked him.

"I don't think so."

Jonas reached up and wiped away the blood on Madison's temple. "What about you?"

She looked up at him with those big brown eyes of hers. "It's not my blood."

He hesitated. "This wasn't how I was expecting to see you again."

"I know. Me either." Her eyes flitted between him and Tucker, who stood just behind Jonas. "This is Judge Saylor," she added.

Jonas helped the man up, careful to avoid his injured arm. "You were overseeing the Cervantes case?"

The judge nodded.

"There's a back exit with a staircase," Jonas said, putting off what he really wanted to say to Madison. Like how much he'd missed her. And how much he wanted to pull her into his arms and kiss her. "We need to get you out of here."

"Why don't the two of you head out with the judge," Tucker said. "I'll cover and make sure no one follows."

"Can you walk?" Madison asked Judge Saylor.

He nodded. "I think so."

Jonas didn't miss the look of panic in the judge's eyes in the middle of the chaos going on around them. Back when Jonas had trained law enforcement officers, he'd always taught them to be prepared for the unexpected. Today was one of those days.

He and Madison escorted Saylor out the back door of the courtroom, to the private passageway that led to a stairwell.

"I need you to stay between us," Jonas ordered as they made their way down the narrow hall.

"Get him to the basement." The order came from his comm. "We'll have a car meet you at the southwest corner so they can escort him to a safe house."

"Roger that."

They just had to get him there alive.

Jonas pulled open the door to the stairwell, checking the area before giving the all clear signal. They started down the stairs, their footsteps echoing against the cement steps.

A door slammed below them, and a shot fired up the stairwell, hitting the wall behind them.

Jonas fired back, then quickly stepped out of the line of fire.

"We're cut off," Madison said. "Is there another way out?"

"Back up the stairs," the judge said. "There's an exit on the floor above us that connects to the parking garage through a tunnel."

"If we can make it to the tunnel, we can have him picked up in the parking garage," Jonas said.

"My car is parked there," Madison said. "If nothing else, we can drive him out of here."

Jonas nodded, but no matter what they did, it was going to be a risk. He ushered the judge through a door and down the hallway that led to the exit.

"I need a car waiting for us at the southeast entrance," Jonas said into his comm as they reached the tunnel.

He paused. There was no response.

"Thompson, can you hear me?"

Nothing.

"Madison, they're not answering. Try your comm."

She shook her head a moment later. "Mine's not working either."

If their communications were down, they were on their own.

They rushed the judge through the tunnel. Several people skittered aside as they passed, getting out of the way when they saw the marshals' weapons. This might have been their only option, but it was a scenario they always tried to avoid. There were limited exits, and they could easily get trapped.

"Where's your car?" Jonas asked as they entered the parking garage.

"Just ahead. On your left."

"I see it."

A van squealed around the corner. Seconds later, a man emerged wearing a black mask. Jonas's heart sank. The masked man pulled a blindfolded hostage out with him, a gun held to her head.

Jonas looked behind them.

Two more men emerged from the tunnels, carrying guns. They'd penned them in.

The man from the van stepped forward. "I need you to drop your weapons. Now. Both of you. Then let Judge Saylor walk toward me."

Jonas clicked on his comm again. Nothing.

Madison held her gun steady. "We're not going to do that."

"Please." Their hostage was sobbing in front of them. "Please let me go."

"Hand over the judge now or this woman is dead."

"There's no way out," Jonas said. "You do realize that. You won't make it to the next block."

"I didn't ask for your input. Just do as you are told. And I'm telling you to put your weapons on the ground. I'm going to count to three. And if you haven't complied, she's dead."

FOUR

Options raced through Madison's mind as the man started counting. Every scenario she came up with ended with the very real possibility of someone getting shot—primarily, their hostage. There were three of them, all wearing black masks and carrying weapons. Negotiating might be an option, but from what she'd seen so far, these men weren't here to talk. They were here to follow through with their agenda, no matter the cost, which meant her and Jonas's role at the moment had to be to help calm down the situation.

But something else struck her. Something had to have gone wrong inside for them to have taken a hostage, and more than likely grabbing the woman hadn't been planned. This was their last chance to gain the upper hand. A desperate act because they needed something that was worth the risk of someone dying.

"What do you really want?" Madison asked, not ready to follow the order to drop her weapon.

"I told you want I wanted."

"What do you want with me?" Judge Saylor spoke up, his voice shaky.

"I don't have to answer your questions." The man pressed the gun against the woman's head. "Put down your weapons now or she's dead."

Madison pressed her palm against the judge's arm. He needed to stay out of the conversation. It didn't take much for explosive situations like this to blow up, because the possible outcomes were limited. The men could surrender. Law enforcement could sweep in with a tactical assault. Or they could give in and meet the demands—which, as far as she was concerned, wasn't going to happen.

"He's right," Madison said, keeping her voice even. "It's over. No one has to get hurt."

The man's expression darkened. "That's where you're wrong. We're willing to do *whatever* it takes to get what we want."

A chill shot through her. Negotiating was about persuasion and a willingness to listen to the hostage taker's side. And while the man could be bluffing when he said they were ready to do anything—even to kill for their cause—if talking didn't work, their law enforcement tactics had to shift as well.

"US Marshals." The shout came from behind them. "Drop your weapons now."

Madison turned around as the marshal who'd entered the courtroom with Jonas rushed toward them. One of the masked men fired his weapon at the marshal, but his aim was off. The marshal fired back, dropping the man to the ground. But there was no time to dissect what had just happened as the man with the hostage rushed toward her.

Madison swung her elbow out, hitting him across the jaw and stopping him from approaching the judge. The man stumbled backward, losing his grip on the hostage.

At least their odds had increased.

"Get them out of here. Now!" Jonas shouted.

Madison grabbed the woman's arm, removed the blindfold, then motioned at the judge as they ran toward her vehicle. She clicked her car unlocked.

"Both of you get in the back and stay down."

As soon as they were in, she slammed the door shut then slid into the driver's seat. She threw the car in reverse, clipping the back bumper of the car next to them in the process.

Madison shifted into drive, then pressed down on the accelerator. "Are either of you injured?"

She could hear the woman sobbing behind her. "I don't think so."

"Judge?" Madison asked.

"Besides my arm, I'm okay."

Madison glanced in the rearview window, praying for Jonas and the other marshal as she headed for the exit. The van was on their tail, racing through the parking garage after them. She honked her horn, and a couple jumped out of the way as Madison took the corner.

A shot from behind blew out her back window, shattering glass across the seat.

"Hang on."

Madison pressed the accelerator even more, but the van was closing in on them. It rammed into her bumper as they neared the exit.

The horizontal boom of the tollbooth loomed ahead of them. Her tires squealed as she took the sharp right, slamming through the barrier. Another shot fired from behind her.

Her comm still wasn't working, so she punched the call button on her steering wheel and phoned Michaels.

"I'm heading east out of the parking garage and need backup immediately," she said as soon as he answered. "At least two of the shooters are on my tail. I have Judge Saylor and a hostage they took with me."

"We're tracking your phone," Michaels responded. "Keep heading east, and I'll have law enforcement intersect your position."

Madison gripped the wheel, pulse racing as she stuffed down the panic. They'd expected the possibility of someone going after Cervantes and freeing him, but why did they want the judge?

She could hear sirens approaching from behind as she turned into traffic. She blasted her horn and ran the red light, barely missing an SUV as she raced toward the freeway.

Madison glanced in her rearview mirror again. They were still on her tail. "What do they want from you, Judge Saylor?"

"I don't know."

His voice quivered as he spoke, and she couldn't blame him. They'd breached his courtroom, he'd been grazed by a bullet, and now the men who'd wanted to exchange a hostage for him were right behind them.

If they'd wanted to scare the judge, they'd done a good job, but she was certain they planned to take it further than that. Clearly whatever they wanted was something they were willing to risk their lives for.

Madison gripped the steering wheel, trying to stay far enough ahead of the van in case they were shot at again. Two squad cars came up behind her, one forcing its way between her and the van. Madison pulled off onto the side of the road and stopped. Her hands were shaking as the van shot past them with the squad cars still surrounding it.

A third police car stopped behind her and two uniformed officers ran up to them as she slid out of the driver's seat.

"Are you okay?" one of the officers asked her.

"I think so." She pointed to the back seat. "The two of them need to be checked out at the hospital."

"An ambulance is on the way now. But it looks like you need to be checked out as well."

"The blood on my shirt isn't mine," she told him.

"What about your hand?"

She looked down at the cut on the back of her hand. She hadn't even felt it. "I'm fine. I need to check on my passengers."

She opened the back door and held it open. "You're both safe now."

"I can't stop shaking," the woman said. "Thank you for getting me out of there."

"That's our job. Judge Saylor?"

The judge's face was ashen as he stared at his phone.

"Are you okay?" Madison asked.

"Yes. I'm just trying to get through to my wife."

Madison nodded, then turned back to the woman who was starting to hyperventilate. She crouched down beside her and squeezed her hand. "What's your name?"

"Tiffany."

"Tiffany, I want you to take a couple deep breaths. Nice and slow. You're safe now. I'm going to make sure an officer stays with you while the paramedics check you out, then the authorities are going to want a statement."

The woman nodded, then started sobbing again. "I was just heading to work. I got out of my car, and they were there."

"I know this was traumatic, but you're okay now. Is there someone you can call to meet you at the hospital?"

"My husband's at work. And yes, I need to call him." She reached into her coat pocket, then stopped. "I don't even have my purse. If he hears what happened at the courthouse, or if my photo somehow ends up on TV . . ."

"You can use mine." Madison pulled her phone out, then handed it to her.

Two ambulances pulled up as the woman was making the call to her husband. Madison motioned them over to the car, then quickly updated the paramedics on what had happened. One of them had just finished cleaning and bandaging the cut on her hand when Jonas pulled up.

He jumped out of his car and hurried toward where she sat on the curb near her car. "Hey . . . are you okay?"

"My car has seen better days, but yeah . . . I'm okay."

He glanced at the bandage on her hand.

"It's nothing." She held it up. "Really. It's just a scratch. Didn't even need stitches."

"It doesn't look like a scratch to me."

"Forget it," she said, more worried about how he'd fared. "What happened when I left?"

"They jumped into the van and headed after you."

"Why were they so determined to get the judge?" Madison asked. "Why take a hostage?"

Jonas shoved his hands in his back pockets and shrugged. "We need to find that out."

"And your friend who saved our lives?" she asked.

"We definitely owe him, and trust me"—Jonas let out a low chuckle, his gaze flitting toward his friend, who was heading their way—"Tucker won't let us forget. I'm just . . ." His smile faded as his gaze caught hers. "I'm glad you're okay. This isn't exactly how I thought it would be seeing you again. I missed you."

"I missed you too."

She caught the intensity in his eyes and wished she had time to explore what she was feeling right now. He'd promised her he'd wait until she was ready for them to move forward in their relationship, but seeing him again made her question any reservations she'd had. Revenge, though, was an ugly beast, and she knew that whoever had killed Luke wanted to hurt her. She couldn't let something happen to Jonas because of her. Not until she knew who was behind Luke's murder. Not until she found closure.

She shoved the conflicting thoughts aside to analyze another day. "Tucker seems capable for the job, but he took quite a risk back there."

"It was a risk, but we knew enough about Cervantes to know that his men wouldn't have hesitated in shooting their hostage."

"Unfortunately, I agree."

"You're not talking about me, are you?" Tucker patted Jonas on the shoulder, then held out his hand to Madison. "Tucker Shaw. I was in SOG training with Jonas, though we've known each other for years."

"Welcome aboard." Madison stood up, then shook the man's hand. "It's nice to meet you, and it looks as if we're in your debt. That was a tough call."

"Careful." Jonas chuckled. "Like I said, Tucker here isn't someone you want to be indebted to."

"Very funny." Tucker glanced at Jonas. "He mentioned you once or twice over the past few weeks. I feel almost as if I already know you."

"Really?" Madison tried to read Jonas's reaction. "I'd like to hear what went on in those conversations."

Jonas shook his head. "I think we'll save that for another day."

"I'm going to hold you to that," Madison said, "but just so you know, Tucker, Chief Deputy Michaels loves throwing people into the deep end. Jonas's first day involved a plane crash and a cross-country fugitive chase."

"Wow. Something tells me today is far from over."

Tucker's phone buzzed and he pulled it out of his pocket. "That was Michaels, and you're right," he said after hanging up. "He wants us back at the office for a briefing ASAP."

***

Thirty minutes later they walked into the US Marshals' office in downtown Seattle. Madison quickly changed out of her bloody blouse then joined them in the squad room where Michaels was waiting for them.

"Three of the shooters are in custody," Michaels said, getting straight to the point, "but the others managed to overpower the guards and escape. They took Cervantes with them."

"What about the one I shot?" Tucker asked.

"He's in surgery but stable. The hospital will contact us as soon as he's awake so we can question him. The other two who went after Madison in the van are in custody and currently being questioned in interview rooms as we speak."

"And the situation at the courthouse right now?" Madison asked.

"The courthouse has been locked down and swept for explosives," Michaels said. "There were no casualties, but four are in critical condition in local hospitals, including an assistant district attorney."

"We need to find Cervantes and his men," Jonas said.

"That's why you're here." Michaels nodded at Tucker. "I'm sorry for the rough start to your first day, but there will be an investigation into the shooting incident that happened at the courthouse. As soon as you've given your statements, Jonas and Madison, you'll be working alongside local law enforcement to find our three fugitives. We need them off the streets now."

Madison rested her hands on her hips. "What about Judge Saylor? He was clearly targeted. There has to be a connection."

"I've arranged for him and his wife to be placed into temporary protective custody until we can determine what's going on. He went with officers to his house to pick up his wife."

"What do we know about our fugitives?" Tucker asked.

"Our intern, Piper, has been pulling things together from officials involved in the case." Michaels signaled at the criminal justice major who had been interning in their office the past few months.

Piper shoved her thick, black-rimmed glasses up the bridge of her nose, grabbed a file off the desk where she was working, then hurried over to them.

"They have been able to identify four of the five suspects, all of whom have been tied to Cervantes's organization." Piper switched on the large screen above them and brought up photos of the men. "As you already know, Cervantes was arrested for not only drug trafficking across the Puget Sound region but also for a long list of crimes including drive-by shootings, money laundering, and murder. Law enforcement had been investigating him for eighteen months when he was finally arrested, but since his arrest, there have been numerous threats made toward a number of people involved in the case."

"Including Judge Saylor, according to a statement by him this morning," Jonas said.

"That is correct," Piper said.

Michaels's phone rang, and he told them to continue while he stepped out into the hallway.

"What can you tell us about our list of fugitives?" Jonas asked.

"The US Attorney and his investigators who built the case against Cervantes are sending that information now," Piper said. "But each one of them has been on the state's radar for quite some time."

"We've got another problem." Michaels stepped back into the room. "Law enforcement just showed up with Judge Saylor at his house. They found his wife inside."

"Is she okay?" Madison asked.

Michaels dropped his phone back into his pocket. "No. She's not. Myra Saylor is dead."

FIVE

There were three marked police cars as well as a van from the medical examiner's office parked in front of Judge Saylor's residence when Jonas and Madison arrived. The three-story house was located a couple blocks from Puget Sound, in a well-established community in West Seattle that offered both beaches and incredible cityscape views.

An officer in uniform approached them as they made their way up the long drive that was flanked by a tall privacy hedge to the left and an exquisitely manicured lawn to the right.

Jonas and Madison held up their badges and quickly introduced themselves.

"Detective Jade Victoria," the woman said, stopping in front of them. "I was just informed that the US Marshals were coming."

"We were at the courthouse when it was attacked and believe that the two assaults could be related," Madison said. "We're trying to track down the suspects that escaped."

The detective nodded. "My partner and I were in the area and were the first on this scene. We actually arrived at the same time as Judge Saylor."

"So the judge was here when you discovered his wife's body?" Madison asked.

"We insisted the house was cleared before he went inside, but yes."

Jonas frowned. "Did you find anything that might be related to the intruder?"

"There were no signs of a forced break-in and no murder weapon. The front door was closed but not locked, and Myra's body was in the front living room."

Which didn't fit with the scenario they'd been working with. Why would Myra let in one of the men connected with the attack at the courthouse?

"We're waiting for CSU to arrive," Detective Victoria said. "I've also assigned a couple officers to canvass the area, but so far no one they have spoken to saw anything."

Madison glanced back down the drive. "That isn't surprising considering how far the house is set back from the road."

"What about video surveillance on the property?" Jonas asked, spotting one of the driveway cameras on the outside corner of the three-car garage.

"We've already got someone accessing the footage."

"Good," Jonas said as they started toward the house again. "We're going to want to see the crime scene and then talk to the judge."

"Anything you want," she said. "I was told to give you complete access."

They followed the detective into the entryway of the house that was just as impressive on the inside as it was on the outside. Sunlight streamed through floor-to-ceiling windows. To the left was a formal dining room, and to the right, a formal living room, where she was found. Ahead of them was a floating steel-framed staircase that led to the second story.

"Where was the victim killed?" Madison asked.

"In the front living room. The medical examiner's there now."

They followed Victoria to the formal living room, which had a matching, pinkish-orange-colored couch and love seat, reddish walls, and a fireplace. The westward-facing windows offered views of Puget Sound and the Olympic Mountains, but Jonas's attention was fixed on Myra Saylor, who lay on her back on the thick carpet with a large blood stain on her chest.

"We're with the US Marshals Service," Madison said, addressing the ME, as he stood up and stretched his back. "We were with Myra's husband at the courthouse earlier this morning during the attack."

"And you want to know if the two attacks were perpetrated by the same people," he said.

Jonas nodded at the man's assumption.

The older man pulled off his gloves and stepped away from the body. "I can't tell you if the two cases are tied together, but I can tell you that it appears as if Myra was killed by a single shot to the chest. I'll know more after the autopsy, but there are no other visible signs of trauma."

Jonas worked to put together the fragments they had gathered so far. Threats had been made against the judge, and he'd stated he was worried Cervantes's followers would come after his wife. What didn't make sense was why Myra would have let her attacker into her house.

Madison turned away from the body to face Victoria. "Where's the judge now? We're going to need to get him out of here and into protective custody."

"He's in the kitchen, but there is something I think you're going to want to hear before you speak to him."

Jonas's brow rose. "Okay. What is it?"

"We received the BOLO with photos of the suspects from the courthouse shooting, but you need to hear a 911 call that came in from this house around nine thirty this morning. I was sent the audio file, and it was a woman on the line."

"Myra?" Madison asked.

The detective shook her head as she put her phone on speaker and played the audio.

"911, what is your emergency?"

"I need help. Please . . ." A woman's voice broke. *"She's been shot."*

"Ma'am, I need you to slow down and tell me your name."

"I . . . I can't. But she . . . she's been shot."

"Okay . . . Tell me who's been shot."

"Myra. Myra Saylor."

"Can you tell me where you are?"

There was a muffled sound, as if the phone was dropped, before the audio picked up again. *"I'm at her house. Judge Robert Saylor's house."*

"Ma'am, I need you to tell me if she's alert and able to speak."

"No . . . she's not moving." The woman was crying now. *"Please . . . you need to send someone here. She can't die."*

"I'm sending someone now. Can you tell me where she was shot?"

"In . . . in her chest. There's so much blood. Please . . . I don't know what to do."

"I'm going to walk you through what to do, but I need you to stay on the line. Do you understand?"

"I just don't know."

"What's your name, ma'am?"

The call ended.

"So we don't know who she was?" Madison asked.

"No." Detective Victoria dropped her phone into her pocket. "According to the notes I received, dispatch tried to call the number back, but there was never an answer. And as you heard, the woman never gave her name. By the time they got to the scene, Myra was already dead, and whoever made the call—on Myra's phone, by the way—was gone."

"We should check the phone for prints, because whoever made the call was with Myra when she was dying," Jonas said.

"And very likely was her killer," Madison finished for him.

It might be too early to make assumptions, but now at least they had a lead on a suspect—whoever had been on the other end of that call. But while the attack at the courthouse had been well coordinated, there was no indication that any of those suspects were women.

"We need to talk with the judge," Jonas said.

The detective motioned for them to follow her. "Just know he's pretty upset."

"I can't blame him." Madison's face was unreadable as they followed the officer to the kitchen, but her shoulders seemed to stiffen.

Jonas reached out and gently touched her arm. "You okay?"

"Yeah . . . Home invasions just hit close to home."

He caught the tension in her jaw. Four months ago, Madison had been shot in her own home. He'd found her lying on the kitchen floor in a pool of blood. The bullet had hit her upper right abdomen, causing a laceration across the liver. But the most puzzling part of her injuries had been the partial amnesia she'd been left with. She still didn't know who had pulled that trigger.

Judge Saylor was leaning against a large kitchen island with a coffee mug in his hand, staring at the wall when they walked into the open kitchen. Jaw tense. Lips pursed. He turned around and threw the mug, slamming it against the backsplash behind the stove. Glass and liquid scattered across the countertop.

Jonas cleared his throat. "Judge Saylor?"

The older man turned around and gave them a blank look. "I'm sorry. I . . . I didn't hear you walk in."

"It's okay," Madison said.

"No, it's not." The judge's hands shook as he dropped onto one of the island's barstools, ignoring the mess he'd just made. "She's dead, and I have no idea how to process this."

"We're sorry for your loss," Madison said. "I know this is a very difficult time for you, but we do need to ask you a few questions. We want to find whoever killed your wife, and we believe it's possible that her death is tied to the attack at the courthouse."

"It's the only thing that makes sense to me." The judge pressed his fingers against his temple. "I'm just still trying to wrap my head around everything. When I got up this morning, I never imagined I'd have to deal with planning my wife's funeral. I'm still waiting for her to come down the stairs and ask me what I want for lunch. She can't be dead."

A woman wearing a modest knee-length skirt and simple white blouse walked into the kitchen and immediately started cleaning up the broken glass.

The judge walked over to her. "Angela, you don't have to—"

She laid her hand on his shoulder. "I told you, I'm here to help. It's not a problem."

The judge cleared his throat and turned to face Jonas and Madison. "This is Angela. She works for us several days a week. Today . . . today was supposed to be her day off."

"Angela," Jonas said, "we're with the US Marshals. When did you get here?"

"Just before you did. Judge Saylor called me and told me what happened. I had to come."

"So you weren't here when the 911 call was made," Madison said.

"No. I was at home. When I got here, there were police everywhere and Mrs. Saylor . . ." Angela glanced at her boss, then continued picking up the shards of glass that were scattered across the counter, without finishing her sentence.

"I should have been here," the judge said while Angela cleaned up the mess. "I could have stopped this."

Madison shook her head. "This isn't your fault. You had no way of knowing what was going to happen."

"You're wrong." The judge stared at the granite island countertop, his shoulders slumped in defeat. "My wife is dead because of me. I should have done more to make sure she was safe."

"I know this is hard, but can we see the message you received?" Madison asked.

"Sure." He reached into his pocket and fumbled for his phone.

"Do you receive threats often?" she asked as he searched for the message.

"Ninety-nine percent of the threats are simply someone saying to me what they never would say face-to-face. They're cowards. If I stayed home after every threat I received, I wouldn't go in to work."

"But clearly today was different," Jonas said. "They not only tried to kidnap you but they possibly came after your wife as well."

Judge Saylor pushed the phone across the island to Jonas.

Think carefully about how you decide this case.

There is more than just your life at stake.

Jonas handed the phone to Madison to read. "That's a pretty direct threat."

The judge's shoulders slumped. "And now Myra is dead."

"We can work with your mobile phone company and try to track down who sent this, but did you tell anyone about the message this morning?" Madison asked him.

"I showed it to court security, then called my wife, telling her to turn on the security alarm and stay home." He combed his fingers through his hair. "I should have told her to go to her sister's in Portland. I thought she'd be safe here. She promised me she'd turn on the alarm."

"There is something that doesn't make sense," Madison said, working to ease the conversation forward. "There were no signs of a break-in, which means if she did what you said—turn on the alarm—she had to have let in her killer."

"Wait just a second and I can tell you," the judge said, taking back his phone. "Our system keeps a record of all alarm activity." He opened up one of the apps then hesitated. "I don't understand."

"What does it say?" Madison asked.

"I called Myra about seven fifteen, and she turned on the alarm like I told her." A vein on his forehead pulsed. "Two hours later, she turned it off."

"That was not long before the 911 call."

He set the phone down on the island while Angela dumped the glass into the trash can. "Why did she turn it off?" he asked.

"We might have an answer for that," Victoria said, walking into the room. "I'm sorry to interrupt, but you need to come see what we found on the security camera."

Madison glanced at Angela, then laid her hand on the judge's arm as the older man stood up. "You don't have to come right now."

"No . . . I need to know who did this."

Jonas nodded. He was right. They needed to identify the intruder, and there was a good chance that if Myra had known the person she'd let in the front door, the judge would too.

His office was located at the back of the house. The large room had vaulted ceilings, wood flooring, a fireplace, and a heavy wood desk situated in the middle of the room. On top of the desk, a computer monitor was split into four security camera angles. The detective quickly zoomed in on the top left of the screen.

"Most of the cameras in the security system are outside and at points of entrance," Victoria said, "so while there isn't a camera in the living area, there is a camera at the front door, and one that offers a good view of the front of the house and yard. Both of those cameras show Myra opening the front door and letting someone in a few minutes before the 911 call."

They watched a few seconds of the footage of Myra letting in a woman, then Victoria froze the screen.

"Judge Saylor? Do you know who this is?" Jonas asked, taking a step backward so the man could get a better view.

The man's face paled as he stared at the computer screen.

"Judge Saylor," Madison prompted when he didn't answer.

"This can't be my wife's killer. Have you checked the time stamp?"

"It's the right time," Victoria said. "She was in your house at the time of the murder and more than likely made the 911 call."

Judge Saylor walked over to the floor-to-ceiling windows overlooking the backyard. "That's not possible."

"What's not possible?" Madison asked, joining him at the window.

"Her name is Becca Lambert." The judge twisted the ring on his finger. "She's the mother of my son."

SIX

Madison studied the judge's sullen expression. The confession he'd made was not what she'd expected but knowing the identity of the woman was going to make it easier to find her. It also had the potential to shift the entire trajectory of their investigation.

"Who is she?" Madison asked, quickly texting the updated information to Michaels. "An ex-wife?"

"No." Judge Saylor dropped into one of the wingback chairs beside the window, clearly not wanting to talk about the woman. "Becca . . . we had an affair. She got pregnant."

"Did your wife know about the affair?" Jonas asked.

"I didn't think so."

"How old is your son?" Madison asked.

"Six weeks old." The judge shifted in his chair. "The last few weeks have been difficult, and while I'll be the first to confess I made some mistakes, I've wanted a son for so long. Easton was the one bright light in this mess. I just . . . I didn't know how to tell Myra. Now I wish I had."

Madison sat down in the matching plaid chair next to the

judge while Victoria slipped out of the room. "Where did you and Becca meet?"

"At the restaurant where she works. I had dinner there one night, and I don't know . . . we connected. She ended up sitting and talking with me after she got off her shift. The affair was a mistake and I take full responsibility for my actions, but I did love her."

"Did?" Madison asked.

"Maybe I still do. I don't know." His fingers gripped the armrests. For a man who was used to passing judgment on others, the role of the defendant clearly left him unsettled. "Becca isn't the most stable person. She had a hard childhood. I never should have gotten involved with her. You might not approve of my decisions, but I love my son and if anything happens to him . . ."

"Has Becca ever been violent?" Madison asked.

"No. Never." Judge Saylor rubbed a hand over his face, fatigue coloring his expression. "She could be . . . demanding, but never threatening, though I know she was frustrated with me. Becca was convinced I'd leave Myra and we'd start over together somewhere."

Jonas leaned on the desk. "Did you ever promise her that?"

The judge clasped his hands in front of him. "I know I said things I shouldn't have, but I'd been clear from the very beginning that could never happen. We were just two consenting adults having a bit of fun. No commitments. No long-term obligations . . ."

Madison frowned. "But that wasn't what she heard, was it? Becca wanted more from you."

Judge Saylor slumped against the back of the chair. "Becca wanted us to be a family. But while my wife and I might have had problems, leaving her . . . I never could have done that."

"So when you didn't leave Myra," Madison said, trying to keep the irritation out of her tone, "is it possible Becca decided to take things into her own hands?"

"No." The judge blew out a sharp breath. "Becca might have wanted Myra out of the way, but not this way." He ran his fingers across his wedding band again. "I realized I needed to end things with Becca, but I still tried to make things right. I promised her I would own up to my responsibility of taking care of Easton. Schooling, medical . . . whatever she needed, and I meant it. I needed . . . wanted to be in his life. I thought I made that clear to her."

"Did you ever actually cut off the relationship with Becca?"

The judge tugged on his collar, looking trapped. "I was just waiting for the right time. Becca was going through some post-partum depression. I didn't want to make things worse for her."

Madison glanced around the room while the judge composed himself. Like the rest of the house, it had been ornately decorated with a blend of solid wood furniture, antique pieces, and rich textiles, but clearly money couldn't buy everything. Something had pushed this man into the arms of another woman. When had his marriage to Myra shifted to become one simply of convenience and an attachment to a lifestyle, instead of two people truly committed to each other?

"When is the last time you spoke with Becca?" Jonas asked, pulling Madison back into the interview.

"A couple days ago. She called me at work, upset. She wanted to talk with me about something. I'd had to cancel on her a couple times, but now . . . now I wish I hadn't put her off again. Maybe Myra would still be alive if I'd just listened to her. I knew our relationship was changing, but I assured Becca I wanted to be in Easton's life. I didn't feel that he should suffer for what we did." He pressed his fingertips against his temples and closed his eyes again.

"Judge Saylor?" Madison asked.

"I'm sorry." He opened his eyes and looked up at her. "I'm just trying to understand why she would have done this. What did she want? Unless . . . unless all of this had been nothing more than a long con."

"What do you mean?" Madison arched a brow.

He stood and crossed the room, then pulled a large, framed painting off the wall and set it on the ground. Behind the photo was a wall safe.

"I keep cash in here." The judge punched in a code and opened it, then gasped. "It's all gone."

"How much?" Jonas asked.

"About thirty thousand."

"Did your wife know about the money?" Madison asked.

The judge started pacing the gray area rug. "Yes, but if Myra gave her that money, then Becca . . . she's long gone."

"Do you have any idea where she might go?" Madison asked. "Does she have family? Friends?"

"Not really." The judge shoved his hands into his pockets and stopped. "She was an only child who grew up in the foster care system. And as for friends . . . I don't know. We never met together socially, though there is another waitress from the restaurant that she's close to. Her name is Ava Middleton. She takes care of Easton while Becca is at work. There is also a woman Becca knew from her time in foster care. One of her caseworkers."

"Do you remember her name?" Madison asked.

He took off his glasses and rubbed the bridge of his nose. "Liz . . . no . . . Elizabeth. Elizabeth Adler. Yes. I remember Adler because that was my mother's maiden name."

Madison sent another text to Michaels with the updated information.

"What we've just learned is going to change our role in the investigation," Jonas said. "Our job is to apprehend fugitives, not investigate murders. I'm sure Detective Victoria will have further questions for you."

"I understand," the judge said.

Madison's phone rang, and she pulled it out of her pocket. "Excuse me, I need to take this call."

She slipped out of the office and walked down the short hallway.

"Local PD are at Becca Lambert's apartment now," Michaels said. "There has been no sign of a murder weapon, but they did find a pile of bloody clothes in her trash. They're sending samples to see if the blood is a match to our victim."

"What about Becca and her baby?"

"The apartment was empty. Local PD has requested that you help track them down since we have reason to believe the child's life is endangered."

Madison glanced back at the judge's office. "And our suspects from the courthouse?"

"We've reassigned a joint task force to track them down. You can start with talking to Elizabeth Adler, and I'll send someone else to the sitter. We were able to verify that Adler was one of Becca's caseworkers while she was in the foster care system and that they still stay in close contact."

"And Judge Saylor?" Madison asked.

"I'll let Detective Victoria handle things. She is arranging for him to be put into protective custody."

Madison ended the call, then headed back to the office. "That was our boss, Chief Deputy Michaels," she said to the judge.

"Jonas and I have been assigned to stay on the case and find Easton."

"Good." The judge rested his hands on his hips. "Tell me what I can do. I'm still working to establish paternity with the courts, but I'll do anything. If she hurts him . . ." He let his sentence trail off, but his opinion was clear. His son's life was in imminent danger.

"If we need any information from you, we will reach out, but in the meantime, you'll be going into protective custody," Madison said.

"I don't need—"

"The murder of your wife might not be related to the courthouse attack," Jonas said, "but there are still people after you."

"Fine." The judge held up his hand. "I understand."

"I do have one last question." Madison walked over to the large, glass gun cabinet on the west wall of the office. "You have quite a gun collection. A Colt Single Action Army revolver . . . Glock 36 semiautomatic pistol . . ."

"My father loved guns. Quite a few from my collection were actually his."

"You have some stunning pieces," Madison said. "What about Becca? Do you know if she owned a gun?"

"I . . . I bought her a handgun and made sure she knew how to use it. She lives alone, and I wanted to make sure she was safe. But now—"

"And your wife?" Madison interrupted him. "I'm assuming you did the same for her?"

"She didn't like guns, but yes. I made sure she could use one if she needed to." The judge shifted his attention out the window, lost in thought about something.

"What are you thinking, Judge Saylor?" Jonas asked.

"I don't know. I can't shake the feeling that I missed something."

"Meaning?" Jonas prodded.

"I can't help but question how well I really knew Becca. If she killed Myra . . ." His voice trailed off as he shoved his hands into his pockets. "What if this was just one big con and I fell for it. Could that be possible?"

"I can't answer that question at this point," Jonas said.

"Unfortunately, I can't either. What I do know," he said, "is that I just lost everything."

Detective Victoria walked back into the room. "I've arranged for you to be taken to a safe house, Judge Saylor."

"Thank you." Jonas nodded at the detective. "Your team can finish up with CSU and the crime scene, while we try to track down Becca Lambert."

"Yes, sir. And we'll be sure to pass on any updates."

"And please," Judge Saylor said, "let me know when you find Easton."

Madison slipped under the crime scene tape in front of the house, then headed to the car with Jonas. It was the twist neither of them had expected. A married man gets a woman pregnant, makes her promises, then he refuses to leave his wife for her and still wonders why she's mad.

"Maybe I'm naive," she said once they were both inside Jonas's car, "but I can't help but wonder what he expected to happen. Especially when his wife found out. It's like he was expecting a happily ever after, despite his deception."

Jonas pulled onto the street, heading for the address Michaels had given them. “All I know is that there are three sides to every story. Your side, my side, and the truth.”

“Well, I’d like to hear Becca’s side,” Madison said. “Not that anything excuses what she probably did, but given the circumstances, it’s not hard to see how she got to this point.”

“My question is the same as the judge’s,” Jonas said. “Was this a love triangle or a con job that ended in murder?”

SEVEN

Elizabeth Adler lived in an older home in a neighborhood that backed up to the Schmitz Preserve Park, a forested park in the middle of the city that many Seattleites didn't even know about. Madison, though, had once lived in a house nearby and had gotten used to taking advantage of the jogging trail and the chance to get away from the normal city rush.

She and Jonas made their way up the stone walkway that weaved through the middle of the overgrown yard. The house itself was worn, but from age rather than neglect. Madison stepped to the left of the door while Jonas rang the doorbell.

"Elizabeth Adler?" Madison held up her badge when the woman finally opened the door.

Her expression darkened. "Yes."

"I'm Madison James, and this is my partner, Jonas Quinn. We're both with the US Marshals. We understand you're close friends with Becca Lambert?"

"I am." The woman hesitated, her gaze still guarded. "What's going on?"

"When is the last time you spoke with Becca?" Jonas asked without answering her question.

"We . . ." Elizabeth reached up and touched the hollow of her throat. "We had lunch together last week."

"So you haven't spoken to her today?" Madison asked.

She shook her head. "No, but please tell me what's going on. If Becca's in some kind of trouble . . ."

"She's a person of interest in a murder investigation, and we believe that her child could be in danger."

"A murder investigation?" The woman's face paled. "I think you need to come inside."

She motioned them into the living room and then invited them to sit on a long couch with a colorful afghan thrown over the back. The rest of the room was an eclectic mishmash of fabrics and patterns, but the combination came across as homey and inviting. The kind of place that would put a vulnerable teen at ease.

Elizabeth folded her arms across her chest. "Please tell me what's going on."

"A woman named Myra Saylor was murdered," Madison said, "and we have evidence that Becca may have been involved in her death—"

"No . . . no, that's not possible." Elizabeth started pacing the multicolored rug in front of them. "Becca would never hurt anyone."

Jonas leaned forward, his elbows on his thighs. "Then you need to tell us anything that might help us find her and Easton."

Elizabeth perched on the edge of an armchair. "That's the problem. She doesn't know where Easton is."

Madison looked at Jonas, then turned back to the woman. "What do you mean?"

Elizabeth pressed her palms against the cushion. "I wasn't completely truthful."

"You spoke with her today?" Madison asked.

Elizabeth nodded. "Something happened at Myra's. She wouldn't tell me, except she was almost hysterical. I tried to get details out of her, but she was so upset she wasn't making any sense."

Jonas shook his head. "Why didn't you call the police?"

"I was going to, but she said she'd be in trouble if I called. I was trying to figure out what was going on—why Becca was so upset—before I called the authorities. And before I could, you showed up."

"You need to tell us where Becca is. Becca and her son."

"Becca doesn't know where Easton is. That's why she was so upset."

Madison caught the panic in Elizabeth's voice. "If that's true, then that's just another reason for her to turn herself in and get help from law enforcement."

"I know, but she wouldn't listen to me. She's scared. Myra was obsessed over having a child. She'd gone through all kinds of treatments in the past, but nothing worked. And I think . . ." Elizabeth's hands clenched at her sides. "I think she was determined to have both her husband and her husband's child and make sure Becca was erased from the picture."

"Becca told you this?" Jonas asked.

"Yes. You have to understand that Becca has had a hard life, but she's managed to pull herself together. I don't get to see the fruit of my work as a caseworker often, but there was always something special about Becca. She's been working hard to provide for Easton and has even started to take some online classes. She would never sign away her rights to her baby, just like she would never kill anyone."

"Then help us," Madison said. "Tell us everything you know about what happened."

Elizabeth tugged at a loose string on her sweater. "I don't know what happened at Myra's, but Becca told me she left there and went to her friend Ava's apartment to pick up Easton. Ava's a close friend of hers who takes care of Easton when she works."

"And they weren't there?" Madison prodded.

"No." Elizabeth shook her head. "She tried calling Ava's cell phone, but Ava didn't answer, which isn't like her."

"And then she came here," Madison said, watching the woman's response.

Elizabeth's chin lowered. "Yes. She needed money. She told me she couldn't go back to her apartment."

"Did you give her any?"

"Three hundred dollars. I know it's not much, but it's all I had."

Madison tried to determine if the woman was lying again. Something wasn't adding up. If Myra had given Becca the money out of the safe, why come here for money as well? Three hundred dollars was chump change compared to the thirty thousand in the safe.

Jonas shifted on the couch beside her. "When did she leave?"

Elizabeth grimaced before answering. "Just a few minutes ago, but you have to understand," she rushed on. "Becca's terrified and doesn't know what to do. She told me she didn't want me to get involved and wouldn't tell me where she was going, just that she was going to be okay."

"Where do you think she would go?" Madison asked, standing up.

Elizabeth shook her head as if she were trying to get rid of the guilt of betraying her friend. “I don’t know where her car is, but she walked out the back when you knocked on the door. She’s probably headed to the preserve. She knows that place like the back of her hand. Used to spend a lot of time hiking when she was a teenager when she wanted to get away. I can’t tell you how many times I found her there.”

Madison sighed. And now Becca had a solid head start on them.

“I know I should have insisted she turn herself in, but all she could think about was finding Easton.”

Madison headed for the back door with Jonas, who had pulled out his phone. “What was she wearing?” Madison asked.

Elizabeth pressed her hand against her chest. “Tan pants and hiking boots. A white shirt and a . . . a light-blue cardigan, I think.”

“An officer will be here in the next couple minutes to take an official statement,” Jonas said, slipping his phone into his pocket. “In the meantime, we’re going to do a search.”

Madison pulled out her own phone as they hurried out of Elizabeth’s house and toward the trailhead. Piper answered on the second ring.

“Piper, we’re going to need backup sent to the exits of the Schmitz Preserve area. We have confirmation that Becca Lambert is there, and we’re assuming she’s armed, but there’s a lot of ground to cover.”

“Copy that. I can coordinate with local PD. Anything else?”

“Any luck on using her phone to get a location?”

“We’re waiting on the warrant.”

“Okay.” The temperature dropped slightly as they slipped into the shade of the forest. “In the meantime, find out everything you can about Elizabeth Adler.”

"Already on it."

Madison jogged down the trail beside Jonas, hopeful they were on the right track, but from here, Becca could have gone anywhere. They were close to the freeway, and even without a car, public transportation was easily accessible.

"Do you believe Elizabeth," Madison asked Jonas, "or do you think we've just been sent out on a wild-goose chase?"

"My gut tells me that Elizabeth believes what she told us, but I can also see her covering for the girl. We know Becca was at that house, and the connections to her involvement in Myra's murder keep getting stronger."

Jonas was right. A surprising number of people, when faced with protecting a guilty friend or relative, tended to make up stories in an attempt to safeguard them—even when they knew they were guilty. On top of that, people tended to believe what they wanted to about a situation, even when the evidence spoke to the contrary.

"If Elizabeth is lying," Madison said, "and Becca has the money from Myra, she has enough cash to disappear with her son for a long time."

"True, but if Becca was telling the truth—if she really doesn't have Easton with her—then she won't be going far until she finds him."

A row of tall ferns brushed against Madison's leg as they pressed deeper into the park. The preserve was fifty acres of old-growth forest. When she lived closer, Madison and Danielle used to jog the preserve's trails that were lined with cedars, Douglas firs, and maple trees. The green foliage was dense, allowing nothing more than slices of sunlight to break through the canopy.

A jogger approached them. Jonas held up his badge and signaled for her to stop.

"We're looking for a woman you might have passed," he said. "Early twenties, wearing tan pants and hiking boots."

"Sorry." The woman stopped in front of them but kept jogging in place. "It's been pretty quiet this morning. I haven't seen anyone except for an older couple a few minutes back."

"Thanks." Jonas stepped out of her way, and she continued her run.

"There's a fork in the trail up ahead," Madison said, "but if she's here, that jogger should have seen her."

"Maybe your gut was right, after all." Jonas slowed his pace. He dropped his hands to his side, the frustration on his face noticeable. "If she's not here, we're wasting our time."

"Yes, but this preserve is easy to get lost in. She could be anywhere."

Madison's phone rang, and she pulled it out of her pocket. "Piper, what have you got?"

"I was able to get ahold of a former supervisor of Elizabeth," Piper said.

Madison put the call on speaker as they kept walking down the trail. "Go ahead."

"Elizabeth retired eight months ago, and like she has with Becca, she stays in touch with a number of the foster kids she worked with. But her supervisor said that Elizabeth was never one to work *inside* the box."

"Meaning?"

"Meaning she wasn't above bending the rules if she believed it was necessary for her kids' welfare, which apparently got her in trouble with a number of the judges over the years. On the other hand, the supervisor said that she'd never worked with someone so engaged and for the children as Elizabeth."

"So there's a good chance that Elizabeth lied to us," Jonas

said. "About giving her money, not knowing where Easton is, and even where Becca is."

"It's just an educated guess," Piper said, "but from what the woman told me, it definitely wouldn't be out of her character. What do you want me to do?"

Madison glanced down the quiet trail. "We could spend hours looking for her inside the park and she could be halfway to Portland by now."

"Agreed," Jonas said. "I think we need to go back and have another talk with Elizabeth. But, Piper, keep a patrol car at each of the trailheads, just in case Becca did go through the park."

"Hang on a minute," Piper said. "Thanks to a warrant, we just got a GPS location on Becca's phone."

"And?" Madison's heart rate escalated. "Where is she?"

"Maybe Elizabeth wasn't lying, after all," Piper said. "Unless she dumped her phone, it looks like she's there in the park."

"Is the phone moving?" Madison asked.

"At the moment, no. Looks like she's just south of your location."

"We're on our way," Madison said. "Stay on the line."

They hurried forward in the direction Piper had indicated, but there was no one in sight.

Madison started turning in a slow circle. "There's no one around, Piper."

"Are you sure? I've got your location as well, and there's a strong signal just ahead of where you're standing."

Madison considered this. If Becca heard them coming, she could have slipped off the trail, but navigating the denser undergrowth and fallen trees wouldn't be easy. It was also possible that she'd dumped the phone.

"Do you see anything?" Piper asked.

"Madison." Jonas held up something.

"Give me a second, Piper." Madison hurried over to where Jonas was holding up a black smartphone.

"She dumped her cell," Jonas said.

"Okay," Madison said, "but she can't be that far ahead of us. She has to be heading to the bus stop."

And from there she could disappear.

They started back down the trail, picking up their pace. Madison was thankful it had been dry the past week. With any rain, the trails would have been too muddy to navigate quickly.

As they made it to the bottom of a hill, the marshals recognized her immediately. Becca was walking fast, her head down and hands in her pockets as she headed toward the trail exit.

Madison pulled her Glock out of its holster. "Becca Lambert? US Marshals. I need you to stop and put your hands in the air where I can see them."

Becca looked back, then started running away from them down the narrow trail. On the other side of her, coming toward them, was a female jogger.

"Becca . . ." Jonas stepped closer, his own Glock raised.

Becca paused as the woman got closer. Her arm shook as she grabbed the older woman from behind, forcing her to stop, then pressed the barrel of a gun against the woman's head.

EIGHT

"Becca." Madison took a step toward the two women. "My name is Madison James, and I'm a US Marshal. I need you to put the gun down and let her go."

Madison had seen Becca on the security feed at the Saylor home, but she still hadn't expected her to look so young. She didn't look a day over eighteen. Dark hair hung across her forehead, but it was her eyes, peeking out from below her long bangs and red from crying, that revealed the truth. The girl was terrified. But instead of obeying the order, Becca held the gun steady against the woman's head, unmoving and determined, as if she were attempting to convince them that she was in charge of the situation.

"Becca," Madison continued, "this isn't the way to solve things."

Wind blew through the trees above them, making an eerie, haunting sound as branches creaked and leaves rustled. The older jogger stood motionless, gun against her temple, eyes wide with panic. Madison might not have been in the Saylor home when Myra was killed, but she was here now, and she wasn't going to let anyone else get hurt.

Becca's hand started to shake as she kept the gun pressed against the jogger's head. "I don't want to do this, but I don't have a choice."

Madison took another step forward while Jonas let her take the lead. "I know you don't know what to do, but you do have a choice, and this isn't the answer."

"If your child's life was in danger, you might not jump to judgment so quickly."

"Then let us help." Madison shifted her gaze to the jogger. "What's your name?"

"L-Lila." The woman's chin quivered.

"Lila, I'm going to do everything I can to help both of you, but I need you to stay calm for right now. Because"—she turned back to Becca—"Becca, I know you don't want to hurt anyone, and just like you, Lila has friends and family she cares about."

Becca wrapped her arm around Lila's shoulder and pulled her back a couple feet. "You don't understand what's going on. I have to find my son."

"Easton," Madison said.

Becca's eyes narrowed.

"Why did you go to Myra's home this morning?" Madison said, working to keep her voice even.

"You talked to Elizabeth?" Becca shook her head. "I told her not to call the police. I told her not to get involved."

"We were already involved," Madison said, trying to walk a thin line between being honest and yet not pushing Becca over the edge. "She only wanted to help. She wanted to make sure you got your baby back safely. That's what we want as well."

Becca tightened her grip around Lila's arm. "She shouldn't have talked to you. She's just like everyone else. In the end, all they do is betray you."

"She talked to us because she does care about you, Becca. Listen, you're scared, I get that. But you have to put the gun down and let Lila leave so we can talk. Just you and me. Let's figure out a way to find your son together."

The internal conflict Becca was battling against reflected on her face. "You can't help me."

"Why do you think that? Because of what happened at Myra's house?"

"I didn't mean to hurt her, but what would you do if someone had taken your child? You'd do anything, wouldn't you?"

Madison worked to keep the frustration out of her voice. "I would want to."

"Do you have a child?"

"No, I don't." Madison paused, still treading carefully. "But I know what it's like to be betrayed by someone. I know what it's like to lose someone you love."

Becca shook her head. "You can't understand what it's like to have no idea where your child is."

"Do you know what a US Marshal does?"

Becca shrugged.

"My job is to find people. Especially people who are in trouble. And my partner, Jonas . . ." Madison motioned back at him. "Together he and I can help you find your son."

Becca tightened her grip on Lila. "Why? Because you feel sorry for me and want to help or because my son's now considered in danger because you think I murdered someone?"

"Where is he, Becca?" Madison pressed, still uncertain if the woman was telling the truth. "Just like you, we want to find him."

"I don't know. Myra told me she'd taken Easton. Told me he was somewhere safe."

Another piece of the puzzle clicked together. "I thought you left him with Ava?"

"I did, but I haven't been able to find her either." Becca shook her head as confusion over the situation seemed to outweigh her determination. "I think Myra might have taken both of them. It's the only thing that fits."

"You think she was using Easton as leverage?" Madison asked.

"Yes, but now she's dead." The terror was back in Becca's eyes. "If I turn myself in, can you promise they'll give Easton back to me? Because I didn't go there to kill her. I didn't want her to die, but she had a gun and tried to kill me. I shot back in self-defense. And then . . . all I could think about was running."

"If you're innocent, why did you run? Why take a hostage?"

"I didn't know what to do. I knew what you'd find. I was covered with her blood . . . she was dead . . ."

Madison considered Becca's assumption, but she wasn't ready to buy into the woman's conspiracy theory. There were simply too many things that weren't adding up for that to make sense. What they did have was solid evidence Becca had been at the scene. Evidence that she'd been with Myra after she'd been shot. And the bottom line was that the details of the case, including Becca's guilt or innocence, weren't for her to determine. Her job was simply to bring Becca in and make sure no one else got hurt.

"I promise, I'm going to make sure someone listens to your story," Madison said finally. "But you can't do this on your own. You need help."

"Help from who? Another government agency?" Becca's voice held a strong tone of mistrust. "The foster system never helped me. And now . . . All I wanted was what was best for Easton. I thought of giving him up for adoption, but when I held him in the hospital, I knew I couldn't do it. And I won't lose him now."

"We will listen to your story, I promise, but first you have to let Lila walk away."

Lila was sobbing quietly now, but Becca made no move to step away from her.

Madison glanced at Jonas as she slowly lowered her weapon to her side. He nodded slightly.

Madison turned back to Becca. "What can I do to help you?"

The question seemed to take the young woman by surprise.

Madison caught the slight shift in Becca's posture.

"I just want to find Easton. That's all." Becca's shoulders relaxed slightly. "Everyone tells me they want to help, but in the end, I've learned that I'm the only person who can really take care of me. I'm the only person who can take care of Easton. It's up to me to find him."

There was still hesitation in Becca's eyes as she took another step backward. She lowered the gun slightly, removing it from Lila's temple but keeping it trained on Madison, while she kept a grip on the woman's arm.

"You're doing the right thing, Becca," Madison said. "Let her walk away, then we can concentrate on finding Easton. I promise."

A dog barked in the distance, momentarily seizing Becca's attention. She looked back, still hesitating. A couple pushing a baby stroller and trying to handle a hyper boxer on a leash were headed toward them.

Madison walked forward, needing to get Becca's attention. "Becca—"

She whipped back around. "I want to believe you, but I . . . I can't take that chance. I have to find Easton on my own."

Instead of putting the gun down, Becca shoved Lila away from her, then dashed into the cover of the trees.

"I've got Lila," Jonas said, rushing to where the jogger had stumbled to the ground. "Go."

Madison ran after Becca through the dense tree line. The brush off the trail was thicker, including fallen branches, large ferns, and mossy undergrowth that made spots slippery. She watched her footing as she kept Becca in sight. From what she could piece together, the young woman was running with no plan of action, fueled only by pure adrenaline. But in reality, the situation was like jumping into quicksand. Every move just pulled you farther and farther into the pit until you were crushed and could no longer move. And for Becca, she was certain the girl felt as if there was no way out.

Madison slid on a patch of dewy grass, then grabbed a tree limb to catch her balance. The uneven ground and debris were slowing her down. She looked up again. Becca had disappeared.

Madison listened for the rustling of leaves ahead of her. Becca couldn't be far. She had to be struggling on the uneven terrain too. And even if Madison did manage to lose her here, all the exits were blocked off by local patrol by now. A bird was singing, undisturbed by what was going on around him. Madison breathed in the smell of damp moss beneath the cathedral of leaves above her, while sounds of rushing water from a nearby stream met her ears. A flash of pale blue flickered in her peripheral vision. Becca had turned left, toward the other main trail. Getting there, though, wasn't going to be easy.

Madison made her way up another hill, quickly trying to

traverse across the loose soil before she lost Becca again. If she could get ahead of her and cut her off on the adjoining trail . . .

A spiderweb brushed across her face as she raced forward. She reached up to pull it off without slowing down. She was gaining on Becca, moving diagonal across the terrain. Sunlight seeped through the trees as she stepped onto another trail, then turned around as Becca emerged on a clear path.

"Becca . . . stop running. It's over."

She faced Madison, hands out in front of her, clasping her handgun. Her arms shook and her shoulders heaved forward from crying as she pointed the gun at Madison. "You don't understand. Myra was right."

Madison raised her own gun and held it steady. "What do you mean?"

"Do you believe that I didn't kill her?"

"I want to."

"She told me no one would believe me. She told me that it would always be her word against mine. I'm a nobody. I have no family. No money to hire a lawyer to erase this nightmare."

"But if you're telling the truth," Madison said, "if you do the right thing, right now, I told you I would listen."

"If I go with you, I'll never see him again. They'll take him away."

"And if you don't go with me now?" Madison said. "Or if someone else gets hurt? Then what happens to Easton? Think about it, Becca. It's only going to get worse."

"All I ever wanted was a family for him." Becca dropped her hands to her sides as tears spilled down her cheeks. "All I ever wanted was to give him all the things and opportunities I never had. If they find him before I do, they'll take him away and put him in foster care. He'll never have a home.

Never know me. Never have the stability I've always wanted for him."

"If you want a chance of seeing your son again, you need to trust me and do what I say. Drop the gun and come with me. I promise we will help you find your son, but there's nowhere to go. It has to end here."

Becca slumped to her knees and placed the gun on the ground next to her, then stood back up and put her hands behind her head.

Jonas emerged from the trees and kicked the gun away before handcuffing her. Madison dropped her own weapon to her side. A mother facing the possibility of losing a child was heartbreaking, but there were still consequences to choices. And Becca was right, Madison had no input in how this was going to end.

Still. "You did the right thing, Becca."

"Did I?" Her lips tightened into a thin line. "Because I hope that doing the right thing doesn't cost me my son."

NINE

Deputy Chief Michaels met them inside the US Marshals' office squad room at half past two. The gray-haired man was not only a boss to Jonas but also a longtime friend and mentor, someone he looked up to. Michaels somehow managed to handle the stress of his job with a level of grace and strength Jonas only hoped he could one day achieve.

"I had Becca Lambert taken to an interview room," Michaels said, slipping his reading glasses into his suit jacket pocket. "And I just finished questioning the judge."

Jonas leaned against a desk. "Did you learn anything?"

"He's insisting he knew nothing about the text message Becca claims his wife sent, and there were no messages from Myra to Becca on her phone."

"What about Becca's phone?" Madison asked.

"IT's looking at it now, but she erased all her messges before dumping her phone." Michaels signaled for Piper to join them. "I want the two of you to finish interviewing Becca and see what else you can get out of her. If we really are dealing with a missing child, that's going to change things significantly."

Piper pushed up her glasses, then handed Madison a file. "Michaels asked me to do a profile and background check on Becca Lambert. She's twenty-five years old and currently works as a server at a local restaurant. Her mother passed away when she was nine. After that she was raised by her father, until he was convicted of burglary and assault. She was in and out of foster care until she was seventeen and has been on her own ever since then."

Madison nodded. "That matches what both Elizabeth and Becca told us."

"What else?" Jonas asked.

"She had a few minor run-ins with the law when she was in foster care, but she's stayed clean since then. Nothing is on her record as an adult. Until now, anyway." Piper glanced up from her notes. "CSU just finished going through her apartment. Forensic technicians were able to match the blood on her clothes to our victim, but they also found a stash of heroin—"

"Heroin? Wait a minute . . ." Madison's frown deepened at the information. "Does she fit the profile of a drug user?"

"I'm saying they found drugs in her apartment," Piper said. "Though CSU said there's enough for the prosecution to claim intent to sell instead of simple possession."

"What about Ava Middleton, the sitter? What do we know about her?" Jonas asked.

"Not much, actually, which is strange in this day and age." Piper handed the file to Madison. "We know she lives in the same apartment building as Becca, and she works at the same restaurant. I'll keep looking, but that's all I've been able to confirm. When local PD went by to check on her, as requested by our office, they confirmed that no one was there. They're currently canvassing the area to see if anyone saw anything."

Jonas stood, stretching his arms behind his back. "Let us know if you hear anything else."

Piper nodded. "Will do."

Madison was quiet as they headed toward the elevators. Jonas had sensed her mood shift on the way over as she processed, he guessed, what had happened in the park. Their primary role in the situation had been to preserve lives, which was exactly what Madison had accomplished. He'd let her take the lead in the situation, because he knew firsthand her strengths and her ability to connect as a negotiator. But even though things had ended the way they'd wanted—with no loss of lives—Madison still seemed unsettled.

"You think Becca's innocent," he said, pushing the elevator button.

"I think things aren't adding up."

He waited for her to continue as they stepped inside.

She sighed. "It's clear she's made bad choices with her life and is now paying for it, but murder and drugs? When I was talking to her inside the preserve, all I saw was a desperate mother. There were no obvious signs of drug use."

"That doesn't mean she's not guilty. It also wouldn't be the first time an affair ended in murder. And if she needed extra cash . . ."

The doors opened again, and they headed down the hallway.

"Maybe." Madison stopped in front of the closed interview room where Becca was waiting and looked up at Jonas. "How far would you go in order to save your child?"

"That's a loaded question," Jonas said, not sure he could even attempt to answer it. He might not have been in the room when Myra was shot, but what happened in there seemed pretty obvious. "All I know is that if she lied about the missing money, for example, there's a good chance she's lied about other things as well."

Madison folded her arms across her chest. "You think she knows where Easton is?"

Jonas gauged her reaction. "I think Myra's dead and can't defend herself, so Becca can pretty much say whatever she wants."

"But what would be the point of following through with a charade like this if she knows where her son is?" Madison asked. "It doesn't make sense."

"It does if she's conning him." Jonas typed in the room's access code. "Thirty thousand dollars is missing, and as far as we know, that could be the tip of the iceberg."

Inside the interview room, Becca sat slouched against the back of a metal chair. Her hands were clasped tightly in her lap and her cheeks were red. "Have you found my baby?" She straightened up as they entered and sat down across from her.

"Not yet," Madison said. "We need to ask you a few more questions."

Becca gripped the edge of the table with her fingers and leaned forward. "I'll tell you whatever you want to know, but please—I need to be out there looking for him."

"Right now, we need more information from you," Jonas said. "Starting with your relationship with Judge Saylor. And we need you to tell us the truth."

Her lip quivered as she started talking. "I'll be the first to admit that I made a lot of mistakes. I believed Robert when he told me he loved me, and that he would leave his wife for me."

"But he didn't," Madison said.

Becca pressed her lips together. "Shortly after Easton was born, he started standing me up. When I did see him, he always seemed excited to see Easton, but with me he . . . he was distant. I started wondering if he'd gotten tired of me, but honestly, I think the problem was Myra. He'd always been so attentive to me, but suddenly he started putting me off and making excuses about the divorce proceedings. He kept telling me that the timing was wrong and that I needed to be patient." Becca grabbed a tissue from the box next to her and blew her nose. She held up her hand. "I'm sorry."

The wall clock ticked above them as they waited for her to collect herself.

"Becca?" Jonas prodded.

"I'm sorry. I knew I was compromising, and maybe even deep down knew that our relationship couldn't end well, but I just didn't care. Especially when Easton came along." Becca smiled for the first time.

"What was Robert's reaction to having a baby?" Madison asked.

"I was smitten with Easton, but surprisingly, so was Robert. Honestly, I'd expected him to be angry when I told him I was pregnant, but instead he was thrilled. His wife hadn't been able to have children, and now he finally had a son. I'd never seen him so happy. The only problem was I couldn't tell people who the father was. Robert made me swear that from the very beginning."

"So you had motive," Jonas said. "And we have video evidence that you entered the Saylor's home, not to mention the clothes we found in your apartment were covered in blood."

Becca leaned forward, clutching the tissue in her hand. "Why would I want to cut myself off from Robert? He clearly wasn't ready to leave Myra, and I don't make enough to support my son. Robert promised from the beginning that he'd help me raise Easton. I might have wanted to make a family with him, but I also needed him financially."

"So this was about money," Jonas said. "Robert's wealthy and could support you and Easton far better than you could on your own."

Becca's lips thinned into a flat line. "It helped, but I was with Robert because I loved him. Not simply for the money."

"But you didn't take money from Myra when you were there today?"

"No. She said she was going to pay me if I would walk away, but I refused."

"Interesting." Madison tapped on the file in front of her. "Because thirty thousand dollars went missing from their house this morning—"

"You aren't listening to me." Becca blew out a sharp breath. "I didn't go there to kill Myra, or to ask for money. I certainly didn't take money from her. Why do you think I went to see Elizabeth? It was because I have a hundred dollars in my bank account."

"Then start at why you went to the Saylor house in the first place," Madison said.

"I received a text from Robert. Or, at least I thought it was from Robert. He said he needed to see me, and he wanted me to come to the house. I thought it was odd, because I'd never been there, but he told me he needed to talk. I thought maybe he wanted to apologize for getting so angry with me a couple nights before."

"But he wasn't there when you arrived."

Becca shook her head. "No. *She* was there. Waiting for me."

Jonas tapped his finger against the table. "Tell us exactly what she said."

"Myra threatened to take Easton away from me. Told me she knew about Robert and me and the baby and that I had no choice but to do what she said." Becca's voice rose in pitch. "She . . . she told me that I had to sign over my parental rights to Robert and walk away. She even had papers for me to sign."

"And if you didn't sign?" Madison asked.

"She said she had the power to prove to the courts that I wasn't a good mother." Becca's shoulders trembled as she started crying again. "She said there was no way I could win."

"Becca . . ." Jonas leaned forward. "This is very important. We need to know everything she said to you."

"She . . . she said if I tried to fight her . . . that I would lose."

Jonas moved the tissue box in front of Becca. Tears streamed down her face. The woman could be lying, covering for Myra's death, but if she was, she was quite an actress. And it was certainly possible that the judge really didn't know what his wife was doing. More than likely the truth lay somewhere in the middle.

Becca grabbed another tissue. "She said she'd make sure Easton was taken away from me. She'd discredit me as a mother, and I'd lose him. She . . . she knew I'd left him with Ava this morning, but when I went there, they were gone." She wiped her eyes with the balled-up tissue. "And what terrifies me is that if Myra had something to do with their disappearance, she's the only one who knows where they are, and now she's dead."

"Did you try to contact Ava?"

"Yes. Of course. I went to her place, but she wasn't there, which isn't like her. She always tells me if she's going somewhere. Always answers her phone."

"Do you think Ava could somehow be involved in Easton's disappearance?" Madison asked.

"I don't think so, but . . ." Becca's face paled. "Myra did say something I didn't understand."

"What was that?" Jonas asked.

"She knew I'd left Easton with Ava this morning, and she said that Ava had been very . . . useful."

"Myra used that word?" Jonas raised his brow. "Useful?"

Becca nodded. "I didn't understand what she meant. Whether she planned to use her as a pawn or if Ava's somehow involved . . ."

"What do you really know about her?" Jonas asked.

The question seemed to throw Becca off. "I don't know. She . . ." Becca gripped the edge of the table again and sat back as if processing her answer. "She's never really talked about her past. She moved here from back East, wanting a fresh start. Her parents passed away a few years ago. And if I remember right, her aunt recently died and left her a small inheritance. It gave her that chance to start over."

"Do you think it's possible that Myra hired Ava to take Easton somewhere?" Jonas asked.

"No. Not voluntarily. She was my friend," Becca said.

"We weren't able to find her on social media at all," Madison said, not trying to hide the doubt in her eyes, "which is unusual."

Becca shrugged. "I don't know. I never really thought about it, but now that you mention it, she never wanted photos taken of her. Honestly, I never asked her why. We'd worked together for a few months when Easton was born, and she offered to keep him for me when it worked out for our schedules. She was like a sister to me. I would trust her with my life. And I did trust her with Easton's life."

Jonas pulled the file toward him. "I have one other question. You told us Myra had a gun."

"She did. She shot at me. I only shot back in self-defense."

Jonas glanced at Madison. "The problem with your story is that no gun was found near Myra's body."

Becca shook her head. "That's not possible. I don't know what happened to it, but I swear she had a gun."

Jonas leaned forward. "We also found heroin in your apartment."

Her brows scrunched together. "Heroin? That's not possible. I've done a lot of dumb things, but never drugs. Please. You have to believe me when I say that none of that was true. None of it. If you found drugs, they were planted."

"By Myra," Madison said.

Becca shrugged. "She threatened to discredit me as a mother. Can you think of a better way?"

"I want to believe you," Madison said, "but do you know how easy it would be to sway a jury into believing you murdered her with what we know? Even premeditated murder."

"I said I was there, but I didn't go there to kill her. She lured me there. I even called 911. I didn't have to do that." Becca slapped the table with her palms, her eyes brightening for a moment. "And I might have a way to prove those drugs were planted."

Madison exchanged a look with Jonas. "We're listening."

"Not long before Easton was born, Robert bought me a nanny cam, one of those cameras where you can watch the baby. You have my phone. It keeps ten days of video history. At the time, I told Robert it seemed a bit obsessive. But now, I hope it worked."

"We'll look at it," Jonas said, "but why did you leave after Myra was shot?"

"I . . . I panicked and ran." Becca rubbed her temples. "They have money and power. I'm a nobody. And if Robert didn't back me up, no one would believe me."

"You don't think Robert would have stood up for you?"

"I doubt it. She's his wife. He wanted to have a high-profile life, with the big house and the beautiful wife. I'm just the mistress he never could leave his wife for. On top of that, I can't afford to hire an attorney. I have no way to fight back. But she had a gun, and she shot at me with it. That's the only reason I fired my own gun."

Becca's chest heaved as she started to hyperventilate.

"Becca," Madison said, "take a couple deep breaths. You need to try to calm down."

"How can I calm down? She took my baby. And now she's dead and there's no way to find him. What am I supposed to do?"

Madison pushed back her chair and stood up. "Is everything you've just told us the truth?"

She looked up at her. "Everything. I swear."

"I hope so," Madison said. "Because it's the only way we're going to be able to find your son."

Michaels was waiting for them on the other side of the one-way glass where he'd been listening in on the interview. "I'll arrange for her to be taken to the cell block, at least temporarily, and we'll get someone on that video footage." He looked back and forth between them. "I've also got a couple updates, starting with a call from CSU at the Saylor house. They just found the thirty thousand dollars from the safe."

Madison folded her arms across her chest. "Where was it?"

"In Myra's purse."

"So Becca was telling the truth," Jonas said. "Myra never gave her the money."

"She was telling the truth about that," Michaels said, "but there's still no evidence of a second gun or a second shot, as she claimed. I checked again with CSU, and there were no casings or additional bullet holes found in the Saylor home."

"Did you ask the judge where Myra's gun is?" Jonas asked.

Michaels motioned toward the elevator, and they started walking. "We'll verify what he said, but according to Robert, she'd had some issues with her grip when she'd been out target practicing with him. He said she'd taken it in to have the grip upgraded."

"And unless Robert's not telling us everything, that puts a hole in Becca's story about there being a second gun," Madison said.

Michaels punched the elevator button, then took a step back. "Local PD also talked with one of the tenants at the apartment building where both Becca and Ava live. He was working on his car in the parking lot, and he saw Ava and Easton get into a van with a man."

Jonas frowned as he took in the information. "Under duress?"

"The witness said he didn't notice anything unusual at the time, but he was not really paying attention. She definitely went with him though."

The elevator dinged and the doors slid open.

"It does fit with Becca's story," Madison said, stepping in ahead of the men. "If Myra arranged for someone to grab them as further leverage, we're looking at a kidnapping."

"That's exactly what I'm thinking," Michaels said. "I'm working on getting a description of the driver from our witness, and we already have the make and color of the van they got into. I want you both to go visit Ava's apartment and see if you can find something they might have missed. I've already informed local PD that you're coming."

"Becca was right about one thing," Madison said. "We need to find Easton."

Michaels nodded. "Agreed. It's time we put out an Amber Alert."

TEN

Ava climbed out of the back of the van onto the slick drive that was partially covered with patches of slippery moss. Easton whimpered in her arms as she fought to keep her balance.

"Where are we?" she asked, grabbing the diaper bag before pulling the baby tighter against her chest to block his cheeks from the wind.

"This is where you'll be staying the next couple days," her captor said, not exactly answering her question.

She studied him for a moment—dark eyes, thinning hairline, and a scar above his brow. She was certain she'd never seen him before.

Wind whipped through her jacket as she surveyed the heavily wooded property. There were no visible signs of neighbors from where she stood on the isolated stretch of terrain. No one who would hear her if she started screaming or who could help if she tried to run. It would have been different if she were on her own, but with Easton, she couldn't take that kind of risk.

Her captor grabbed a bag out of the back seat, then barked at her to follow him.

Wooden steps leading up to the cabin's porch groaned beneath her as she obeyed the order. Flower boxes filled with pansies sat in the windowsills, still in full bloom. If she'd been looking for a rustic, isolated getaway for the weekend, the spot would have been perfect, but this was no holiday. DeMarco, the man who wanted to stop her from testifying, had found her.

Inside the cabin was a bed, a couch and table, a wood stove, and a tiny kitchen. A ladder led up to a loft with a second bed, and there was a door to her left that she assumed went to the bathroom.

She pulled Easton even closer, trying to stop his whimpering. "We can't stay here. It's freezing inside, and once the sun sets—"

"Stop your complaining. I'll turn up the heat, and there are blankets in the closet. I'm also leaving you some food and water."

She dropped the diaper bag onto the counter. "You're leaving us here alone?"

It was a foolish question, but the thought of him deserting them in the isolated cabin terrified her almost as much as his staying with them.

He dropped the bag of groceries and car seat he'd carried in on the kitchen table. "As long as you don't try to leave, you'll be fine. The nearest neighbor is a couple miles away, and the temperature is supposed to drop tonight, so I wouldn't advise leaving."

He glanced at the baby, his point clear. She had no options, and he knew it.

"Why did they want you to bring me here?" she asked.

He turned up the heat, before looking back at her. "I'm just the deliveryman."

Ava frowned. She needed information. Anything that might give her a clue as to what their intentions were. "Do you know when they're coming?"

His brow furrowed, but he didn't answer the question. Maybe he really didn't know anything, but she knew better than most what DeMarco was capable of doing, in or out of prison. What she didn't understand was why, if he'd found her, she was still alive.

"You can't just leave me here," Ava rushed on, bouncing Easton in her arms while frantically trying to come up with a way out of this. "I'll pay you. I have money stashed away. All you'd have to do is take me somewhere safe, then tell them I got away—"

"Stop." His nostrils flared as he stepped in front of her. "There's no one here to help you. No one. No cell coverage, and no one who can hear you scream or hear the baby cry. So just be quiet." He headed toward the exit, then turned back to face her. "And trust me, if you try to run, you'll end up lost or frozen to death out there."

"Please, if you'll just—"

The slamming of the door after he stomped out of the cabin swallowed her question.

She heard the click of a lock on the front door, then a few seconds later, the roar of the van's engine.

"It's going to be okay." She kissed Easton on his forehead. "I promise."

He cooed up at her, but she had no idea how she was going to keep her promise.

First, she had to find a way out. She set Easton in his car seat, then went to tug on one of the windowpanes. It was stuck, locked from the outside. She looked around, then rushed to the door and slammed her shoulder against the wood, but it didn't budge.

Ava pressed her hand against her chest. Apparently, her abductor wasn't taking any chances. Her heart raced as the familiar feelings of panic spread. She sat down on the couch and reached for the diaper bag, willing her mind to still. She'd prepared for this. No matter what happened, she wasn't going to let them win.

She reached for the burner phone she'd hidden inside the bag. Her abductor might have said there was no cell service out here, but she wasn't going to take his word for it. She turned on the phone and waited for it to come on. Hand shaking, she held it up, praying for at least one bar.

Nothing.

She tried holding it next to the window. Still no service.

Easton started crying. She scooped him into her arms, then started pacing the carpeted room. She counted to ten, then turned around and crossed the small space, trying to get him to fall asleep on her shoulder. She accidentally bumped into a chair and the grocery bag tumbled over, spilling crackers, tuna, peanut butter, and granola bars across the table.

Ava frowned. DeMarco had a plan, she was sure of that, and not one that would end well for her. Which was why ensuring she had food struck her as odd. If his goal was to silence her, why worry about something as trivial as food while she waited?

Fear welled as she tried to come up with a way to escape, because she wasn't the only one she had to think about. Becca would be frantic by now. She'd get home from work, expecting to pick up Easton, not expecting to have to call the police and tell them something had happened to her baby.

Easton's eyes fluttered shut as he faded off to sleep, his thumb in his mouth. His mother had become like a sister to her, an unexpected blessing that had helped to strip the feelings of being alone when she first moved to Seattle. Through Becca she'd made a few friends, but the knowledge that DeMarco wanted her dead was never far from the front of her mind.

Water dripped from the kitchen faucet, a constant trickle in the background. The wind had picked up, and a tree limb tapped against the window. She shut the curtains, feeling scared and exposed.

Familiar feelings of guilt swept through her. She'd gone as far away from home as she could, believing DeMarco would never find her in Seattle. Putting Easton's life at risk—or Becca's, for that matter—had never been her plan.

But neither had running from her old life.

She missed the beaches and the lighthouses. Tiny fishing harbors with lobster buoys bobbing in the water. She'd thought she'd be safe here. They promised her she'd be safe. And the fact that she now knew she wasn't safe terrified her.

If DeMarco's crew was keeping her here—keeping her alive—there had to be a reason. Whatever it was, she didn't want to stick around and find out. But even if she was able to find a way out of the small room, where was she supposed to go?

She'd prayed for so long to be able to put this nightmare behind her. Every shadow and strange noise had kept her from sleeping through the night for months. She'd gone to the range and learned how to shoot a gun and even took self-defense classes. She took precautions most people would never even think of, but for her they'd become second nature. She was always aware of what was happening around her. She never played on her phone while out on a walk and always looked for things that seemed out of place, like cars making the same turns as her or seeing the same person more than once.

Becca had commented on some of her odd habits, but Ava didn't care. She rarely took the same way home, and if she felt she was being followed, it was always worth the extra time to turn around and go a different route. And yet even with all the precautions she took, they still hadn't been enough. DeMarco had promised her that he'd never stop looking for her, and now he'd found her. And it had taken only one wrong move on her part.

She drew in a deep breath. As risky as it was, she needed to go for help, because only one thing made sense. The only reason she was still alive was because DeMarco needed something from her.

ELEVEN

The apartment complex where Becca and Ava lived sat on the edge of a bustling neighborhood in West Seattle, within walking distance of a number of shops and restaurants. It included four large, three-story buildings, which surrounded a courtyard with a swimming pool and playground.

Madison's phone went off as Jonas parked the car. "Hold on," she said. "I've got something coming in from Michaels."

She clicked on the text message and read it.

"What is it?" Jonas askedd.

"Michaels had Piper go through the footage from the nanny cam, and it looks like Becca was telling the truth. They found video of an unidentified male going through her house."

"Could be a friend," Jonas said.

"Could be." Madison clicked on a still from the video Michaels had sent. "Becca doesn't recognize him, and he appears to be looking for something."

"Can they tell if he took anything?" Jonas asked.

"They've got IT working to sharpen the images to make sure they don't miss anything, but it doesn't look like it."

Madison climbed out of Jonas's car and scanned the parking lot.

Their witness was working on his car engine in the shade at the edge of the parking lot, exactly where they'd been told to look for him. She hurried next to Jonas to the end of the lot.

"Daniel Pollard?" Madison asked.

The man nodded, then grabbed a rag next to the open hood of his car and wiped his hands. "I'm guessing you're with the police?"

"US Marshals," Madison said, holding up her badge. "We understand that you saw one of the other tenants, Ava Middleton, get into a van with a man this morning."

"I did, but like I told the officer who interviewed me earlier, I feel bad, but I was more focused on the car than paying attention to what was going on around me. If she was in trouble, I didn't notice."

"So she didn't look as if she was in distress?" Jonas asked.

"Not that I saw. When I looked up, they were walking toward a van here in the parking lot. She was carrying a car seat with a baby and had a bag over her shoulder. I remember looking up again, and he'd opened the side door for her. She looked serious, even intense, but I never got the feeling she was in trouble."

Madison held up her phone and showed him the photo of the man Piper had pulled from the nanny cam in Becca's house. "Is this the man you saw?"

Daniel leaned in closer to get a better look. "Yeah. That's definitely him."

"Have you ever seen him around here before?" Jonas asked.

"No." Daniel shoved the rag into the back pocket of his jeans. "I'm pretty sure I've never seen him, or the van. I wish now I'd taken note of the license plate, but I never imagined she was in trouble."

"What about Ava?" Madison asked. "Do you know her?"

Daniel shrugged his shoulders. "Not really. I've seen her around the complex. Said hi to her in passing. She's always seemed friendly but reserved. I've seen her take the baby for walks in a stroller some afternoons, but that's really it."

"We appreciate your help," Jonas said, hovering his hand over the side of the buffed-up car before taking a step back. "She's a beauty, by the way."

"It was my father's baby, a second generation 1964 Chevrolet El Camino, but he died recently, and now I have to decide if I want to fix it up or sell it."

"V8 engine?" Jonas asked.

"327 cubic inch and over 300 horsepower."

"Looks to me like he kept it in pretty good shape," Jonas said.

"I never quite understood why he loved the car so much except maybe the memories that came with it, but he never could get rid of it."

"Thanks again for your help," Jonas told Daniel. "So," he said as he and Madison headed toward the sidewalk leading to Ava's apartment, "the man who took Ava and Easton is the same man who was in Becca's house."

"I'm not surprised," Madison said. "If we take what Becca said as the truth, Myra hired the guy to plant incriminating evidence inside Becca's apartment, then took Ava and the baby for the leverage she needed against Becca. But then why do we have a witness telling us Ava went with him willingly?"

"I don't have an answer for that, and until we ID him, it's going to be hard to track him down, especially considering Myra is dead."

"I didn't know you had a love for classic cars," Madison said, shifting the conversation as they started up the stairs to the second-floor apartments.

"My father had a Ford Mustang that I was always clamoring to drive."

"Did he ever let you?"

Jonas chuckled. "Not very often."

A policeman was standing in the breezeway of the apartment when they reached the second floor. Jonas held up his badge and introduced them.

"Officer Carl Merrill. The detective and CSU team have already left, but I was asked to wait and let you in."

"Thanks," Madison said. "We appreciate it."

"We were told there were no signs of a forced entry," Jonas said, stepping inside the small one-bedroom apartment.

"That is correct. From all the evidence, it seems as if Ava left willingly."

Madison studied the small space. On the surface, the apartment was neat, with only minimal pieces of furniture. There was no TV or any pictures of family or friends, but there was a tall bookshelf filled with books.

"What can you tell us about her?" Madison asked, slipping on a pair of gloves as she scanned the bookshelf that was primarily filled with classics.

"Besides the obvious fact that she's a voracious reader," the officer said, "not much. We found her car keys and wallet, though no purse."

"As if she'd left in a hurry," Madison said. "Or it's possible she knew the man."

"Maybe, but all it would take was a threat to the baby or Becca, and you could see why she didn't put up a fight."

"Or it goes along with the theory that she was in on it," Jonas said.

Madison wasn't sure. "Possibly, but after listening to Becca, I have a hard time believing that she would betray her friend over a handful of cash."

"We don't know much about her, but we can't ignore that she had financial problems." Jonas pulled open the kitchen drawers one at a time. "I'm always surprised hearing what people will do for money."

What they didn't know was where the man had taken her and Easton. There were dozens, if not hundreds, of white vans registered in the area. While they had a description of the driver, they still had no idea who he was, and it could take days to come up with an ID. The only thing they did have on their side was the Amber Alert that had gone out. They had enough of a description of the man in the van in order to do that, and someone at some point had to see something. Especially now that they had the photo from the nanny cam.

Madison picked up the hardback copy of *Return of the King* that was laying on the coffee table. "She must be a Tolkien fan. She's got at least a dozen of his books."

She glanced around the room, trying to sort out the pieces of the puzzle they'd been given. Ava Middleton was new to Seattle, lived alone in an apartment with nothing personal beyond perhaps her library. To her neighbors, she was friendly yet reserved. She had no presence on social media, and even her closest friend didn't know much about her past or where she'd come from.

Where are you, Ava, and who are you hiding from? Madison thought. *If you were so worried about your safety, then why did you let someone in?*

She turned toward the middle of the room. Maybe she had simply been trying to start over, but how did that fit into what happened today? Her aversion to danger had to have come from somewhere, but then why had she opened the door to a stranger and gone with him?

Something fell to the floor from inside the book in Madison's hands. She reached down to pick it up. "Jonas, look at this."

"What is it?"

"A strip of pictures from a photo booth," she said, holding it up. "It's Ava and a little girl."

There were four silly poses, and both of them looked as if they didn't have a care in the world. The only odd thing was the charred edges of the photo strip.

"I thought she didn't have any family or kids?" Jonas said.

"I thought so too, but that's definitely Ava, because it's the same person in the photos we got from the restaurant where she works. The little girl looks a lot like her. A daughter? Maybe a niece."

"Maybe, but why keep the photos in a book and not framed where she can look at them?" Jonas asked.

"I was wondering the same thing."

For some reason, the photo seemed significant. Like Ava was trying to keep her life private and yet she still needed to hang on to something. But none of this was going to help them find her or who she'd walked out of the apartment with.

Something rustled in the bedroom.

Madison set the book down and turned to the officer. "I thought you said all of your people had left."

Merrill's eyes focused on the bedroom door. "They did."

"Someone's here." Jonas's hand went to his holster.

Madison pulled her own gun out, then strode down the short hall to the bedroom. A shadow shifted as she got to the doorway, and a man wearing track pants and a T-shirt swung a weapon toward her and fired it. Madison pulled back instinctively as the bullet slammed into the wall behind her.

"US Marshals," she shouted from behind the doorframe. "Drop your weapon and put your hands in the air now."

The man responded by firing off another shot, this time hitting the bedroom ceiling.

Madison gauged the threat of moving forward into the room versus staying out of sight. Clearing corners and doorways involved high risk and called for sharp judgment. If she could see the suspect, he could see her, and the man was armed and clearly willing to shoot.

"He's going to jump," Jonas said, pressing in behind her.

She spun around as the suspect pulled the balcony door open. "We need to cut him off on the ground level."

They ran back into the living room and out the front door, ordering Merrill to stay in the apartment and make sure the intruder didn't come back inside.

Madison turned the corner with Jonas right behind her. There were only a couple places the man could go, but somehow he'd slipped from their sight. "Where is he?" she asked, scanning the back of the property.

"I don't know," Jonas said. "Head left toward the second breezeway, and I'll try the other direction."

Madison started to turn, then stopped.

A red dot hovered on the back of Jonas's jacket.

"Jonas!"

She lunged forward and pulled Jonas down, slamming him into the sidewalk as a bullet smashed into the brick wall beside them. She fought to catch her breath as she searched for the source of the bullet. Taking the shot didn't make sense, especially since they'd lost him. Why had he shot at them again?

"Are you okay?" she asked.

He was lying flat on his back. "Thanks to you, I am."

Sirens rang in the background.

She pulled her hands away from where they'd landed on Jonas's chest and helped him off the sidewalk, before searching the open area adjacent to them for movement. The intruder didn't have much of a lead, and they had to find him.

"There he is," she said.

Their suspect emerged from a parallel breezeway and was now heading toward the parking lot. She started after him, lengthening her stride. What they didn't want was another hostage situation. She'd never believed that Becca was going to shoot her hostage in the preserve, but this man had already shot at her and seemed to have no hesitation in engaging law enforcement.

She turned the corner, following the sidewalk and bridging the distance between them. Ahead to the left, three kids played at a playground while their mom looked on. Madison's heart beat faster, not only from the exertion, but from the possible scenarios running through her mind. Their suspect was armed and clearly had no intention of surrendering.

She glanced behind her. Jonas was a dozen feet behind, and she knew he was thinking the same thing. The man dodged sideways across the grass and into the playground area. He scooped up one of the toddlers and kept running.

The mother screamed as Madison charged past and motioned for the woman to stay back with her other kids.

Madison's mind raced as they approached the parking lot, needing to stop the situation from escalating any further than it already had. Another stray bullet might hit someone, and now there was the crying toddler's life at stake as well. But that wasn't the only thing she was worried about. This wasn't the same man who'd broken into Becca's house or who Ava had gone with. So, who was he and what did he want?

The man turned around, dangling the child in front of him with one arm, while holding out his weapon in the other. "Stop where you are," he shouted.

"Put him down," Madison said, leveling her own weapon.

The man walked backwards, still carrying the boy.

Jonas stopped next to Madison as a tan, four-door Chevy pulled up to the curb. The driver threw open the passenger door, and the man set the child down on the curb, then jumped inside. Tires squealed as they peeled out of the parking lot toward the highway.

The boy's mother rushed up from behind Madison and scooped up her crying toddler.

"I got the license plate number," Jonas said, pulling out his phone. "I'm calling it in."

Madison holstered her gun, then knelt down next to the woman's other two crying kids. "Is he your brother?"

The redheaded little girl whimpered. "His-his name's Sammy. He's two. I'm five, and Darcy . . . Darcy's three."

"And what is your name?" Madison asked.

"Sh-Shalin."

"Sammy's going to be okay. You're all going to be okay. The bad guy's gone."

"Are you going to catch him?" Shalin asked, wiping away her tears.

"Yes, we are. And I want you both to know you were very brave." The little girls smiled as Madison stood up and turned to the mother. "Are you okay?"

"I think so," she said, pulling the little boy even tighter against her chest. "But I don't think I've ever been so terrified."

"Madison?" Jonas motioned her over. "Michaels needs to talk to both of us."

Madison called over Merrill, who had just descended the stairs, to take a statement from the mother and make sure they were okay, then she hurried to where Jonas was standing.

He put the phone on speaker, then held it up between them. "What's going on, boss?"

"We have a problem." There was a short pause before he continued. "I just got a call about our Amber Alert from WITSEC. Ava Middleton's photo never should have hit the news cycle."

"Wait a minute." Madison's stomach clenched. "She's in witness protection?"

"Yes," Michaels said.

Suddenly all the pieces clicked into place. Why Ava didn't talk about her past, why there was a hidden photo of a little girl in the book she was reading. Madison groaned. They'd just plastered her photo across the news. "How did we miss the connection?"

"I don't know," Michaels said, "except that the records are kept separate to protect the witness."

That might be true, but this shouldn't have happened.

"They're sending her files over right now," Michaels said, "but from what I was told, she worked for a large corporation and is providing evidence at an upcoming trial. She was placed in witness protection after several threats to her life and one actual attempt. I'm trying to connect with the marshal in charge of her case. We've taken her photo down in connection to the Amber Alert, hopefully before the bad guys can put two and two together."

Madison glanced at Jonas. "I think they already have."

TWELVE

"We need to talk with the WITSEC inspector tasked to keep tabs on Ava," Jonas said. "She was supposed to have been protected."

He weighed the implications of what had just happened. A mistake like this should have been avoided.

"Agreed," Michaels said. "I've got Piper on the line with Witness Security Division right now. Hold on, she's got something. I'm handing her the phone."

"What I have isn't good," Piper said. "Ava's contact within the marshal division is missing."

"What do you mean, missing?" Madison asked.

"The last communication they recorded from him was that he was heading to her apartment because he hadn't been able to get ahold of her. Now he isn't answering his phone."

"Who's her contact?" Jonas asked.

"Inspector Peyton Wyse."

"I've met Wyse," Jonas said, though he didn't know much about him except that he was married, had a couple kids, and had worked with WITSEC for almost a decade. "What kind of car does he drive?"

"Give me a sec . . ." Piper said. "A black Ford Escort."

Jonas stared down the two rows of cars sitting parallel to the front of the apartment complex. "And his license plate number?"

Piper read it off.

"We'll call you back," Jonas said, dropping his phone into his pocket.

They hurried down the middle of the two rows of cars, looking for the Escort. If Wyse was here, why wasn't he answering his phone? Jonas studied the many vehicles. Three cars ahead was a dark Escort. He read the license plate.

It wasn't him.

"There's another Escort up here." Madison checked the plate. "It's him."

Jonas walked up to the driver's side then looked into the window. The vehicle was empty.

Where is he?

He scanned the parking lot, trying to determine where the man would have gone. And why he wasn't answering his phone. If he'd gone up to the apartment, he would have checked in with the officer in charge. This didn't make sense.

"Wait a minute," Madison said, hurrying down the row of cars. "Piper just sent me the GPS location on his phone. We're close."

He followed a few feet behind her as she closed in on the GPS location.

She stepped between two of the cars, then stopped. "I've got it," Madison said, picking up a smartphone. "He must have dropped it."

Jonas strode to the front of the vehicle near Madison, stopping next to the driver's seat.

Wyse lay slumped over the steering wheel.

Jonas pulled open the door and checked the man's vitals. "He's got a pulse and is breathing, but he's unconscious."

"I'm calling 911 now," Madison said.

"Wyse!" Jonas shook the man's shoulders while Madison made the call. "Can you hear me? Wyse!"

The man groaned, opened his eyes, then started to sit up.

"Whoa, buddy. Can you tell me what happened?"

"I don't know." Wyse's speech was slurred, and his coloring off. "There was a . . . a woman." He reached for his neck then winced. "I don't know. I was trying to help her."

"I just found a syringe," Madison said, stepping up to the driver's window.

Jonas turned back to Wyse. "Do you know who the woman was?"

"No . . . I'm sorry. I . . ." He pressed his hands against his temples. "My head is pounding . . . I can't think."

Jonas shifted his attention to the agent's neck and found what he'd expected. A red mark. "He was definitely injected with something. Get Michaels on the line and give him an update. We need to have this area canvassed immediately. Someone had to have seen something."

Sirens wailed and lights flashed a few minutes later as the ambulance approached the complex.

"Hang in there, buddy," Jonas said, crouching beside Wyse while Madison went to flag them down. "We're going to get you help."

"Where is . . ." Wyse paused, his breathing labored. "I need to find her."

"Ava?" Jonas asked.

"Can't . . ."

"I'm a US Marshal as well. We're trying to find her."

Wyse shifted his head slightly and looked at Jonas. "I promised her . . . keep her safe . . ."

Flashing lights reflected in the rearview mirror as the ambulance arrived.

Jonas stepped away from the car as two paramedics hurried to the vehicle. "We're pretty sure he was injected with something," he said. "There was a syringe on the ground, and there's what looks like a needle mark on his neck."

"Copy that," said one of the paramedics. "We'll make sure he's stable, then get him to the hospital."

"We need to talk to him," Jonas said. "It's urgent."

"If you want to follow us, you can talk with him as soon as he's coherent, but first we need to make sure he's okay."

Jonas grabbed the keys out of his pocket, then headed to where Madison was talking with a police officer.

"Did Wyse give you anything?" Madison asked as the officer headed back to his vehicle.

"No. He's too out of it."

"We need to head to the hospital with him, but I've given local PD the information they need. They'll canvass the area and report back with any information they come up with."

Jonas nodded, then hurried to the car with her. So much for the romantic dinner he'd been looking forward to. He hoped they'd have a chance to catch up before he was thrown back into the deep end with work, but that's not how it usually happened in this line of work.

"I think you're going to owe me dinner," Jonas said as he pulled out onto the main road and headed for the hospital. "Which is disappointing, because I was really looking forward to that chicken parmesan and chocolate cake you promised me."

Madison laughed. "To be honest, this day isn't exactly turning out the way I'd planned. Plus, I didn't even get a chance to go grocery shopping, so we'd be looking at mac and cheese or takeout."

As long as they were together, he couldn't care less about the food. He peeked at her profile. Man, he'd missed her.

"How's your father?" he asked, changing the subject.

"He has good days and bad days." She stared out the window as they drove toward the freeway. "We're trying to make sure the majority are good ones."

"I'm sorry. I know this isn't easy for you."

"How's your mother?" she asked, shifting the attention back to him.

Jonas took the on-ramp and merged into the middle lane. "She started taking a swim class at the local gym and loves it. She's still thinking about downsizing." He stole another glance, hoping to catch her reaction. "And she wants to meet you."

An almost undetectable blush crept across Madison's cheeks. "I'd like to meet her. And Danielle wants to have you over for dinner now that you're back."

"I'd like that. My mom doesn't cook anymore, so it's been a long time since I've had a home-cooked meal. Though I might be able to talk her into making her legendary chicken fried steak and mashed potatoes."

"Now I definitely will have to come. And your training—I can't wait to hear all the details."

"The short version is just imagining all the training we've had rolled into one and multiplied in intensity by a hundred."

"But you made it through."

"I did."

"Any regrets?"

Just being away from you.

"No." He cleared his throat as he took the hospital exit. "You were right. I'm glad I did it. Especially now that it's over."

He wasn't in the mood for small talk, but maybe there was no way to avoid it right now. They were avoiding the unspoken subject hovering between them. During the past month of training, he'd managed to stay focused on his job while he'd been able to call her only a couple times. But it didn't mean he hadn't thought about her. She'd been in the back of his mind when he woke up and when he went to bed exhausted. She'd even been in his dreams. Seeing her again had reminded him how much he'd missed her. It had been a long time since he'd allowed his heart to think about love, marriage, and a family. But despite the obstacles, he knew without a doubt that she was the one he wanted to spend the rest of his life with.

He pulled into the hospital parking lot, hesitating before asking the next question. "Any updates on Luke's murder?"

Her fingers gripped the armrest between them, and he knew he'd hit a nerve. While the pain of his death might have faded some, the loss would always be a part of who she was.

"There are still more questions than answers, but Edward has been following some leads," she said finally. "I'll catch you up once this is over."

"Okay," he said, not wanting to push. He pulled into a parking space, then shut off the engine. "And your memory?"

She pushed her hair over her shoulder, then shook her head. "Still nothing. I went to my psychiatrist again. He told me to be patient, but it's frustrating."

He studied her somber expression, wondering if the nightmares had continued as he suspected. Her quest to find closure to her husband's death had left her on unstable ground, but it was her strength he saw. And one day, that closure would come. He was certain of it.

They waited almost an hour inside the emergency room before the doctor finally allowed them to talk to Wyse. He'd been put in a private room with a guard standing outside until they could find out exactly what had happened, because unfortunately, canvassing the apartment complex for a second time had come up with nothing.

Wyse opened his eyes and looked over as Jonas and Madison stepped into the room and introduced themselves.

"You were at the apartment complex," Wyse said.

Jonas nodded. "We were there for the same reason you were. To find Ava Middleton."

"I'm still trying to put the pieces together." Wyse reached up and touched his neck. "The doctor told me I'd have a headache for a while, and I guess he's right. I still feel so groggy. Apparently I was injected with some kind of fast-working sedative. But yes, we have to find her. If we don't . . ."

He didn't have to finish the sentence. They all knew what was at stake.

"What's the last thing you remember?" Madison asked.

Wyse closed his eyes for another moment. "I was going to Ava's apartment, and when I got there, this woman flagged me down. She was pregnant and needed help starting her car. I got in to try and start it, and then . . . I don't know. I don't know how I could have been so stupid."

"Can you describe her?" Jonas asked.

"Twentysomething. Blond hair. She was wearing a . . . burgundy sweater and jeans, I think."

"We'll work to ID the woman," Jonas said.

"Ava and I were supposed to go over some things for the

upcoming trial she's testifying at," Wyse said. "I always phone to confirm our meetings, but she wasn't answering my calls, which had me worried."

"Has that ever happened before?"

Wyse shook his head. "No. Never. It took some convincing to get her to testify, but when she finally said yes, she was all in and took her role as a witness very seriously. She knew the risks and what they would do if they found her. She'd never just stand me up."

"And then you saw the Amber Alert," Jonas said.

"Not until a few minutes ago when my boss called me." Wyse let out a low groan. "I still can't believe this happened."

"Local PD told us that your car had been broken into and searched. Did you have anything in there that someone might have wanted?"

"I don't keep anything important related to the job in the car, but whoever attacked me wouldn't know that. If they're trying to find Ava, maybe that's what they were looking for. Something to help them find her."

"Do you have any way to track her?" Madison asked.

"No." He pressed his hands against his temples. "This just doesn't make sense. She knows she's risking her life to testify and would never leave with someone unless she had a very good reason. If you'd heard what they threatened to do to her . . ."

"This seems personal," Jonas said.

"It is, because my job is to keep her alive." Wyse looked up at them. "Someone broke into Ava's house in the middle of the night. They shot her husband, then set the house on fire. She lost everything, including her daughter. We announced to the media that the entire family died in the fire."

"But Ava didn't die."

He shook his head. "It's strange. She told me a number of times that she knew they'd eventually find her, but I always promised her she was safe. And if it weren't for that Amber Alert, she would be."

"What about some kind of retraction." Madison glanced at Jonas. "Something to make them believe that the authorities made a mistake by posting the wrong photo."

"I don't think they'd buy it," Wyse said. "If DeMarco's men believe there's even the slightest chance she's alive, they'll put everything they have into finding her. That's how condemning her testimony is to their case, and they know it."

"How did she get involved in this?" Madison asked.

"She was a personal assistant to Bradley DeMarco. He managed to keep most of his illegal exploits hidden from her, but there were things that made her start to question. When she found evidence of corruption, he tried to silence her and ordered her family killed."

"What kind of corruption?" Jonas asked.

"The DA is gathering evidence on an organized crime ring he's been tied to through a chain of hardware stores back East," Wyse said. "They use the legitimate business as a headquarters for laundering money, drug trafficking, fraud, tax evasion, extortion . . . you name it. The FBI has had them in their sights for years, and finally has come up with enough evidence to arrest DeMarco—primarily because of Ava's testimony. He's refused to ID the boss who runs the crime ring."

Madison leaned against the windowsill. "So DeMarco is just a player in a bigger game?"

"Yes. I . . ." Wyse closed his eyes again. "Everything's still a bit fuzzy. All we know is that their crime boss is known as Púca, which is *Ghost* in Irish Gaelic. We have one blurred photo of him on file, but that's it. He has no digital footprint, and every time the authorities get close, he vanishes with his men—including DeMarco—who are willing to take the fall for him. Three of them, including DeMarco, were arrested on a list of felony charges, but even with the deal that we offered DeMarco, he refused to talk."

"Here's the thing," Jonas said, drumming his fingers against his sides. "We don't think DeMarco or his men have Ava."

"Who else would be after her? They need to stop her from testifying."

"We understand," Madison said, "but she was taken before the Amber Alert went out—the disappearance of the child with her was the reason for the alert."

"Then who has her?" Wyse asked.

"We're not sure, but we're certain that her disappearance is connected to the murder of a judge's wife this morning."

"Okay, but the alert still let DeMarco know she's alive."

"Exactly." Jonas nodded. "Which is why you were attacked and why someone was in her apartment. They're searching for her."

"And why we have to find her first," Wyse said.

Madison's phone rang, and she checked the caller ID.

"Do you need to take the call?" Jonas asked.

"Yeah, I'm sorry." Her jaw tensed as she looked up at him. "It's Edward."

THIRTEEN

Madison stepped out of the private room and started walking down the hallway, away from the noise of the ER. Heart racing, she took the call. Edward Langston was a retired police detective who worked on cold cases during his spare time, and he had agreed to look into Luke's unsolved murder.

"Edward?"

"Can you talk?" he replied.

"Yes. I've got a few minutes." She walked through a set of double doors, following signs to the chapel. "Did you find something?"

"I was going to email you, but this seemed easier." Edward paused. "It's about Thomas Knight."

She took a deep breath, eager to hear what he had found but equally nervous. Last month, Edward had found a connection to an arrest Madison made while still a police officer. Thomas Knight was already heading down a bad path when she'd arrested him after a convenience store robbery that had ended with murder. The DA added murder to the charges, and after a three-day jury trial he was given life in prison with no chance of parole. He was killed in prison not long after he arrived.

After that, Edward had hit another dead end. Which shouldn't have surprised her. The case had gone cold years ago. The reality was that she needed to come to peace with the fact that she might never know who killed Luke.

"As you know, I've been doing some digging," Edward said. "Trying to see if I can come up with a new lead, and I've been struggling to find something we missed. Someone who hasn't been on the radar up to this point."

Madison stepped into the small chapel, thankful it was empty, and sat down on a wooden bench in the back. She knew the problems he was facing because she'd faced the same roadblocks. There wasn't enough evidence to pin down a suspect, which had become both frustrating and discouraging. On top of that, someone had continued stalking and taunting her. But who? Both of Thomas Knight's parents had alibis for the time of Luke's murder. His father had been in prison, and his mother had been in and out of a psychiatric hospital that year. Even his sister had an alibi, as she was back East at the time, living with her aunt.

"Have you found someone?" she asked.

"Maybe. I started looking deeper into Thomas's girlfriend at the time of his arrest."

Madison leaned against the back of the bench. "Sabrina Rae."

"Yes. What do you know about her?" Edward asked.

"Not much. She didn't really play into the trial. I was told by the DA that they'd broken up a couple weeks before Thomas was arrested. She'd been questioned, but she wasn't in the picture anymore, and she had an alibi. She was studying at the library with her best friend."

"What if she lied about that?"

Madison stood up and walked to the stained-glass windows, her heart hammering inside her chest as she stared at the collage of colors. "What do you mean?"

"Did you ever hear speculation that there was someone else with Thomas the night of the robbery?"

"Yes, a getaway driver, but we were never able to identify the second person, and Thomas wouldn't give them up."

"That's what I'd read in the police reports, but I managed to dig up some evidence that Sabrina's best friend lied about her alibi."

Madison's lips tightened. Darkness had settled over the city, but even through the stained glass, she could see the lights from cars passing. Everyone seemed to be in a rush to go somewhere. Life continued around her no matter what was happening in her personal life. But she wasn't going to get her hopes up on another lead. She'd been through this too many times. Which had her questioning what Edward was doing. What if this was just another rabbit trail leading down another dead end? Maybe it was time to admit that they were never going to find whoever had killed Luke. Too much time had passed, and there wasn't enough evidence. Why did she think that would change?

Madison took a steadying breath. "What kind of evidence?"

"Cara Peterson was Sabrina's best friend back then, as well as her alibi for that night. The cops questioned both of them separately, and their stories matched up."

"How did you find this out?" she asked.

"I was down in Portland recently, visiting an old friend of mine. Cara lives in Portland and is the manager at a coffee shop."

"So you showed up and talked with her."

"She was one person on my list that I didn't know much about other than the fact that she was Sabrina's alibi. Turns out, she's been holding on to this lie for years, and it's been eating her up. She was reserved for the first couple minutes, but when I mentioned we'd tied Luke's death to Thomas's arrest, she fell apart."

"She lied about Sabrina's alibi?" she asked.

"Yes. She and Sabrina also lied about the fact that Sabrina and Thomas had broken up. According to my conversation with Cara, the two were planning to get married, though they were keeping it a secret. I think we might be able to go a step further and tie Sabrina to your husband's murder, because she definitely had motive."

The news hit her like a punch in the gut. If what he was saying was true . . .

Madison ran her finger across the dusty windowsill. "Can Cara testify that Sabrina was involved in the robbery?"

"No. All we know at this point is that she lied about her friend's alibi. She did it as a favor, after Sabrina swore to her she had nothing to do with the robbery."

"Then where was she?"

"She told Cara that she'd forgotten one of her books she needed to study," Edward said. "That's all Cara knew."

"So Sabrina needed an alibi."

"Exactly. She begged Cara to tell the police that she'd never left the library when they started asking questions. Cara believed her at the time, but now . . . now she's not sure."

Madison paced the length of the room, afraid to hope and yet desperate to believe this wasn't another dead end. "Thomas was trying to protect her."

"I think that's exactly what happened," Edward said. "He kept her from going to prison, and she went along with it. But I think she expected him to serve a few years then get out. According to Cara, Sabrina was still very much in love with Thomas at the time, and his arrest hit her hard."

Madison stopped pacing. "So she was looking for that happily ever after."

"Yes."

A chill swept through her. "If she blames me for his arrest, and ultimately Thomas's death . . ."

"It's just a theory, but it all adds up."

"What do you need from me?" she asked.

"Everything you have on Sabrina and her friends. I want to see if I can get another one of them to corroborate Cara's story. Then I'll feel like I'm finally on to something we can move forward with."

"I don't have much, but I know I have a transcript of her interview with the police. I'll see what else I have in my files and get them to you right away."

"Sounds good, and Madison . . . I hesitated calling you. This is a long shot, and I know probably upsetting for you, but if this leads us closer to the truth—"

"It's fine. Really," she interrupted him. "I just hope you know how much I appreciate what you're doing."

"Like Jonas told you, I'm sure, I have this thing for cold cases. And it keeps me busy. Retirement gave me too much time on my hands. This keeps me active and feeling like I'm still doing some good in the world."

Madison said goodbye, then disconnected the call, shoved her phone in her pocket, and headed back toward the ER.

Revenge ran deep. She'd experienced the results firsthand.

But it was also a reminder that she'd been right about one thing. Whoever had killed Luke wanted her to suffer. Which meant while Jonas might be back again, giving him her heart could prove to be a fatal mistake.

Jonas was on his cell outside Wyse's room when she got back. She slowed down at the sight of him, not missing the stir of her heart as she studied his familiar profile. Dark hair, cut short on the sides and slightly longer on the top. A hint of a beard across his jawline, broad shoulders . . . But it was the man inside that drew her to him. His inner strength and integrity. His hunger to fight for justice. And the way he looked at her.

She stopped in front of him as he finished his call.

His expression darkened. "Is everything okay?"

"Yeah." She nodded, but she was still trying to process what Edward had told her. "I'll fill you in later. Who was that?"

"Michaels. A message just came in on Becca Lambert's phone, but they can't read it."

"What do you mean?"

"I'm not sure. Michaels just said it was in some kind of code. He wants us to talk with Becca again in case it's somehow significant."

"Have they recovered any of the deleated text messages?"

Jonas shook his head. "Not yet."

Madison glanced back at Wyse's room as they headed for the exit. "What about Wyse?"

"They've decided to keep him a couple more hours for observation, but I think we have all we need from him."

"Is he doing okay?" she asked.

"I think he'll be fine. They just want to make sure the drug is out of his system and there are no complications."

"Sounds good." She smiled weakly. "Let's head out."

***

Evening rush hour was easing slightly by the time they got back to the marshals' office where Becca was still being held.

She jumped up from the chair when they walked into the interview room, nearly knocking it over. "Have you found Easton?"

"No, I'm sorry, but a message came in for you on your phone." Madison set the phone on the table in front of Becca. "We need you to translate it. It's in some kind of code."

Becca frowned as she stared at the screen. "It looks like part of the text didn't get through, but it's from Ava."

"You're sure?" Madison asked.

"Positive. She was always doodling and writing out her thoughts in her own personal code." Becca glanced back at the text. "Though . . . the number isn't hers."

"She could have borrowed a phone," Jonas said, "though no one answered when we tried to call the number."

"Maybe, but I know she had a couple burner phones. I found one in Easton's diaper bag one day. Couldn't figure out where it came from until I asked her. She told me it was hers, just in case, and shrugged it off like it was no big deal."

Becca picked up the phone and studied the text. "Besides doodling, she had lots of odd habits, like always checking the locks two or three times, never taking the same route home, never answering calls unless she knew the person. She always shrugged it off and told me it was her OCD, and that I should just ignore it. But she also liked to write everything down. It was her way of thinking through a problem. She'd either scribble a bunch of notes—usually coded—or make sketches."

Madison glanced at the phone, knowing that Ava's actions

had nothing to do with OCD. The coded messages, burner phones, and paranoid behavior all pointed to the fact that Ava had clearly been terrified of being found.

"What about the message?" Jonas asked.

"I'll need your pen and paper."

Jonas slid the requested items across the table.

"It's just a basic algorithm," Becca said, starting to write below the message. "But the cipher rotates, depending on the day of the week."

Jonas glanced at Madison. "Doesn't sound that basic to me."

"Like I said, she told me she did it for fun, even though I was convinced she was paranoid about something."

"Like she wanted a way to send you a coded message if the occasion ever arose?" Madison asked.

"I don't know. I never thought about it that way, but yeah. That would make sense." Becca studied the message and started scribbling something down the side of the paper. "She must be where cell reception is bad, because parts of the message are gone."

"Can you read any of it?" Madison asked.

Becca scribbled a few more words. "It says . . . *E is fine.*" She pressed her hand against her mouth before looking up. "E is fine!"

"Easton?" Jonas asked.

Becca nodded, tears filling her eyes. "Then it says, *Trying to get . . . King Street . . . nine . . .* I don't know. It doesn't make sense. There are too many words missing." Becca sucked in a deep breath, her hand trembling as she pushed the paper back toward the marshals. "If Easton is okay, Ava must be as well, but for how long?" The fear in her eyes was back. "Someone was after her, weren't they?"

"Yes." Madison glanced at Jonas. "Ava was in the witness protection program."

"Wait a minute . . . so . . ." Color drained from Becca's face as her eyes welled up with fresh tears. "So when the Amber Alert went out, they found her, which means this is all my fault. And if her life is in danger, then Easton's life is in danger."

Madison's voice softened. "I know you're worried and scared, but you need to trust that we're doing everything that we can to find them."

Becca shook her head. "And if they—whoever's after her—find her and Easton before you do?"

Jonas pushed back his chair. "We're going to make sure that doesn't happen."

Madison walked out of the interview room with Jonas, praying he hadn't just made a promise he couldn't keep. The message Becca had encoded was vague, and without a real lead, it was as if they were on nothing more than a wild-goose chase. But Becca had been right about one thing. They had to find Ava and Easton before DeMarco's men did.

"Assuming Ava did escape from whoever grabbed her this morning," Madison said, holding up the paper Becca had scribbled on, "I'm still not sure we have enough to go on."

"Maybe we do." Jonas looked at his watch, then signaled at Piper, who had been waiting in the observation room. "Find out what buses and trains are arriving at the King Street Station in the next hour."

"That's reading a lot into the message," Madison said as Piper started a search on her laptop.

"Then let's pray that we're right," Jonas said.

"I've got it." Piper grabbed her phone off her desk. "There

aren't any trains scheduled in the next hour, but there is a bus arriving from Tacoma at nine. I'm texting you the details now."

Madison thanked her, then grabbed her coat as they headed back outside. "If Ava's in trouble, why didn't she just call the police?"

"Your guess is as good as mine," Jonas said, following her onto the elevator. "But if her WITSEC handler couldn't keep her safe, I'm not surprised she doesn't trust anyone."

Worry threaded its way through Madison. "At some point, she's going to have to trust someone."

FOURTEEN

King Street Station was an iconic building that served as a transit hub in downtown Seattle. The last time Jonas had been inside the three-story brick building, with its looming clock tower and Italian-inspired elements, he was seven, but he still remembered how impressed he'd been with the grandness of the station.

He and Madison stepped inside the large waiting room that had since been restored with high-back wooden benches, bronze chandeliers hanging from ornate vaulted ceilings, and inlaid mosaic tiles.

"I remember this place as being impressive when I was here as a kid, but the restoration they did is pretty remarkable."

"It's like we stepped into a European train station," Madison said. "I always wanted to travel across Europe by train. Though now I wouldn't mind just a weekend up to, say, Vancouver for a bit of R & R."

"Especially after this day."

The station was quiet with most of the passengers already departed for the day. An announcement sounded above them, echoing off the walls of the old station.

"Looks like the 9:03 bus is going to be late," Madison said, looking up at the schedule. "Though there's no way to know how Ava's arriving."

She was right. Everything they interpreted from Ava's text message had actually been nothing more than an educated guess. The clues they'd received had been too sketchy, and there was no way to know if she was arriving by train, taxi, or on foot, because they had no idea where she was coming from.

But having Becca meet her at the city's train station did make sense. It was easy to get to no matter what mode of transportation you wanted to take, and on top of that, it was a public space. With the King Street Station acting as a major transportation hub for the city, if for whatever reason Ava felt uncomfortable, it would be the perfect place for her to disappear.

There was one thing Jonas did know for certain though—Ava was scared. From her message, they were assuming that she'd gotten away from whoever had taken her, though why she'd gone with her abductor without a fight was still unclear. She did have Easton to protect, and maybe that had been her motivation. But she was alone and on the run with probably little idea of everything going on. It was possible she'd seen her own face on the news in connection with the Amber Alert before it had been taken down. Either way, she had to be scared. She'd been looking over her shoulder for months, and now her worst nightmare had just come true in being found, leaving her vulnerable and exposed.

To Jonas's left, a man sat on one of the benches, talking too loudly on the phone. A couple carrying backpacks headed toward the line at the ticket counter. There were a few dozen more passengers scattered throughout the waiting room, most of them on their phones. A few were reading books or sleeping. But there was still no sign of Ava and the baby.

While Madison had been on the phone, Wyse had shared with Jonas Ava's struggle to trust, which was probably the reason behind her contacting Becca instead of 911. And Wyse had been worried about something else. Ava had trusted him to keep her safe, and yet DeMarco's guys found her. Despite mistakes that had been made, that never should have happened. What Ava didn't know was what had happened to Becca.

Jonas's shoes clicked against the tiled floor as he searched the passengers scattered throughout the station. Wyse had given them a better photo of Ava than the candid snapshot from her work they'd used for the Amber Alert, though a woman traveling with a baby was going to stand out and narrow it down for them.

It would also make it harder for her to disappear and stay safe knowing DeMarco's men were after her.

An infant started crying behind him, and Jonas turned around. A man was patting a baby on his shoulder while pacing, trying to calm the infant down while a woman rummaged through a diaper bag.

Jonas let out the breath he didn't even know he'd been holding. They were a few minutes early. If they'd interpreted the message correctly, she'd be here soon, but until then all they could do was pray.

Madison approached him from the direction where she'd been checking out the restrooms.

"Anything?" he asked.

"No. Nothing so far. But I . . ." She left the rest of her sentence hanging as she stared across the large space another second, then walked forward a few steps and stopped. Something had caught her attention near the entrance.

"You okay?" he asked.

"Yeah . . . I . . . sorry." She shook her head and turned back to him. "I just thought I saw someone. It's nothing."

He gauged her expression. She seemed jumpy and on edge, like something had shifted her focus, which wasn't like her. From the first time they met five years ago at a shoot house training he'd taught, he'd been impressed with her laser sharp focus in everything she did. She was fast, smart, and had this ability to problem solve, even when they hit a wall. His gut told him her distracted nature had something to do with her conversation with Edward, but she still hadn't opened up about what he'd said. Which was fine. She would when she was ready, and he wasn't going to push her. But he was concerned.

On the other hand, they'd both been shot at today, which was always unsettling, even for people with all their experience. She had saved his life. And she knew what it was like to lose someone she loved. Maybe that had been the trigger that left her on edge tonight.

Another announcement came over the loudspeaker for the bus they were waiting for. They headed to the stop, arriving before passengers began to debark.

"Why don't you take the back exit and I'll go in the front," Jonas said. "If she's on this bus, we'll find her."

Jonas held up his badge for the bus driver a moment later, then boarded the vehicle. "I need to do a search. I'm looking for a woman traveling with a baby."

"Oh, we've always got one of those," the driver said, motioning Jonas in with her hand.

"Have you seen her?" Jonas asked, holding up the photo of Ava.

The woman stared for a few seconds at the photo, then shook her head. "Sorry. I don't recognize her, but I'm lucky if I can remember my own name by the time I get home at night. There are always at least one or two babies on every ride. I usually just hope they're quiet."

He stepped aside and let passengers pass by while he searched faces, but there was no sign of Ava and the baby. Toward the back of the bus, a woman was getting a couple bags down from the rack above her seat. A baby cried below her, but he couldn't see the woman's face.

Jonas headed down the narrow aisle, passing a few straggling passengers who were still gathering their things. "Ava?"

The woman turned around and looked at him, eyes questioning. "I'm sorry. You must have the wrong person."

He took note of the woman's dark hair and eyes. Definitely not Ava. "You're right—wrong person. Sorry about that." He glanced down at the baby, who was now cooing in the car seat, and smiled. "Can I give you a hand?" He helped her get the bags down, then turned back toward the side exit where Madison was waiting for him.

"She's not on the bus," he said, stepping onto the pavement.

"She didn't get off back here either."

"Maybe we had it wrong." He scanned the dispersing crowd as they headed through the waiting room, but there was no sign of Ava anywhere. "Becca could have easily deciphered the message wrong."

All they really knew was that Ava was trying to get somewhere, but where?

King Street . . . nine . . .

What if she wasn't in Seattle? What if it was an address, like 9 King Street, or what if it meant something entirely different? They needed more, because, while their theory had been plausible, they'd been wrong. Which meant they were now back to square one with no leads, unless they could come up with something else or their tech team could decipher the rest of Ava's message.

Outside, the wind had picked up and the temperature had dropped a few degrees. Jonas and Madison walked toward the car, crossing through Jackson Plaza. With its large planters and cherry blossom trees, the plaza was a welcome oasis of nature in the center of the city.

"I don't know if there's anything else we can do tonight," Jonas said, shoving his hands into his pockets. "Security here at the station have all been notified and are watching for her as well as local PD across the city and state. Facial recognition is still being run on the man who took her, and we can . . ."

He turned around, realizing Madison wasn't beside him anymore. She had stopped to watch a little boy whose helium balloon had escaped his grip and now floated above him out of reach.

"The trajectory . . ." she said, as the boy started crying. She turned to Jonas. "The trajectory was off."

Jonas walked up to her. "What do you mean?"

She zipped up her coat, then walked over to sit on one of the benches surrounding a large planter. Jonas sat down next to her, waiting for her to continue.

"Something's been bothering me since we were at Ava's apartment," she said, watching the balloon drift into the night sky, "but I haven't been able to figure it out until now."

"Okay . . ." he said, urging her to continue.

"What if there was a second shooter?" she said, turning to him.

"I'm not sure I understand."

"I know CSU is still processing the evidence, but we all assumed that the shot outside the apartment complex was also from the intruder in Ava's place."

"True," Jonas said.

"If that were true, the trajectory wasn't right. He was farther to our left when we found him again."

"It could have been his partner, whoever was driving the car that picked him up."

Madison shook her head. "I don't think so. A witness said he drove up but never got out of the car." She looked up and caught his gaze. "I know I'm sounding paranoid, but tonight isn't the first time I've felt that someone was watching me."

He nodded. "Inside the train station. You thought someone was following you."

She rubbed her temples with her fingertips. "Maybe I'm just imagining things."

"Maybe, maybe not," he said, resting his forearms on his legs. "How long has this been going on?"

"A few weeks."

"Why didn't you tell me?"

"I thought I was being paranoid."

A stab of guilt pierced him. He'd been gone. "You've gone through enough to know you're not just paranoid, Madison."

"Then what if there were two shooters? What if the second shooter wasn't there because of Ava? What if they were there because of me?"

Jonas worked through her theory. They would have CSU double-check the trajectory of the bullet that had slammed into the brick wall of the apartment building and determine if her theory had any validity. If it did, things just got a whole lot more complicated. Because they couldn't forget why they were here.

Ava was out there in critical danger because of a mistake they'd made. And all they had were a bunch of dead ends. They had no idea where she and Easton were. No way to confirm who had them. The motivation for finding a fugitive was mixed with the urgent need to make sure no one else was hurt and that the perpetrators were where they deserved to be—behind bars. But searching for someone who was both missing and endangered put an even deeper sense of urgency to finding them. Just like searching for someone who wanted Madison—or maybe both of them—dead.

"What can I do to help?" Jonas asked.

"Honestly, I'm not sure." She shifted in her seat. "I'm worried about Ava and the baby. But I also can't put your life at risk."

He knew what she was thinking. Unexpected loss ran deep, and Madison had experienced her own loss. Healing had come slowly, but without closure, he knew the struggle of putting Luke's death behind her was hard. She wasn't prepared to lose someone else, but sometimes watching her struggle seemed almost as difficult.

But competing with her dead husband wasn't something he was willing to do either. He'd promised he'd wait, convinced the day would come when she'd be able to let Luke go and let him in completely. But some days it felt like a losing battle, and he wasn't convinced that day would ever come.

What he did know, though, was that every day he'd been in training, he'd missed her. She'd made him willing to risk his heart again, something he'd believed wasn't possible. And he wasn't willing to give up on her.

He glanced at his watch. "How about I pick up a late dinner and then take you home? We both need to eat, and I have a feeling it's going to be a short night."

She stood up, ready to go. "I appreciate the offer. I really do, but I think I'll just grab something at home and try to get a few hours of sleep. You understand, don't you?"

"Of course." He forced a smile to mask his disappointment.

Silence enveloped them on the way home. She was pushing him away again. He could see it in her eyes. The pulling back and protecting her heart so she didn't get hurt. So neither of them got hurt. Maybe it was time to acknowledge the fact that at some point, he might have to let her go.

FIFTEEN

Madison bit back her frustration as she shut the front door of her house behind her and locked it. She'd seen the confusion in Jonas's eyes as she'd pushed him away once again. She hadn't intended to, and yet somehow, she'd allowed a day she'd planned to welcome him home end with her putting distance between them. She knew he'd wanted to talk to her about what was going on in her head, but she couldn't go there. Not after everything that had happened today. How could she even begin to explain to him what she couldn't even understand herself?

She started for the kitchen, then hesitated. She'd planned to shop for groceries today, but she hadn't had the chance and was too tired to figure something out. Anything frozen or microwavable didn't sound good either. Maybe she should have taken Jonas up on his offer to pick up something for them. Today had worn on her, but it was more than just her job.

It was also Jonas and the inevitable conversation they'd been needing to have that was gnawing at her. His SOG training had given her an excuse not to give an answer right away about how she felt toward him. He'd promised her as much time as she needed to explore her feelings, but she hadn't been able to make him any promises in return. Even now, her heart was torn. With Luke's killer and her attacker still on the loose, it would be dangerous for him to be with her. She'd already lost one person she loved—she wasn't going to risk losing him too.

But what if I never find closure?

That was a question she still didn't have an answer to.

She headed to her bedroom to change. Up until today, she'd always been able to compartmentalize her work and her personal life—at least for the most part. Luke's death had shaken her, but it had also made her more determined to continue doing what she did—making the world a better place by ensuring evil was pulled off the streets. Not being able to bring justice to a situation—like with what happened today, or with Luke's murder—wasn't acceptable.

She quickly changed into a pair of sweats and a T-shirt, pausing only to run her hand across her stomach where the bullet had struck her a few months back. Then she stopped in the bathroom to replace the bandage on her hand. She knew fear was behind her pushing Jonas away, but her fears weren't based on simple speculation or the unknown. Luke had died. She'd been shot. Her family threatened. Keeping those she loved safe was more important than giving in to her heart. Didn't that in itself prove how much she loved him?

Leaving her bedroom door ajar, she headed to the extra room she'd converted into an office and stopped in front of the eight-by-four-foot bulletin board mounted to the wall. On it she'd posted evidence from Luke's murder. She had it all memorized. The time lines and photos. Police interviews. Names of patients who might have held a grudge against Luke.

There were copies of interviews and additional files in her rolltop desk.

She'd spent five years combing through the evidence. The police had ended up with no suspects and no witnesses. Just a random shooting in a parking garage. But she knew it wasn't random. She'd been targeted.

Both Jonas and Danielle had continued to remind her that Luke's death wasn't her fault. But even if they were right, this wasn't simply an obsession to find the truth. She was being toyed with, and she wasn't going to let anyone else get hurt in the process. Which meant she had to find a way to discover the truth.

She pulled a photo of Sabrina Rae off the board. The girl had been only eighteen when the photo was taken. She was smiling innocently at the camera for the picture, but if Edward was right, she was far from innocent. But had Sabrina fired the weapon that had killed Luke? Had Sabrina been the one who shot Madison in her house?

She dropped the photo onto her desk, then pulled back the chair. The fact that someone had been in her home had unnerved her. That they'd left a rose on Luke's grave every year—black roses that were used as a symbol of death and placed at the graves of their victims. Then they'd left another one beside her while she bled out on the floor of her kitchen.

Maybe she had become obsessed, but there was no way not to make this situation personal. Healing was hard to find when there were so many reminders of the pain around you. Each time she encountered one, it was like ripping off the healing scab that had started to form. And that was another thing that had held her back from moving forward with Jonas.

She pulled open one of the folders on her desk and flipped

through until she found the file on Sabrina. A gamer like Thomas, she'd managed to stay in school—unlike Thomas who had dropped out his senior year. She'd gone on to college, eventually graduating with a degree in interior design.

Had she been involved in the string of armed robberies like Edward believed, as well as Luke's death?

Madison closed her eyes, trying to bring to the surface the repressed memories of the day she'd been shot. Her pulse raced. If Edward was right . . .

She forced herself back to that moment, four months ago, in her kitchen. She needed to be there again. Needed to see who was holding the gun that had shot her. Someone had been taunting her ever since Luke's death, playing a sick game of cat and mouse and somehow managing to leave no evidence behind. If Jonas hadn't come after her, she would have died.

Nothing.

It shouldn't surprise her. Her psychologist had assured her that everything she was going through was a normal part of the healing process. Four months later, she could still feel the panic of that moment she'd faced off with her shooter. But the actual memories refused to surface.

She started looking through the photos she'd collected, willing them to somehow jog her memory. Her phone beeped, and she grabbed it off the desk. There was a text message. No name, just a phone number.

Purple's really not your color.

An icy shiver ran through her as Madison looked down at the purple T-shirt she'd just put on, then shifted her gaze to the window. The curtains were shut. She'd shed her coat at the door, then changed into comfier clothes. It had to be a coincidence. Someone's idea of a sick joke. Madison blew out a sharp breath before replying.

Who is this?

Doesn't matter and don't bother looking. You're not going to find me.

Her stomach clenched. It was Luke's murderer. She knew it. This wasn't the first time she'd been taunted, but how had they managed to outsmart her all this time?

Madison called the number, but it went straight to voice mail. She hung up the call without leaving a message, then sent another text.

Enough of the games. Who are you?

Im surprised you still don't remember. I was in your house. In your bedroom. In your kitchen. We spoke face-to-face.

And then the woman had shot her.

A memory flashed. Madison fought to hold on to it. She needed to see her face. Madison closed her eyes. She could see a blurred silhouette. A short, thin figure, with a ponytail falling over her shoulder as she held a gun on Madison. She picked up the photo of Sabrina. There was something familiar about her eyes. The woman she'd seen at the train station had been heavier and her long hair had been darker. But the resemblance was definitely there. Was she just seeing what she wanted to see, or was Sabrina the one who'd been taunting her?

Her phone dinged and a photo came through from the unknown number. It was her and Jonas at the King Street

Station. Panic pressed against her chest. Her stalker had been there.

Madison looked around the office. Nothing seemed out of place. Nothing seemed to be disturbed, but she'd been spied on. Stalked. And right now, it was as if the stalker was in the room.

Another text came through.

> I warned you once to consider your next move. Told you that I have more reach than you think and know what would hurt you most. Your sister. Jonas.

Madison squeezed her eyes shut, praying for the long-buried memories to finish surfacing.

"What is going to happen?" Madison had asked the intruder standing in front of her in her kitchen as she tried to plan out her next move.

"We'll talk a few more minutes, then I'm going to shoot you."

A piece of the puzzle clicked into place.

"Like you did to my husband?" she asked.

"Would you like me to say I did? It would make you feel better, wouldn't it? Finally finding the person who shot him. The person who was there when he said his last words. And who watched him take his last breath. So many unanswered questions. It drives you crazy, doesn't it?"

Madison pushed back the emotions. She needed to keep her talking. Needed to find a way to disarm the woman. She could rush her. Try to take the gun away from her. But she was still standing too far away.

Madison took a step forward. "Why did you kill him?"

The gun had leveled. "I wouldn't take another step if I were you. As for your husband . . . it's complicated."

"Then why are you here? What do you want?"

"To know why you never found me. I'd like to think I was that good, but you're a marshal. It's what you do day after day and yet you couldn't find me. You weren't even up to the challenge."

Madison opened her eyes. She could see her clearly now. Almost as if the woman were standing in front of her. Memories suppressed for so long rushed to the surface. She remembered it all. The woman's face. Her long hair pulled back into a ponytail. Jeans and a long-sleeve T-shirt. And the last thing she remembered her saying.

"I wanted you to suffer like I did when I lost Thomas."

Madison sucked in a sharp breath. She knew who it was. Edward had been right. Sabrina Rae had killed her husband.

Nausea swept through her. More memories flooded her mind. She'd lunged forward to stop the woman, but instead had felt the impact of the bullet followed by numbing, then a burning sensation as she fell to the ground. Her head had hit hard against the tile. She'd tried to scream, but nothing came out. Tried to move, but she couldn't. A wet sensation bubbled around her midsection where she'd felt the burning of a bullet rip through her.

Now she knew.

Her husband's killer was Thomas Knight's girlfriend. The same woman who had shot her. The same woman who was somehow watching her. She tried to slow her breathing, but her pulse still raced. Sabrina blamed her for her boyfriend's arrest and subsequent death.

Madison looked toward the door of her office. She had to have been here, in her house. Watching her.

The break-in.

Just over a month ago, someone had broken into Madison's

house. The police had assumed that it was connected to a rash of robberies in the neighborhood, but they'd been wrong.

A knock on the front door yanked her back to the present.

She reached automatically for her gun on the desk, then headed for the front door. She wasn't going to be caught off guard. Not this time. Not ever again as far as she was concerned. Not when there was someone out there who wanted her dead.

She glanced through the peephole a moment later, then pulled open the door. "Jonas?"

"Hey . . . I'm sorry." He held up a bag of takeout. "I know it's late and I'm intruding, but I knew there was probably nothing decent in your fridge and you'd end up eating a bowl of cereal. And besides that, I could tell . . ." He hesitated. "Madison . . . are you okay? You look as if you've seen a ghost."

Her jaw tensed as she let him in without answering. She locked the door behind her before motioning him to be quiet. How did he always seem to know when she needed him? Gut instinct or whatever it was, she didn't care. She needed him and he was here. She grabbed his hand and pulled him down the hall with her, into the bathroom.

She shut the door, turned on the sink, then let the shower run full blast before sitting down on the edge of the tub. He sat down across from her on the toilet seat, clearly confused. She closed her eyes and drew in a deep breath, almost wishing she could forget the memories she'd tried for so long to remember. "You always seem to know just when to show up."

"What do you mean?" His voice matched her whisper.

"There are several things that happened since you dropped me off, but right now, all you need to know is that I remember everything. It was Thomas Knight's girlfriend, Sabrina. She shot me."

"Wait a minute . . . Are you sure?"

She took in a deep breath and stared at the running water. "I received some text messages on my phone a few minutes ago. They're from her. She was at the apartment building and the train station tonight."

He leaned forward to grab her hands and squeezed them. "Slow down. What kind of messages?"

She hesitated, then pulled out her phone and showed him the texts.

"She's watching me. Following me somehow. She knew the color of the shirt I changed into."

Jonas read them, then switched off the phone and pulled out the battery. "We need to get you out of here until we can sweep the house for bugs and figure out how she's tracking you."

"And the break-in," Madison said. "It was her."

Jonas nodded. "Until we find out how and where, you need to be careful. On top of bugging your house, she could be tracking your phone, your car—"

"She also knows who I'm close to. And how to hurt me." Madison swallowed hard. She wasn't used to this kind of fear. The kind of fear that bubbles up inside and threatens to swallow you whole. "She's made it clear that she wants to hurt you . . . my sister . . ."

"I'm going to call Tucker," Jonas said. "He's worked intelligence. He'll have resources to make sure we find all the bugs in the house."

She nodded.

"We also need to get you somewhere safe. Maybe even to a safe house."

She turned away, avoiding his gaze. He was right—she knew that. She couldn't put his life at risk anymore. If anything did happen to him, or her family, she'd never forgive herself. At least identifying the suspect would change that. But no matter how hard she tried, while her heart kept telling her to let go and let him in, her head kept making excuses and telling her to run.

SIXTEEN

Jonas drove around until he was certain they weren't being followed, while Madison called Michaels and told him what was going on. Thirty minutes after they left Madison's home, he pulled into the parking lot of a little restaurant he hadn't been to for years.

"Do you think you can eat?" he asked.

"I'm not sure."

"Come on. I left our takeout in your fridge, but trust me, this is even better," Jonas said, switching off the engine. "It's Thai food, open late, with some of the best noodles and fried crab wontons in the city."

She cracked a slight smile. "Well, if it has the best noodles in the city, I might be able to eat a few bites."

They slipped inside with his hand protectively against the small of her back, while his mind worked through a plan. He was sure they hadn't been followed, but he still didn't feel completely safe with Madison out in the open. Especially when things were happening so fast. His gut told him that some of this had something to do with the reason Edward had called, but she'd yet to divulge the details of their conversation.

Jonas sat down across from her, with a clear line of sight to the door of the small restaurant, glad there were only a couple tables filled.

He cleared his throat. How to start?

"I can only imagine how it feels to have a flood of memories return after not being able to remember for so long."

She pressed her fingertips against her temples. "It's funny. All I've wanted was to remember, but now that I can see her face . . . I almost want to erase the image so I don't have to see her anymore."

Jonas took her hands and squeezed them. "Except now you know who she is. And now that we know who she is, we'll be able to find her. There's already a BOLO out across the city and state. This is going to be over soon."

"I hope so, but what I don't understand is that my choices didn't lead to Thomas ending up in prison. I had nothing to do with his death. Why blame me?"

"I'm no expert, but it makes sense that blaming you gives her reason to seek revenge for what she perceived to have been mistreatment by you. It doesn't make sense to us, but she's definitely feeling paranoid or maybe even persecuted. She's out of control of the situation. And when people feel that way, they often grasp for something, anything, to help put them back in the control seat."

Madison nodded, but from her almost blank expression, he could tell she was still in shock over what had happened.

"I sent Tucker a message. He'll meet us here," Jonas said. "Do you want me to order for you?"

She nodded without saying anything.

He ordered her fried rice with chicken along with his favorite curry and rice with fried wontons and extra dipping sauce. There was something about ordering for her and knowing what she liked that made him smile and reminded him of the friendship that had been growing between them over the past few months. His gaze settled on her lips, but he pushed back the desire to make this about them. She was hurting and even scared. His feelings would have to wait.

"I know what you're thinking," she said as the server left their table. "You're going to try to convince me that it wasn't my fault, that there's nothing I can do to change the past, and I know that. But in my heart . . . I don't know how to let go. I don't know how to forget that Luke shouldn't have died. My actions put his life at risk, and now it puts my family's life at risk along with everyone I love. Including you."

Jonas cracked a smile. "So you do love me."

A blush swept across her cheeks. "That's not the point."

"I know. But seriously, the reality is that it wasn't your actions that killed him. It was the choice of someone else. That's what your sister has told you as well."

"I know."

He reached out and grabbed her hand again. "I'll never pretend I understand what you've gone through, and I'm not trying to dismiss how you feel. But what I do know is that at some point you're going to have to stop blaming yourself for what happened. We're going to find out the truth."

"I know." But doubt remained in her eyes.

"Can you catch me up with everything that's going on?" he asked.

"I'm not sure I know where to start." She let go of his hand and took a sip of her water. "There are a couple things that happened while you were gone. A few months ago, a dive team was searching for a missing person in Lake Washington. In the process, they found a weapon.

"The ballistics report just came back last week," she continued, "and while they weren't able to pull fingerprints from the weapon, they were able to complete the report and tie the weapon to both murders. The man Thomas shot at the convenience store and Luke."

"Wow. So between the gaming ring found at the scene of the crime, believed to belong to Thomas," Jonas said, "and the ballistics report matching the gun to the bullet, you now have the positive connection to Luke's murder you've been looking for."

"Exactly," Madison said. "It confirms the theory that Luke wasn't the target, but instead, his killer—who we now believe to be Sabrina Rae—wanted to hurt me."

"The same way she'd been hurt."

Madison nodded.

Jonas studied her expression. The emotion lacing her words was gone now, as if once again she'd managed to fortify the wall around her heart. She updated him on the case as if she were simply an uninvolved third party, retelling something she'd seen on the evening news. Navigating through healing was often a tangled mess. He knew that firsthand.

"What about the owner of the gun?" he asked. "Were they able to identify them?"

"No. It had been reported stolen from a gun store about six years ago, so there is no legal owner."

"Anything else?" Jonas asked.

Madison nodded. "It's looking more and more like Sabrina drove the getaway car during the robberies. And while we can only theorize at this point, when they crashed, Thomas must have insisted she take the gun and run."

"That would explain the missing weapon," Jonas said. "And how she had the gun that later killed Luke."

"Exactly. What I don't understand is why she would keep it for all of these years. Why not just dump it?"

Jonas searched for an explanation. "Maybe she didn't know where to dump it without it being found. Remember, she was scared and vulnerable."

"I don't know, but I need to call Edward and update him. He needs to know what is going on . . ." She reached for her bag, then stopped. "I can't use my phone." Her chest heaved. The emotion that she'd tried to hide was back.

He hated watching her struggle to find her way out of this. "Slow down, Madison. You don't have to do this by yourself. You've got your family, I'm here, and so are Michaels and Edward. We're going to figure out the truth. I promise. Besides"—he caught her gaze and held it—"we're Deputy US Marshals. It's kind of in our job descriptions to find people."

He waited for a smile, but it didn't come.

Instead, she leaned against the back of the seat and frowned. "Which is my point. I've been searching for Luke's murderer for over five years and haven't been able to find her. And now, until she's behind bars . . ."

"This is almost over," he said, praying his promise was true.

The front door of the restaurant opened, and Tucker Shaw stepped out of the cold. Jonas waved his hand at his friend, then glanced back at Madison. They'd continue their conversation later, but for now, it was time to see what Tucker would come up with so they could keep her safe.

"Thanks for meeting us," Jonas said as his friend took the chair across from him.

"Of course." Tucker took off his ball cap and laid it on the table. "Glad to help."

"Are you hungry?" Madison said as their server set their dishes in front of them.

"Thanks, but I've already eaten. Go ahead. Please."

"What did Jonas tell you?" Madison asked, pushing her fried rice around with her fork without taking a bite.

"Just that there was a break-in at your house a month ago, and you believe the real motivation was to bug your place."

She nodded. "Local PD did come in and sweep for bugs after the break-in, just as a precaution, but they didn't find anything."

"I'm not completely surprised," Tucker said. "Before my job with the US Marshals, I worked in army intelligence, and unfortunately there's not one device that will pick up on everything."

"So, what do we do?" Jonas asked, before dipping his wonton into the sauce and taking a bite.

"We'll need to check for spyware on your devices, but we'll look at your house as well. There could be hidden cameras or mics that were planted. The good ones will have things built in to mask themselves from scanners. On top of that, from what Jonas said, it's possible there are also GPS-tracking bugs on your clothes, your bags, or even your car."

Madison set her fork down and sat back. "I'm going to be honest, this has rattled me, but now I know how she's always been two steps ahead. The thought of knowing she's been listening in and following me . . ."

“I’ve already called Michaels,” Jonas said. “He’s putting patrol cars at both your house and your sister’s.”

Madison started to say something, then hesitated. “My first reaction is to say that I can handle this, but thank you.”

Jonas nodded as Tucker turned to Madison. “What do you know about this woman, Sabrina?”

“Not much, really. She went to college, got a job here in Seattle. I’ve got someone back at the office pulling up everything she can, but it looks like she has a brother who works for a tech company.”

“That connection could explain how she was able to plant a bug that law enforcement couldn’t find,” Jonas said.

“Exactly.” Tucker nodded. “She’s definitely got some kind of connection, but if they’re there, I’ll find them.”

***

Madison hesitated, then stepped briskly across the threshold of her house. Knowing she’d been listened to and watched made her feel violated. But it also made her understand how Sabrina had managed to track her. She was done with the games. Now the tables were turned. Now Sabrina would be the one watched.

“So, what do we do first?” Madison asked.

“Turn off every wireless device in your house,” Tucker said, stopping in the middle of the living room. “Laptops, smartphones, routers . . . everything. A bug needs not only a power source, but a way to deliver the data, which means a hot spot. I’ll also check all the networks and scan for transmitters. Anything that is broadcasting a radio signal should pop up.”

He turned to Jonas and handed him one of the scanners he’d brought. “If you’ll do an initial sweep of the other rooms with this, it should detect frequencies from things like wireless cameras and voice recorders. I'll come behind you in a few minutes with one that searches with infrared lights."

It shouldn't make her feel so nervous. Madison went through the mental list of her devices from her laptop to her phone to her eReader, and started putting the items on the coffee table, trying to distract her mind.

"Once you find these bugs, will it be possible to trace them back to her?" she asked.

"I'm going to try."

She stood in the middle of the room watching Tucker work. He was precise and thorough in what he was doing as he went through each of her devices. No doubt Sabrina was still listening, but at this point, Madison didn't care. Let her know that they were onto her and that her house of cards was about to crash. Michaels had sent out a citywide BOLO to law enforcement to pick her up as a person of interest, but until they found her, Madison knew she wouldn't feel safe. Which irritated her further. She was ready to be the one on the offense. Needing something to do, she decided to put on a pot of coffee.

Tucker held up his hand as she walked back into the living room a few minutes later with a tray of coffee and some cookies she'd found in the cupboard. He was holding two tiny electronic bugs in the palm of his hand.

"Is that all of them?" Madison asked, setting the tray down on the fireplace hearth.

"Unfortunately not," Jonas said, walking into the room. "I found two more. One in the office and one in your bedroom."

"Your electronics are clean," Tucker said, "but I need to do the second sweep on the rest of the house."

"I can't believe she was able to listen to everything in this house."

Jonas went with Tucker to do another sweep, while she waited in the living room.

"And you're sure that's all of them?" she asked when they returned, her untouched coffee now cold.

"I'm ninety-nine percent sure," Tucker said, "though I'm going to borrow one more device and do a final sweep tomorrow as an extra precaution. The bugs we found have been deactivated, but I'll take them in to be filed as evidence."

Madison nodded. "Thank you. Both of you. I really appreciate it."

"Especially your help, Tucker," Jonas said.

"Not a problem," he said, heading toward the door. "I'll see you both tomorrow at the office."

Jonas turned around as soon as Tucker was gone. "I'm staying tonight. I can take the couch—"

"You don't have to stay, Jonas. There are already two officers outside my house."

He shook his head. "I almost lost you once. I won't lose you again."

She tilted her head and smiled at him. "You really need to stop worrying about me. I'm a Deputy US Marshal, in case you forgot. As someone smart once said to me, it's kind of in our job descriptions to catch the bad guy."

"Yes, and I intend to ensure this one gets caught."

Madison's stomach fluttered as her gaze traced Jonas's lips. He wasn't going to wait for her forever. And now that they'd identified Luke's killer, maybe it was time for her to take a step forward.

"Thank you," she said. "Really."

"Go get a good night's sleep. This is almost behind us."

Fifteen minutes later, she felt her body relax as she stretched in her bed and closed her eyes. They still had no idea where Ava and the baby were, or where Sabrina Rae was, but for the first time in as long as she could remember, her sleep was dreamless.

***

Jonas's phone went off at seven, pulling him out of a deep sleep. He grabbed his phone off the coffee table, sitting up as he did. It took him a couple seconds to recognize the stone fireplace and remember where he was.

"Hey, boss," he answered.

"I tried calling Madison but couldn't get through." Michaels's voice sounded worried.

"I'm at her house. Slept on her couch last night. I removed the battery from her phone, and we won't install it again until we're a hundred percent certain it's clean."

"Good call."

"What's going on?" Jonas asked.

"Local PD just picked up Sabrina Rae at her apartment. They're bringing her in now."

SEVENTEEN

Michaels was already in the squad room when Madison and Jonas arrived at the office forty-five minutes later. Madison handed their boss his favorite medium roast coffee they'd picked up on the way. "Thank you for calling us in."

"I knew you'd want to know what was going on," Michaels replied, nodding his thanks for the drink. "I know that this is personal for you."

"Very."

"Jonas has kept me updated," Michaels said, "but I'm worried about you. You've already been through so much. Are you okay?"

There was no simple answer to his question. "I will be. Especially now that we have her in custody."

Michaels took another sip of his drink, then paused. "Jonas also said your memory is back. Are you sure Sabrina's the one who was in the house the day you were shot?"

Madison leaned back against the desk, wishing she could control the flood of unsettling memories. "I'm still sorting through everything, and my mind feels as if it's on overload, but yes. I'm sure it's her. I feel as if it happened yesterday, and I can remember everything."

"Okay, that's all I needed to know."

"Is she talking?" Jonas asked.

Michaels shook his head. "That's our issue right now. She's not confessing to anything. Not to any involvement in the convenience store murder. Not to Luke's murder or to shooting Madison. Not even to being at the apartment yesterday afternoon."

"Then she's lying," Madison said. "It's all connected. She even sent photos of us at the train station. She was there, watching us."

"The evidence is starting to prove that," Piper said, walking up to them. "Turns out you were right about a second shooter. CSU just called. They were able to extrapolate the trajectory of the bullet that almost hit Jonas. It definitely came from a different gun. And that's not all. Results just came in for the gunshot residue test that was done on Sabrina after her arrival."

"And . . ." Madison prodded.

"Sabrina tested positive to traces of gunshot residue."

"So it definitely had to be her." Madison blew out a sharp breath of relief. After weeks and months of dead ends, they were about to put an end to the nightmare that had haunted her for the past five years.

"It proves she was around gun particles," Michaels said, holding up his hand to slow her down. "We still can't definitively prove she was there."

Frustration returned, churning inside her gut. They had to find a way to prove Sabrina's involvement. "Does she have an alibi for yesterday?"

"She works for a home design service and said she drove to

Granite Falls to meet with a client. The company she works for confirmed the consultation job, but according to Sabrina, the client wasn't at the house when she arrived."

"So she can't prove where she was," Jonas said.

"No, she can't. She said she didn't stop anywhere except for the client's house. But don't worry," Michaels said. "We're going to get the truth from her. We're working with the DA to put a case together, though right now . . ." He hesitated. "Right now, I'm just glad you're okay."

"So am I." Madison nodded, appreciating his concern, but her being okay wasn't enough. "But I am ready for this to be over."

Michaels nodded. "I know. And it will be."

"What about the search for Ava?" she asked. "Have any leads popped up during the night?"

"Nothing yet," Piper said. "Still no ID on the intruder in Becca's home, or any sightings of Ava and the baby."

Madison took a sip of her coffee, allowing the hot drink to soothe her nerves, as Piper headed back to her desk. Sabrina Rae might not have confessed yet, but they just had to be patient. The truth would come out. Ava and Easton, on the other hand, didn't have the time she had. If the marshals didn't find them soon, it might be too late.

"Madison?" Michaels's voice pulled her away from her thoughts.

She looked up at her boss. "I'm sorry. I was just thinking." She reined in her thoughts, needing to stay focused. Being distracted wasn't an option.

"I'm headed down to the interview room," Michaels said. "We'll figure this out *and* find Ava and the baby."

Madison paused before she made her request. "I want to talk to Sabrina."

"You know that's not happening," Michaels said.

"Then at least let me be in the interview room when you talk to her," she said, settling for the next best option.

"You can watch from the other side of the glass," he said, making the only compromise she knew he could. "Meet me down there in ten minutes."

Madison watched her boss walk away, trying to calm the storm still brewing inside her. She'd waited for too long, spent too many hours on this to give up now.

Jonas squeezed her hand. "He's right. You can't be in there. This is way too personal for you, and you don't want to say or do anything that her lawyers can use against you when she goes to trial."

"I know," she said, trying to take the boiling agitation out of her voice. "But more than likely this woman murdered my husband. It doesn't get more personal than that."

Jonas placed his hand on her arm. "Just trust the process, Madison. You're not in this alone."

Madison watched from behind the one-way mirror while Michaels and Jonas stepped inside the interview room where Sabrina was sitting, gnawing on a fingernail. Her hair might be longer and darker, but the eyes were the same, along with the stubborn tilt of the jaw. Clearly the woman wasn't going down without a fight.

Madison's chest heaved as she studied Sabrina's face. She closed her eyes, wondering if the memories she'd fought for so long to remember would now stop haunting her. Sabrina standing in the kitchen, pointing a gun at her . . . The sound of the weapon going off . . . The impact of the bullet as it hit her . . . So many lives had been hurt, not just hers. The convenience store manager's family, Luke's family, and hers . . .

She laced her fingers together and started praying. Praying that her anger wouldn't turn to bitterness and that she wouldn't let this woman steal her joy and peace.

Michaels and Jonas sat down across from Sabrina.

"Your gunshot residue test came back positive," Michaels said. "Do you know what that means?"

Sabrina's jaw tensed as she shook her head.

"There was gunshot residue on your hands," Michaels said.

Sabrina shook her head. "That's not possible. I didn't shoot anyone. I've never even shot a gun."

"That's interesting, because we have a witness who can tie you to another shooting. A victim who has positively ID'd you as the shooter in an attempted murder we're investigating. And to make matters worse for you, that shooting has been tied to two other murders. The murder of Dominic Cox at a convenience store by Thomas Knight and, with the same gun, the murder of Luke James in a hospital parking lot. Do you see where we're going with all of this?"

Sabrina closed her eyes and rubbed her temples.

"Sabrina—"

"I don't know." She snapped her head up. "I don't know what else you want me to say."

"Hands down, you're looking at life in prison."

"No!" Sabrina smacked her hands against the table. "You have the wrong person. I never shot anyone. I never killed anyone."

Madison studied the woman's face. She was clearly scared. Terrified even. She had to know how much trouble she was in. Lying was only going to make things worse for her in the end.

Michaels pulled a piece of paper out of a file and slid it across the table toward her. “Then let me start here. This is a sworn affidavit by Cara Peterson, stating that you didn’t stay at the library the night of the convenience store robbery five years ago, but instead left about seven thirty. Later, when the police started asking questions, you made her promise to tell them that you never left the library that night so you’d have an alibi.”

She ran her hands through her hair, then sat back. “I can’t believe this is happening.”

“Did you tell Cara to lie for you?”

Sabrina closed her eyes for a moment. “Yes, but you have to believe me. I swear I never shot anyone.”

“Then let’s start at that night and you can tell us everything that happened.”

Madison held her breath as Sabrina started talking.

“I was in love with Thomas,” Sabrina said. “When he told me he’d held up a few convenience stores, I was shocked. He told me he needed some money to pay some shady creditors he owed a bunch of money to. He was convinced they were going to kill him if he didn’t pay up.”

“Do you know who he owed the money to?” Jonas asked. “Or why?”

She shook her head. “No one was supposed to get hurt. When Thomas got away with robbery once, he decided to do it again. I don’t know how he normally did things, but that night he asked me to drive the getaway car. It was stupid and foolish, but I didn’t ask any questions. I just said I’d help if he promised it would be the last time. I told him we’d find another way to get the money.”

“It ended up being the last time, didn’t it?” Jonas asked. “Because something went wrong.”

Sabrina nodded. She was sobbing now, not even trying to hold back the tears. "The cashier pulled out a gun, and then Thomas . . . he panicked and shot the man. I didn't know what he'd done at first. He just jumped into the car and told me to drive. Then I saw the blood on his shirt. My hands started shaking. I-I'd never been so terrified. I couldn't stop shaking. I remember hearing a siren somewhere behind me, and I-I lost control of the car and ran into a tree."

"Which is where the cover-up began," Jonas said, folding his hands on the table in front of him. "You weren't in the car when the police arrived."

"No, I . . ." She drew in a ragged breath. "Thomas told me to run. He'd broken his ankle in the crash and knew he couldn't outrun the police. But I could. I wanted to stay with him, but he said they couldn't prove anything if I'd promise to be quiet. He told me to take his gun, and go back to the library like nothing had ever happened. So that's what I did."

Michaels glanced down at his notes. "We now know you told two lies during your initial interview with the police. The first being that you and Thomas had broken up two weeks earlier. And the second was that you told them you'd been at the library studying with your best friend."

Sabrina pressed her lips together and glanced around the room as if she were looking for a way out, but there was no escape. "Both were partially true. We had broken up, but we'd gotten back together the day before. And I was at the library that night with Cara."

"Until you left early," Michaels said.

"When Thomas texted me that he needed my help, I told Cara I had to run home and get one of the textbooks I'd forgotten. He didn't tell me he wanted me to be his getaway driver."

"But you trusted him," Jonas said.

Sabrina nodded and shifted in her chair. "Before the police started asking questions, I convinced Cara to back me up and tell them that I hadn't left the library. I also told her not to tell anyone that Thomas and I had gotten back together. Thomas told me to say that."

"In an attempt to keep you from being charged as an accessory to murder," Jonas said.

Sabrina winced but nodded. "He convinced me to stick with my story, promising me that he'd be out soon, and I . . . I loved him, so I promised to wait for him. I convinced Cara—and maybe myself as well—that he was innocent and all this would be over soon."

"But that wasn't true," Michaels said.

Sabrina didn't answer out loud, but she didn't have to. Her guilt was as clear as the ink on the paperwork in her file.

"What did you do with the gun?" Jonas asked. "It wasn't found in or around the convenience store or in the car, but we know you had it."

"Thomas . . . he told me to take it and dump it in the lake."

"But you didn't," Jonas said.

"I was afraid it would be found, so . . . I hid it in my room."

"The gun you were supposed to dispose of has been tied to two other shootings," Michaels said.

"It was stolen."

"How convenient," Jonas said.

"It's the truth. My apartment was robbed and that was one of the things that was taken."

Michaels picked up one of the papers in his file. "That wasn't mentioned in the police report."

"I couldn't tell them about the gun." Sabrina shook her head.

"Listen. I was eighteen years old when that happened, and yes, I was stupid. I thought if I did what Thomas said, then maybe they wouldn't have enough to convict him on, and we could be together. But I never killed anyone. You have to believe that."

Madison frowned as Sabrina's defensive pleas rang hollow. The woman could deny pulling that trigger, but Madison had been there. Another memory rushed to the surface.

She'd tried to reach for her gun, but her weapon was on the other side of the counter. She hadn't recognized the woman holding a gun on her, but Sabrina had clearly known who she was. And what she was going to do.

"What is going to happen?" Madison had asked, trying to plan her next move.

"We'll talk for a few more minutes, then I'm going to shoot you."

Like she'd shot Luke.

"Madison?"

A hand rested on her shoulder, and she jumped. Michaels and Jonas had left the interview room and were standing next to her.

"Are you okay?" Jonas asked.

"Yeah, I'm fine. I just . . . seeing her brings back a lot of memories. I'm still trying to process everything."

"We're going to need to send this case to the DA," Michaels said, "but this is far from over. If she is behind Luke's murder—which, at this point, I'm convinced she is—they'll make sure this goes to trial."

Madison nodded, then took one last look at Sabrina through the one-way mirror, still wishing she could be the one in there asking the questions. Wishing she could be the one asking Sabrina Rae why she'd killed her husband.

EIGHTEEN

Jonas pulled a dollar from his wallet, then stopped in front of the vending machine that was located inside the marshal building.

"I don't think I've ever seen you eat something out of this machine before." Madison stepped up beside him, a grin on her lips.

He hesitated before putting his dollar in the slot. "So, you've never impulsively grabbed a package of M&Ms or a chocolate bar out of this machine?"

"I didn't say I hadn't. I just said I hadn't seen you do it."

"Actually, this is for a craving I've had the last two weeks." He pushed a couple buttons, then waited for the item he'd picked to fall. "This is going to sound crazy, but out of all the things I could have wished for during training, I craved peanut butter filled pretzels. Not plain or cheese filled but peanut butter filled."

Madison laughed. "My craving lately has been Italian. I ordered it in twice last week, something I rarely do."

He turned and flashed her a smile. "Maybe when this is

over, we'll have to order some fettuccini, with a side of peanut butter pretzels."

She matched his smile and made his stomach flip. "Somehow, I'm not really feeling that combination."

Jonas pulled the snack out of the machine, ripped open the package, then popped one into his mouth. He frowned. The taste of stale pretzels was *not* what he'd been craving. There was one combination, though, that would always feel right to him.

"I know nothing's changed since I left, and that's okay." He paused before continuing, as he caught her gaze. "But I missed this. Missed us."

He thought she was going to reach out and touch his arm, but she dropped her hand to her side instead. "It wasn't the same without you here. I missed chasing down the bad guys with you."

He smiled, but going after fugitives together wasn't what he was thinking about.

"Sorry to interrupt," Piper said, stepping up to them, "but we just ID'd the man in the video from Becca's apartment."

"That's what I want to hear," Madison said, heading out of the room with Piper. "We could use some good news."

Jonas crunched on another pretzel, then followed Madison and Piper into the squad room, wishing he could freeze time for an hour and talk with Madison without all the chaos surrounding them. He knew he had to wait, and that was fine, but he had so many questions he wanted to ask her. Had she thought about him as much as he'd thought about her while he'd been gone? Had his absence helped cement how she felt about him?

Dating a coworker might not officially be against the rules, but there was always a danger attached in falling for someone you worked with, along with certain consequences. But he was past guarding his heart.

He pulled his mind back to the case as Piper slid in front of her computer and projected a photo of their suspect onto the screen above them.

"That's definitely him," Madison said as the driver's license photo popped up. "Who is he?"

"Callum Burks is thirty-three years old, has some speeding tickets and a couple misdemeanors, but for the most part he's managed to stay out of trouble. He grew up around here and has held half a dozen jobs over the past few years. He never seems to stay with anything too long. He's been working at the docks for almost a year. He goes out to sea for about a month at a time on a ship up to Alaska and back, mainly transporting goods."

"And now?" Jonas asked. "Is he back on land?"

"I called his boss, and he's been back from his last trip for a few days. Which fits the time stamp of when he was inside Becca's apartment. It means he was definitely here in Seattle."

"Okay," Madison said. "If Becca was telling the truth, and Myra hired him to plant drugs in her apartment, there has to be a connection between the two of them."

"Not one that we've found," Piper said.

"With her husband a judge," Jonas said, "she could have had access to names to choose from."

Madison nodded. "That's a good place to start."

"If you give me a second, I can cross-reference to see if one of Burks's cases came across the judge's desk." Piper turned back to her computer to dig further. "You're right. Callum went before Judge Saylor for a traffic violation a year ago."

"So she didn't have to go far for hired help." Jonas folded his arms across his chest. "Let's start at his place of employment and see what we can find out there."

Piper nodded. "From the employment record I pulled, he currently works at Glacier Bay Fish Company."

***

The view of the Seattle skyline never ceased to impress Jonas. Despite a smattering of clouds in the sky, Mount Rainier rose to the left and the hazy outline of the Olympic Mountains rose to the right. It was yet another reason why he was happy to be back in the Northwest. As he and Madison drove into the parking lot near the docks, the scene ahead of them brought its own string of memories.

He used to come crabbing with his grandfather on one of the piers. They'd walk past cycling paths to the water, then hours later head home and cook the crab they'd caught together. Things had changed over the years, with several of the more popular piers closing, but this area used to hold every kind of boat—sailboats, yachts, tankers, ferries.

The sign for Glacier Bay Fish Company led them to a small, weathered building not far from the water. Inside, a man in his late fifties sat behind a counter with an old desktop computer surrounded by stacks of invoices.

"We're looking for Callum Burks," Jonas said, breathing in the smell of fishing tackle and salt water.

The man held up his hand but didn't look up from his computer.

"We're Deputy US Marshals," Madison said. "We need to know where Callum Burks is."

"Callum . . ." The man glanced up, squinted, then pulled off his glasses. "Sorry, he's not here."

"Can you tell us where he is?" Jonas asked.

"Wouldn't know."

Jonas frowned, irritated at having to pull information out of him. The man's cell phone rang next to him, and he reached for it.

"Not so fast," Madison said, holding up her hand. "All we need is two minutes of your time."

The man rubbed his eyes, then put his glasses back on. "I'm sorry, but you caught me at a really bad time. I had two men call in sick, and I'm trying to ensure that our next boat is ready to go out tomorrow morning."

"Will Burks be going out?"

The man glanced at the wall calendar behind him. "He's off for another few days, so unless I can't get anyone else, no. He just got in three days ago."

"What does he do for you?" Jonas prodded.

"He's a deckhand. Works loading and unloading cargo off the boats as well as performing maintenance. Most of our trips are close to a month long and are pretty grueling. Our seamen usually work three trips, then take one off. Which is part of the problem. I interview a lot of people, but most walk out when they realize what is required. Or they're simply not physically fit enough to perform the job. Two-thirds of the job is simply standing watch or taking care of maintenance, but the rest of the trip is spent lifting cargo on and off the boat, and days can easily run twelve hours or longer."

"So you don't know where he goes on his days off?"

The man shrugged. "If he's off, he only comes in to pick up his paycheck, but I haven't seen him today. He does have a boat in the marina he's fixing up. He's there a lot when he's not working. I guess I'd try there."

"What's the name of the boat?" Madison asked.

The man scratched the back of his neck. "*The Dreadnought*. It needs some work, but it's pretty fast."

"It's very important that we talk to him." Jonas handed the man his card. "If he does show up, will you please give us a call?"

The man took the card and nodded. "Just don't count on a call anytime soon."

***

Madison and Jonas stopped to speak to the harbormaster, who said he hadn't seen Callum around but directed them to the slip where *The Dreadnought* was anchored. Callum's boss had been right. The boat did need some work, but from the dock, it looked like it was mainly cosmetic. There was no sign of Callum onboard.

Two slips down, a couple was working on an aluminum fishing boat. Madison held up a photo of Callum as they approached the pair. "Do either of you know this man? He's the owner of *The Dreadnought*, a couple slips down from you."

The woman glanced at the phone. "I'm not sure about his name, but he's here a lot."

"When he's not working," her husband said. "He goes to Alaska a lot."

"Have you seen him here today?" Madison asked.

"Haven't really seen anyone with the weather getting colder," the woman said. "It's been pretty quiet, and we've just been busy painting and cleaning. If he was here, I didn't notice."

"Sorry. Me neither."

Jonas let out a huff of air as he looked around. Waves lapped against the dock, squawking seagulls dove into the water around them, and boats spread out across the marina in neat lines. A man who just kidnapped a woman and baby probably wasn't going to be out working on his boat. If anything, he'd be trying to secure an alibi.

"Where would he have taken them?" Jonas asked as they walked back up the wooden dock toward the shore.

Madison matched his stride. "Somewhere close and yet private. Myra wouldn't want him to get caught."

"They could be anywhere in Seattle, or he could have taken them out of the city, north toward Bellingham, south toward Olympia, or even toward the coast."

"Agreed. Piper is searching for any property connected to either Callum or Myra. I'm thinking she would not have risked the chance of getting anyone other than Callum involved, which means something isolated would make sense."

As they headed back to the parking lot, Madison's phone rang. She clicked the speaker button before answering. "What have you got, Piper?"

"Michaels asked me to call you. Have you found Callum?"

"Not yet," Madison said.

"He isn't at his apartment either," Piper continued. "They're sweeping his place, but so far they haven't found anything."

"We have a BOLO out on him, right?" Madison asked. "I think it's safe to assume he won't go far with Ava and Easton. Maybe he's waiting for Myra to give him instructions."

"That's it!" Piper said.

Madison looked at Jonas. "What do you mean?"

"There's no way for him to know she's dead, right?"

"It's unlikely, unless he was watching the house. We've pushed for it to be kept off the news for as long as possible, though it's going to leak at some point."

"We have her phone," Piper continued. "We can reach out and arrange a meetup between the two of them. Then when he shows up, you can bring him in."

"That's not a bad idea," Jonas said. "In fact, it's quite brilliant!"

Piper laughed. "I'm learning from the best."

Madison worked through the idea in her mind. The plan made sense, and the risk was minimal, giving them a tangible way of reeling him in. "I'm about the same build and height as Myra," she said. "We can send him a message that there's been a complication with their plan and she needs to talk. Maybe even offer him a bonus for another job. We set a meeting place—"

"And we arrest him," Piper finished.

"What do you think, Jonas?" Madison asked.

"He'll know you're not Myra."

"Not if she wore a wig with darker, shorter hair," Piper said. "And we have access to her closet. All you need is to look enough like her to get him to approach you."

Jonas's brow raised slightly at Piper's plan. "Someone's been reading too many spy novels."

Piper laughed, then gushed on, "Actually, I'm reading this book about US Marshals back in 1985. A hundred guests arrived at the Washington Convention Center after receiving a letter that said their names had been selected to receive free tickets to an NFL game. They were also invited to a pregame party where there would be a drawing for season tickets and the Super Bowl."

"I remember that. The Special Operations Group was involved in that sting," Jonas said. "They were told there was a surprise for them, and then the SOG team swept in and arrested them."

"Instead of heading to the stadium," Piper added, "they headed back to prison."

"This might not be quite as epic," Madison said, "but it might bring Callum out of the woodwork, which is all we need."

Because they had to ensure they found Ava and the baby before DeMarco did.

NINETEEN

Madison was tugging on the front of the wig Piper had found for her when Jonas walked up and sat down on the edge of her desk.

"I'm still trying to decide," he said, tilting his head, "but I think I might like this new look of yours."

"Well, don't get too used to it." She tugged it again to the left. "It's hot and uncomfortable and I've only had it on for five minutes."

"The only problem," he continued, "is that the color does seem to be a bit dark for your complexion. I'm wondering if next time you should try a fiery red."

"I don't know." She grinned as she held up a hand mirror so she could see the side, then combed it into place with her fingers. "I've always wanted a fun color like purple, or pink maybe."

He laughed, but the seriousness of the moment wasn't lost between them. "You're sure you're okay with this?" he asked.

She put the mirror down and looked up at him. "You're not going to try to talk me out of it, are you?"

"Would that really work?" He shot her a smile. "Because I have a feeling I couldn't even if I wanted to."

"You know me well, then."

"I'll be honest," he said, stepping in front of her, "there's something about having a partner who can hold her own no matter the situation. I've seen you at the shooting range, and you're even better in action when taking down a fugitive. I know I wouldn't want to go one-on-one with you. I'm much more worried about Callum Burks. He has no idea who he's about to come up against."

She picked up the mirror again and pushed the longish bangs away from her forehead, hoping he didn't catch the blush she knew was spreading across her face. "Very funny."

"It's true," he said. "Just . . . be careful."

She nodded. "You know I will."

Madison knew what he meant and didn't dismiss his concern. They'd both lost people they loved and knew it only took one false move, one deadly second, for everything to fall apart. No matter how much you wanted to control everything around you, it couldn't be done. Sometimes all you could do was move on, one day at a time, and pray you found the right people to move forward together with.

She glanced at Myra's photo, then grabbed a stick of red lipstick off the desk.

"When this is all over," Jonas said, changing the subject, "we're going to have to celebrate over dinner."

She grinned. "Fettuccini and pretzels?"

"Oh, I managed to curb those cravings, thanks to the vending machine."

"Then I'd like that."

Jonas's phone rang, and he picked it up while she applied

the same color lipstick Myra Saylor always wore. She didn't miss the currents that had sparked between Jonas and her as he flirted with her. She'd tried for so long to keep him at arm's length, convinced Sabrina might hurt him to get to her. She knew the idea wasn't too far-fetched. Not after everything the woman had done. Madison had the scars to prove it, both emotional and physical. Bowing to fear wasn't who she was, and yet she'd still given Sabrina the power to dictate how she lived and felt. And she'd pushed Jonas away because of it.

She recapped the lipstick along with the guilt, then checked her work before glancing back up at him. She'd felt a connection between them the first time they'd met in Nashville at a training exercise, but back then it had been more of a sense of admiration and respect for his skills and leadership abilities. She never imagined she'd one day fall in love with him.

Still, she'd tried to push him away.

Before he'd left for his SOG training, he'd reminded her that life wasn't always black and white. That there were things that happened that you couldn't fix because life was messy. But despite her fears and hesitation, he'd promised to give her the time she needed to move on. With him.

Jonas ended the call, then set his phone down on the desk beside him, bringing her thoughts back to the present.

"That was Michaels. The DA is looking at the arrest report of Sabrina Rae. They're going to need more evidence to connect her to Luke's murder, but it looks like he's planning to bring criminal charges against her as an accessory to felony murder for the death of Dominic Cox."

She blew out a breath. "Wow. That's a start. I don't think it will be long before the rest of the pieces come together and they'll be able to add another felony murder charge for Luke's death."

"And your attempted murder," he added.

She nodded. She had waited over five years to see Luke's murderer behind bars, and now, thanks to Edward and her memories coming back, that was about to happen. A sense of relief washed through her. She'd taken on the guilt of Luke's murder. The guilt of knowing that the bullet that had killed him was meant for her. That was a burden she'd never learned how to shake. Maybe now she'd finally be able to take that step forward.

"Any response from Callum?" she asked, standing up, ready to go.

"Not yet, but we dangled a bit of cash out in front of him. I have a feeling it won't take him very long to bite."

Almost an hour later, there was a ding, and Jonas read the message on Myra's phone.

"Bingo." He held it up for Madison to read.

Will meet you, but I'll choose the place. One hour.

A second text came through with a pinned location.

"Where is that?" Madison asked.

Jonas zoomed in on the spot. "It looks like one of those street-end waterfront beaches close to the marina."

"It should be quiet and pretty deserted," Madison said.

Jonas sent another text, confirming the meet.

I'll be there.

And Myra, come alone.

From his texts, Callum seemed anxious or, at the very least, cautious. They had to assume he'd met Myra in person, but even if he hadn't, he'd know what she looked like. There were dozens of photos of Myra and her husband taken at various fundraisers and charity events in the city. The plan had to work, because they couldn't lose him. Not if they wanted to find Ava.

***

Madison drove toward the address Callum had given them, then parked along the side of the road. Backup would be watching, ready to track the man's car if he got away, but so far there was no sign of their suspect. Which was fine. She wanted to get to the meeting place first.

"Can you hear me?"

Madison touched her earpiece at the sound of Jonas's voice. "Copy that. I can hear you."

"We've got our eyes on you. Stay alert."

She walked down the dirt path edged by razor wire that surrounded an exclusive club, her mind now totally focused on the job at hand. The stretch of beach ahead was public property, open to anyone who wanted a quiet spot with a view. She made it to the rocky alcove, then took in the view of Mount Rainier to the south. There were security cameras mounted on tall poles, behind her and ahead, and she could see the wooden bench where Callum had told her to come. Past a patch of wild blackberry bushes, a gnarled tree trunk had fallen across the sand, and in the distance a couple canoes glided by in the water.

"Going radio silent until I make contact," Madison said.

"Copy that." Jonas's voice came through her comm. "As soon as he shows up, we'll take him down."

She set her bag on the bench, then sat next to it and glanced at her watch. He was late. Her adrenaline pulsed steadily, as she stared out at the water. If they were right about him, he'd be here. Not only was he waiting for Myra's instructions, he wouldn't pass up an opportunity to cash in on some easy money.

A couple played Frisbee to her left. To her right, a man was walking his German shepherd. All three were a part of the team they'd brought, trained to blend in to their surroundings.

She checked Myra's phone again, to see if she'd missed another text. Nothing. He was now ten minutes late. Doubt wormed through her. He could have found out Myra was dead and ran. Or he could just be running late. She shivered and then pulled up the zipper of her coat. It was cold for October, with temperatures expected to drop close to freezing tonight. Which worried her. Wherever she was, Ava couldn't have prepared for this cold snap. And even though Myra would have wanted to keep the baby safe, her death had just altered the whole scenario.

"I wasn't expecting you to want to meet me in person," Callum said, sliding onto the bench next to her. "You always said it was too dangerous."

Madison stared out at the water. "Things have gotten complicated."

"Just tell me what you want me to do, and as long as you pay me, I'll do it."

"I would, except"—she gave the signal for the team to move in—"you're under arrest."

He glanced at her held-out badge, then reacted automatically by shoving her hard off the bench and running. A jolt of pain shot through Madison as she hit the ground.

She gasped, then managed a shallow breath. "He's heading toward the marina," she yelled.

"Madison, are you okay?" Jonas's voice sounded through her earpiece.

"I'm fine. Go after him."

She pulled herself back onto the bench, then stood up. For a man in his thirties, Callum was still far more fit than she'd anticipated. Working on the boat twelve-plus hours a day had clearly given him a level of fitness she didn't encounter often.

She sprinted after him along the shoreline.

"We've got this, Madison," Jonas said.

"So do I. He's heading toward his boat."

Jonas somehow managed to get to the marina first, with the rest of the team close behind. By the time she hit the dock, Callum was already in his boat and pulling away. She raced down the wood dock, irritated at herself for letting him get the upper hand.

The couple they'd spoken to earlier was on the deck of their boat, painting one of the rails.

"We need to borrow your boat," Jonas said, motioning them onto the dock as he held up his badge.

By the time Madison had jumped onto the watercraft, Jonas had the engine going and was ready to maneuver his way out of the marina.

"I'm radioing in assistance from the coast guard," she said, shouting above the rumble of the engine as he plowed past a row of boats.

Jonas continued gaining on the other boat as they hit the open water and Madison received confirmation that the coast guard was on their way. In the distance, the Space Needle rose above the downtown skyline, while dark storm clouds hung above the horizon south of them. They followed Callum farther out into the open water of the bay, until his boat suddenly slowed down and stopped. Jonas maneuvered them next to the boat that was now dead in the water.

"I've got him," Jonas shouted to her. "You take the wheel."

Jonas jumped onto the other boat and ordered Callum to put his hands in the air.

The man hesitated, then complied as he stepped away from the helm.

"You probably should have done that the first time instead of assaulting my partner." Jonas grabbed a pair of handcuffs out of his pocket, then glanced back at Madison. "You know, even after all my years of working in law enforcement, I'm not sure why people run. It almost always ends up in this same scenario."

"Sorry, but when someone starts running after me," Callum said, growling, "I react."

"As I recall, I wasn't running when you took off," Madison called out as she secured the two boats together. "It also probably isn't a good idea to take your boat out on an empty fuel tank when the authorities are after you. That never works out for a suspect."

"Suspect for what?" Callum asked as Jonas secured his hands behind his back with the cuffs.

"Sit down and we'll have a little chat," Jonas said.

"Right here?"

"Why not?" Madison nodded to the seat next to him. "We have to wait for the coast guard. Besides, I have a feeling you know exactly why you're here."

Callum pressed his lips together and stared out across the water as the boat bobbed up and down.

"We know you were hired by Myra Saylor," Madison continued. "We know she paid you to plant drugs in Becca Lambert's house and to kidnap her son. But right now, all we want to know is where Ava Middleton and Becca's baby—"

"Wait a minute." Callum shifted in his seat, trying to adjust the handcuffs behind him. "I didn't break into anyone's house, and I certainly didn't kidnap anyone. I've been working on my boat."

"That's interesting," Jonas said, "because when we dropped by to talk to you, you weren't there."

"I had to go get parts."

"I don't think so," Jonas said, the tension in his voice cutting through the chilly air. "So I'll ask you one more time, where are Ava and the baby?"

Callum avoided his gaze. "I said that I don't know. You've got the wrong person."

Madison frowned. They didn't have time to sit and argue. "In case you need proof that you're the person we were looking for, know that we found your name in Myra's contact list *and* saw you on security footage inside Becca's house. We also have footage of you planting drugs at her apartment."

This time Callum didn't respond. The boat continued to bob as the waves brushed against the side. Jonas held up his phone and started playing the footage from Becca's nanny cam.

Madison studied Callum's expression before continuing. "I'm guessing your employer didn't tell you about the hidden baby monitor in the room. Turns out the quality is pretty good. Enough to get an ID, in fact. And give us some pretty solid evidence of who was there, along with the time stamp that proves you weren't working on your boat *all* day."

Callum's frown deepened. "Fine. I was paid to break into the house, which is nothing more than a misdemeanor, but I'm not taking the rap for . . . for kidnapping."

"Oh, we're not talking just about a misdemeanor." Madison paused to make sure what she'd said was sinking in. "We already have you on breaking and entering, and on possession of drugs. We also have a witness who puts you at the scene of the kidnapping. And if anything happens to Ava and the baby, it won't be hard to tie you to murder as well."

Madison watched Callum's face pale as she laid out the stakes.

"We can start with the breaking and entering," Jonas said. "Why did you do that?"

Callum's jaw tensed. "Myra paid me."

"To do what exactly?" Jonas asked.

"She's a judge's wife. Sometimes she needs things done so that she doesn't get her hands dirty. She hired me online. I never met her in person. She said it was safer for both of us. That was why I was surprised when I got a text from her that she wanted to meet."

"And what exactly was the job?"

"Like you said, I was to plant drugs in a certain apartment." He gritted his teeth. "I had no idea there was a camera."

"You thought you were meeting with her to get further instructions," Jonas said.

Callum nodded.

Jonas glanced at Madison before he spoke again. "You haven't heard from her because Myra Saylor is dead."

"Wait a minute." Callum started to stand up, then lost his balance and fell back against the chair as the boat rocked. "She's dead?"

"I thought that might get your attention," Jonas said.

"Great. I guess I won't get paid now."

Madison's eyes widened. "Seriously?"

"I'm sorry, but I've never even met her. And I certainly didn't kill her."

"We didn't imply you did," Madison said. "Unless—"

Callum leaned forward. "Hold on. Even I know where to draw the line."

"At murder?" Jonas asked.

"She was a source of income. But I didn't ask questions. I just did what she asked me to."

"What about kidnapping?"

Callum shut his mouth and looked away.

Madison glanced toward the shore and caught a flash of red from the incoming coast guard vessel. They would help transport Callum, as well as the two boats, back to the shore, but until then, they had to get as much information as they could out of him.

"Here's the deal," she said. "This is all unraveling quickly, so the more you help us, the more the DA will be persuaded to go easier on you. But we need to know everything. With a Class C felony, you could be looking at five years' imprisonment. And that's just for starters."

"I was just supposed to keep them off the grid, so to speak, until Myra contacted me again." Callum's voice rose in panic. "I was supposed to make sure they were safe. She insisted that she didn't want them hurt."

"Do you know why?"

Callum shrugged. "I didn't ask. She told me that she and her husband had adopted the child, but the birth mother had illegally taken him. She was just trying to get her child back."

"Maybe you should have done a bit more research before deciding to be a good Samaritan, because that excuse isn't going to fly with any judge I know," Madison said.

"She told me I was helping her out because the authorities weren't taking her seriously."

"And so you agreed to kidnap them," Jonas said.

"She offered to pay me ten thousand dollars to grab the woman and the baby. But it was just supposed to be until she contacted me again. They were never supposed to get hurt."

"Where are they?" Madison asked.

His gaze dropped. "She told me to take them to a cabin north of here. The owners call it the Brambles, I think, but—"

"Are they still there?" Madison asked.

"No . . . I . . . never took them there." Callum picked at a hangnail, still ignoring her gaze. "I figured if I was the only one who knew where they were, then I could get more money out of Myra. I took a risk kidnapping them and deserved to be compensated. I wanted some leverage if things went wrong."

Madison tried to suppress the wall of anger at his confession, but maybe they were finally getting closer to the truth.

"Things have gone very wrong," Jonas said, "and depending on how you cooperate right now, you may or may not be seeing the light of day outside a prison cell. Because if anything happens to Ava and the baby . . ."

Callum shifted in his seat. "I made sure she had food and water, and that the baby had formula. Made sure she had blankets and that the heat was on."

"If they're not at the Brambles, where are they?"

"I took her to a cabin that belongs to my cousin. A couple hours from here, on the coast. I came back to the city, but I left them with food and water and a place to sleep."

Madison frowned as the coast guard approached the side of the boat. "We need the address. And let's hope and pray that they're okay."

***

Michaels was waiting for them when they returned to the marshals' office thirty minutes later. Callum had decided he was done talking and wanted a lawyer, but at least they'd gotten what they needed out of him—the address where he'd taken Ava. The DA could deal with him now.

"I got your update," Michaels said as they stepped into his office, "but we've got a problem."

Madison glanced at Jonas. "I don't like the sound of that."

"I had the local sheriff go to the address you were given by Callum Burks."

"And?" Madison prodded.

"Ava and the baby aren't in the cabin."

TWENTY

Jonas felt the tension in his jaw increase as he sat down in front of Michaels's desk. Another dead end. "So Callum lied to us about where he left Ava and Easton."

"Not necessarily." Michaels leaned back in his chair and folded his arms across his chest. "They did a thorough search of the cabin and believe she and the baby were there but managed to leave. There was a broken window, and it appeared to have been breached from the inside."

"Meaning she managed to get out of the house on her own," Madison said.

"At this point, that's what it looks like, but we can't ignore the possibility that DeMarco's men found her."

"We need to go," Jonas said, standing up. "Even if they don't have her right now, they won't stop looking until they do."

"Already arranged," Michaels said. "I've notified the sheriff and have a helicopter ready to take you." He glanced at his watch. "Your ride to the heliport will be here any minute, but Madison—I want you to know that the deputy district attorney has also filed criminal charges against Sabrina Rae for being an accessory to the murder of Dominic Cox."

"That was fast," she said. "What about Luke's murder and my shooting?"

"He hasn't filed those charges yet, but I feel sure that it will happen. And no bail. Which means you're safe, and that's enough for now."

She nodded and reached to shake his hand. "Thank you for keeping me updated. I appreciate it."

Jonas caught her expression as they turned around and headed out to grab their backpacks and head downstairs, surprised she didn't seem more relieved. But they hadn't had a chance to really talk about what had happened last night. Like himself, she'd learned to separate her personal life from her job as a marshal. But drawing those lines and compartmentalizing wasn't always possible. And judging from the intensity in her eyes, he was sure she was struggling to keep her emotions detached. He couldn't blame her. After months of dead ends, they'd finally found the person who shot her and who, more than likely, was responsible for the death of her husband.

He stepped into the elevator behind her, then adjusted the backpack on his shoulder. "How are you feeling? Not about Ava, but Sabrina?"

She leaned back against the wall of the elevator. "Honestly, I'm going to have to wait to process everything, but initially, both relieved and anxious."

"Relieved you found the person who shot you."

She nodded.

"And anxious?" he asked, needing more clarification.

She hesitated. "Anxious that something will go wrong, and this isn't really almost over like I want it to be. Fearful that they'll have to let her go on some technicality. I know that's a ridiculous thing to worry about—"

"It's not ridiculous at all. You're making perfect sense."

The elevator doors slid open, and they stepped into the lobby and headed outside the building.

"I'm also grateful," she continued. "Grateful for those who have supported me and didn't think I was going crazy when sometimes even I did. I just need to keep the memories at bay for the moment until I can actually sit down and deal with them."

"One step at a time," he said.

"I know."

Outside, the wind had picked up, which added another concern to the situation. A four-door vehicle pulled up in front of them, and Peyton Wyse stepped out of the driver's seat and opened the back door.

"When we were told we were going to have a chauffeur take us to the airport, I wasn't expecting you," Jonas said, letting Madison in first then sliding in next to her.

"I hope you don't mind, but I asked Michaels if I could escort you." Wyse shut the door, then climbed back in. "I feel responsible for what happened to Ava. She trusted me, and I let my guard down. And since the doctor doesn't want me to return to work for a couple more days, this is the next best thing. We need to figure out where she might have gone."

"Anything you can tell us will help," Madison said as Wyse started driving.

"Ava used to talk to me about what she'd do if they found her." Wyse pulled out of the parking lot and headed toward the freeway. "Because she was convinced they would."

And perhaps they had.

Jonas watched the cars pass them on the busy four-lane road as they approached the heliport, praying Ava had managed to somehow stay a step ahead of the people pursuing her. And that they'd be able to find her before she disappeared.

"Did she have a plan?" Jonas asked.

"Yes, though she would never give me any details. Mainly she asked me a lot of questions."

"What kinds of questions?" Madison asked from beside him in the back seat.

"Everything from what she should have in a go bag to leaving a trail of disinformation to how to reduce her digital footprint. I'm pretty sure she has money and a burner phone on her at a minimum, but we also don't know what she was able to grab out of her apartment."

"So she believed this day was coming and was prepared for this scenario."

"As much as she could be, yes, both mentally and physically." Wyse put on his blinker and took the next exit. "But DeMarco has resources and wants her out of the way. Especially if he's concerned she might have information on Púca . . ."

"What she probably wasn't prepared for was having Easton with her when they grabbed her," Jonas said, knowing how helpless Wyse had to feel.

"What about friends she might go to for help? We know she contacted Becca. Is there anyone else?"

"Her work at the café was always in the back kitchen making all their desserts. Which worked out perfect for her. She didn't want to take the chance of anyone recognizing her. The only person she really seemed at home with was Becca."

"Becca mentioned how private she was."

"No photos, no social media, no real socializing, period," Wyse said. "That in itself made her stand out to some. But for the most part she was able to stay under the radar."

"Where was she from?" Madison asked.

"Maine. She'd never been to the Pacific Northwest. We try to relocate witnesses to places where they have no connections. No ties. Somewhere no one would ever think she would go."

"Do you think she would go back to family or friends back East?"

"That's exactly where she wouldn't go. My theory—and I could be wrong—is that her plan was to head to Alaska."

"Why Alaska?" Madison asked.

"It's about as far as you can get from her old life. And being from Maine, she didn't mind the cold. She mentioned once that she'd been watching a YouTube video about surviving in Alaska. I thought it was odd at the time, but now I can't help but wonder how much of a plan she might have actually had in place."

Jonas shifted in his seat as Wyse took a sharp left toward the heliport. The problem was, while Alaska was a good theory, it wasn't enough to go on. They needed a solid lead. Details on what she'd planned. Someone who had actually seen her or maybe even gave her and Easton a ride. But that was where Ava's fear was going to factor in. Wyse had promised her she'd be safe, but despite his efforts, she'd now been thrown into a vulnerable situation, and if Wyse was right, she also didn't know who she could trust, which was going to make it even harder for them to find her.

"She already contacted Becca once," Madison said. "I think that more than likely she'll try again. She knows Becca will be frantic, wondering where Easton is."

"If she won't go to the authorities, then Becca is her best and most likely option. As long as we can keep Becca's name out of the media. Otherwise, there's a good chance that Ava won't trust contacting her either."

Jonas watched as a small plane took off to their right. There was always a wild card. A decision handed to you that you hadn't considered before. The unpredictable twist that left you scrambling for a new plan. The first one had been Easton. Ava might have been prepared to disappear on her own, but she couldn't have anticipated the scenario of having Easton with her. The second wild card had been the Amber Alert that had thrown Ava unwillingly into the spotlight.

Helicopter blades whirled a dozen yards away as they exited the car and spoke to the pilot who was going to be flying them. Moments later, Jonas snapped his seat belt into place, then slid on his helmet, wishing the skies were clearer. No doubt on a cloudless day the views over the peninsula and Olympic Mountains would be spectacular. Today, though, the haze over the city was going to block much of the view, especially if it stretched out over the peninsula.

"What Wyse said makes sense," Madison said once they'd settled in. "If Ava had an escape route planned, she very well might have thought about a plan to throw off DeMarco."

"Which is only going to make it harder for us."

Jonas stared out the window as they hovered above the ground for a few seconds, then started gaining altitude. "Piper is going to continue to try to contact her. Hopefully, she didn't dump the burner phone and we'll be able to connect once she has better reception. They'll also work with the carrier to see if they can track the phone using cell phone towers."

"But until then?"

He turned back to her. "We pray for a new lead."

The cabin where Callum claimed to have left Ava was in an

isolated area in the Olympic Peninsula. The peninsula itself contained Olympic National Park, spreading out across almost a million acres of terrain with a combination of glacier-capped mountains, rain forests, and miles of rugged coastline. If Ava didn't find help, or shelter, the result could be just as disastrous as if DeMarco found her.

TWENTY-ONE

The sheriff's vehicle was parked outside the cabin when Madison and Jonas pulled into the driveway with an escort from the small precinct. The A-frame structure with a front porch was set back from the road and surrounded by a thick forest of trees. On the way over, their escort, Deputy Fields, had told them that they'd already started canvassing the area, but the house's position was far enough back from the road that cars passing by wouldn't be able to see the house or who was coming in and out.

A middle-aged man in uniform walked down the gravel driveway toward them as they exited the car. "Thanks for coming out and helping. I'm Sheriff Lukas Daugherty."

"Any updates?" Madison asked after shaking his hand.

"The house has been searched," he said as they started up the drive. "I'm convinced Ava was here but managed to get away with Easton. My team found a couple things inside that you're going to want to see."

Madison breathed in the earthy scents of damp moss, pine trees, and cedar that were even stronger, she was sure, after this morning's rain. A loose board on the porch steps groaned beneath her as they headed up the wooden staircase and into the cabin. They first needed to verify Callum's story, that Ava had indeed been here. They could go from there in narrowing the search.

"It's small," the sheriff said, stepping inside the cabin ahead of them. "This is the main living area and kitchen, and then there's a loft upstairs with a second bed."

The setup was perfect for someone who wanted to get away from the city and spend a few quiet days on the edge of the peninsula's wilderness. There was a layer of dust on top of the wooden furniture, and the space was void of anything personal, but it still felt warm and cozy with its large windows that held views of the surrounding woods.

But as the officers had said, there was no sign of Ava.

"Who owns this house?" Jonas asked.

"A couple from Seattle. They come here several times a year, mainly in the summer months. Not as often in the winter."

"So it's normally empty this time of year?"

"Unless they rent it out, yes."

Callum had told them that his cousin owned it, so that information would have been easy for him to find out.

"Windows were wedged shut from the outside," the sheriff continued, "and the front door was locked with a padlock on the outside."

That explained the damaged door. And why Callum believed he could leave Ava for an extended period of time without worrying about her escaping.

"This must be how she got out," Madison said, walking to a small, broken window on the side of the house.

Daugherty nodded. "She managed to break the glass and push off the screen. We found both on the ground outside."

"So it was broken from the inside," Madison said.

"Yes," Daugherty said motioning toward the small kitchen. "At first we thought the place might have been vandalized, but we found fresh milk, bread, baby formula, and dirty diapers in the trash."

If Callum had been telling the truth, then the extra food made sense. Myra's plan was to use them as leverage to force Becca to sign the papers, but her intent had never been to hurt them.

"In addition to the dirty diapers, we also found this." One of the deputies handed her a piece of paper. "Though I'm not sure if it's important."

Madison looked at it, then handed it to Jonas. It was a string of doodles and coded notes written on a hotel pad of paper. The same type of code they'd seen before in Ava's message to Becca.

"This is definitely Ava, and the diapers prove Easton was still with her," Madison said, trying to work through the woman's thought process and actions. "From the way Becca describes her, Ava is a visual thinker, and is always sketching and taking notes. I'm not sure what this says, but if she was trying to figure out a plan, writing it down might have helped her come up with a solution."

"That makes sense, but escaping from this house was only step one of the problem. She has the baby with her," Jonas said. "And she probably has no idea where she is. Or, at the very least, it's unfamiliar territory."

"And we have no way of knowing how long ago she left, or where she went," Madison said. She turned to the sheriff. "What's around here?"

Sheriff Daugherty placed his hands on his hips. "There are a number of houses scattered around the area, but the nearest one is almost a mile away. The nearest town, another fifteen minutes by car."

"We can assume she's looking for a phone service or a ride," Jonas said.

"Except she doesn't trust anyone at this point," Madison said. "She's probably going to think it's too risky to get a ride."

One of the deputies hung up his cell and walked over to them. "I might have an answer. We just got a call about a stolen vehicle from the Porters' cabin next door. There's a couple in town that check on the place every week or so, to make sure everything's okay, and the owners' old Jeep Wrangler is gone. Apparently, they kept a spare key on the inside of the bumper."

"That's got to be her," the sheriff said. "Put a BOLO out on that vehicle right now."

"Yes, sir."

"The problem is, she could be anywhere by now." Madison picked up an empty container of formula that had been left on the table. "We have no idea what kind of head start she had. All she needs is money and fuel and she could be back to Seattle or on to Portland for that matter."

"Then let's keep canvassing the area, including the nearby town," Jonas said. "If she stopped for fuel or food, she might have spoken to someone. She's going to have to trust someone at some point, and we need to find that person."

Madison's phone buzzed, and she pulled it out of her pocket. "Piper, what have you got?" she asked, putting the call on speaker so Jonas could hear her.

"Michaels asked me to check in with you both. Any progress?"

"We're talking with the sheriff here at the cabin where Callum Burks brought Ava," Madison said. "They're canvassing the area. She was definitely at the house with Easton but managed to get out, and we now believe she was able to get ahold of an old Jeep Wrangler."

"Anything on your end?" Jonas asked.

"Yes, actually. There has been some credit card activity. Ava purchased a bus ticket from La Push to Port Angeles, and then on to Victoria, Canada, by ferry."

"Wait a minute." Madison worked to process the information. "That doesn't make sense. I can't see her leaving Washington with the baby, and immigration definitely won't let her leave the country."

"Maybe she decided to leave the baby at a church or a police station," Piper said, searching for answers just like she was.

Madison pressed her lips together. Maybe, but something didn't add up. If Ava didn't trust her own handler or the authorities, she certainly wasn't going to trust strangers to take care of Easton.

Or would she?

"Keep tracking her phone in case she turns it back on. Oh, and Piper," Madison said before hanging up, "I'm going to send a photo of a note found at the cabin. See if Becca can make sense of it. Keep us updated."

"I'll arrange to have the BOLO out on her extended to include the bus route up to Port Angeles, as well as the port authority there."

"Great. Thanks, Piper." Madison ended the call.

Wyse had been right. Ava didn't know who to trust. He was supposed to keep her safe, and yet she was once again running for her life. All it had taken was one misstep for her life to be put back on the line again. And the thought that Ava was out there, alone, with someone dangerous after her was terrifying.

The temperature was dropping, and she could be in further danger if something were to happen to the car.

Madison shoved her hands into her coat pockets, then stopped as she felt the photo strip she must've unintentionally taken from Ava's apartment. She stared at the sweet photos of Ava and her daughter. She knew what it was like to lose a husband, but a husband *and* a child . . . how did one begin to deal with that kind of pain? How was it even possible to find your way through the grief?

She slipped the photos back into her pocket, wondering what she would have done in the same situation. The pain was still raw. The options limited. Feelings of being trapped returning. Wondering if you'd ever feel okay again.

Madison walked toward the window Ava had managed to escape from and felt an unexpected connection to the woman. How many times she'd wanted to simply get into her car and run. Running didn't mean having a particular destination. It didn't always matter where you were going as much as it mattered what you were leaving behind.

She ran her fingers across the dusty windowsill, trying to get inside Ava's head. Wyse had mentioned how running also meant leaving a trail of misinformation. Especially when someone was after you. You needed to throw off whoever was hunting you down to ensure that they searched in the wrong places. Sending them on a wild-goose chase meant you had more time to run, until eventually—hopefully—your trail ran cold. If Ava and Wyse had talked about this, then there was a good chance Ava had implemented some kind of diversion into her plan.

Like the bus ticket out of the country?

Madison looked out at the wooded area surrounding the house. It made sense that she wanted to throw off DeMarco, but if Ava was trying to send him on a wild-goose chase, it was going to make it harder for them as well.

"Madison?" Jonas stepped in front of her, pulling her away from her thoughts.

"Sorry."

"You're fine. Daugherty was called back to the station, but Deputy Fields will take us wherever we want to go. I told him we need to head to the bus station."

Madison shook her head. "I don't think she got on that bus."

"Okay . . . why?"

"Wyse mentioned a trail of disinformation," she said, stating her thoughts out loud. "What if that's what she's doing? Charging tickets on her card to throw us off."

"It's possible," Jonas said. "But she's scared and on the run. She knows DeMarco is on her trail and is trying to get as far away from here as possible. She doesn't have time to come up with some master plan."

"She had a plan. She knows we're looking for her, but she also knows DeMarco, and maybe even Púca, is looking for her. And while she might not trust law enforcement, she knows she can't let them find her at any cost. Avoiding them has to be her primary objective."

"Okay. Then what are you proposing?"

"We extend the BOLO and go to the bus station, but stay aware that she could be trying to lead us down a rabbit hole."

Jonas rubbed the back of his neck and blew out a breath of frustration. "If you're right, then instead of narrowing down her location, we've just opened it up to about anywhere on the West Coast. She could have driven all night and be in another state by now."

"I know, but—"

Deputy Fields approached them. "I'm sorry to interrupt, but I think we might have something."

"What is it?"

"A car matching the description of the Jeep was found off the side of the road five minutes out of town. We've sent a patrol car out there, but I thought you might want to go as well."

"Definitely." Madison glanced at Jonas, who nodded his agreement. "Let's go."

TWENTY-TWO

Ava clutched the steering wheel, trying to stop her hands from shaking as the Jeep's engine sputtered beneath her, then died. She managed to turn the wheel enough to make the sharp right turn off the highway onto the paved road that led to the beach, then pumped the brakes until they slid to a stop, partially off the road and into the bushes.

She fought to breathe. Easton cried in the back seat, hungry and scared. Well, so was she. She had to trust someone, but she'd done that before and look where it had gotten her. They'd found her, just like she knew they would. And whoever had brought her here was no doubt still out looking for her.

She pulled out the burner phone she'd used to contact Becca yesterday, still debating if she should turn it back on or not. She'd found a radio in the closet of the cabin and had turned it on, hoping for information on where she was. But instead, she'd heard the emergency that an Amber Alert had gone out for Easton. It had reinforced everything she'd feared could happen. She'd immediately turned off the phone and pulled out the battery, stopping any chance of being traced. She realized that making it harder for DeMarco to find her made it equally hard for law enforcement to find her, but what choice did she have? She didn't trust any of them.

Wyse had promised that she'd be safe. Promised that her testimony would take down DeMarco and the entire crime ring he worked for. Promised that one day she'd be able to stop looking over her shoulder. But that wasn't really a promise he could make or keep, and now she knew none of it was true. Even if her testimony did put them behind bars, they would still come after her. If they couldn't silence her before she testified, they'd find a way to hurt those around her out of revenge. Which meant she'd never really be safe. Never really be free. Now she wished she'd never gone to the authorities. The cost hadn't been worth it.

But like her grandmother used to tell her, wishes only came true in fairy tales.

She held up her hands, wishing she could turn on the heater, but the car she'd found at the neighbor's house yesterday afternoon hadn't been the answer to her prayers like she'd hoped. Not knowing where to go until she had a plan, and figuring DeMarco would assume she'd get as far away as possible, she'd holed up in a hotel, thankful she had some money stashed away in the bottom of Easton's diaper bag. She managed to check in with no mention of the baby. The last thing she wanted was to be recognized—especially if DeMarco's men were still tracking her.

But what now?

She'd still be in the hotel, except she'd needed more formula for Easton. Guilt flooded through her at the reminder that she'd stolen the formula. But she couldn't take any chances of being recognized.

Ava glanced out the car's rearview mirror. She was far enough off the main road that it was going to be hard for a passerby to see her. With darkness starting to settle in, walking back to the cabin wasn't an option. Not with Easton. She didn't want to spend the night along the side of the road, but at the moment—despite the cold—she couldn't think of any other options.

She breathed in deeply, trying to settle her nerves. Chloe would have loved the Northwest. A tomboy at heart, she'd never tired of the rugged beaches of Maine, or the three of them camping over long weekends at Moosehead Lake. It was moments like those that she missed. Going out onto the lake in a canoe or fishing for salmon . . .

Ava shoved aside the memories and instead made up a bottle of formula before undoing the straps of Easton's car seat. She hummed softly to him as she lifted him into the front seat with her and gave him his bottle. Becca had trusted her to keep him safe and that was a promise she had to keep. She would fight to the end to protect him.

Easton stared up at her as milk ran down the side of his cheek. A gurgle followed before he latched back on to the bottle. If only she had faith in God the way Easton had in her. But faith was hard to hold on to when you'd lost everything. Trust was hard to regain when it had been broken.

Headlights reflected off her mirrors, and she heard the crunch of tires as a car slowed down and stopped behind her.

A car door slammed.

"Hello . . . Is anyone in there?"

Ava's heart raced. Instinct warned her to keep Easton quiet, but there was nowhere to run. Nowhere to hide.

It's just someone coming to help you, Ava. You know you can't stay here. You have to trust someone.

The fear in her heart began to dissipate. A good Samaritan

had found her and would take her somewhere safe, maybe a hotel, where she could figure things out. And if they recognized her from the Amber Alert, she'd just tell them they must have the wrong person.

Someone knocked on the window.

Trust.

You have to trust someone.

She looked up to see who was there.

TWENTY-THREE

An unsettling sense of dread surged through Madison as she jumped out of the squad car ahead of Jonas and ran toward the Jeep that had slid partially off the side of the road and into the brush. She could hear the pounding of the Pacific against the rocky shoreline.

A uniformed officer hurried up to them as she held up her badge. "Is she there?"

"No. I'm sorry. The car is empty, and the driver's side window's been shattered."

Madison glanced toward the ocean, her frustration brewing. "Have you searched the area?"

"I've got three deputies out doing a broad search of the beach just up ahead."

"Any obvious injuries?" she pressed, needing answers.

"No traces of blood or damage to the vehicle," the deputy said. "She left behind a car seat. I was just getting ready to do a thorough search of the car."

"Let us know if you find anything."

Anger began to simmer below the surface in Madison, only adding to the frustration she already felt. Their job had been created to hunt down fugitives in order to ensure they stayed behind bars so they weren't able to hurt anyone. But missing person cases like this were different. They searched because lives—normally children's—were at risk and in immediate danger. They searched to save them. And when they couldn't find them . . .

Madison pushed away the thought and followed the trail down the side of the bluff toward the beach below, needing to clear her head.

The beach was cloaked in a hazy fog as the sun began to set, leaving rays of orange sun filtering across the horizon. Spindly pieces of bleached driftwood littered the rocky shoreline, adding to the ghostlike ambiance. The wind blew against her as she made her way down toward the sand, listening to the sound of the surf pounding against the shore. Farther out, waves were crashing against the sea stacks that looked as if they'd erupted out of the ocean floor. Cooling temperatures and fading light, coupled with the fog rolling in, had left the beach eerily quiet, with only a handful of visitors enjoying the view.

Madison picked up one of the hundreds of flat stones sprinkled across the sand and ran her thumb back and forth across the smooth side while staring out at the mesmerizing scene.

"You okay?" Jonas asked, catching up to her.

"Yeah . . ." She dropped her hands to her sides. "Did you talk to the officer?"

"I did."

"I was just trying to clear my head and figure out where she might be." She breathed in the salty sea air, in awe of the view in front of her, despite her frustration. "Our family used to come out here when I was small. It always amazed me that we could explore snow-capped mountains, rain forests, and beaches all on the same trip. My favorite was the Hoh Rain Forest. I would walk down the trails in front of my parents and sister and imagine that I was a tiny fairy living in an enchanted forest. I was completely taken in by the giant moss-covered trees and the thick canopy overhead." She paused to look down at the stone in her hand. "And then we would come here and climb on the sun-bleached logs, search for tide pools, and look for sea anemones. Sometimes we would find sea cucumbers and small octopuses."

Jonas stood beside her, the wind whipping around them while he patiently waited for her to continue.

"We always had a wonderful time until the summer when my sister tried to scare me with a story about a girl about my age who disappeared along this beach, never to be seen again." A shiver slid through Madison at the memory. "I remember turning around at one point on the beach—after she'd told me the story—and my parents were gone. I was terrified. It probably wasn't a minute later that I found them just around the bend behind me, but it was a long time before I left my parents' side after that."

She turned away from the sea and faced Jonas. "What if Ava doesn't want to be found? What if that's the real reason why she hasn't checked in with Wyse? What if her plan all along, if she was discovered, was to run?"

"I don't know, Madison—"

"She knows what it's like to cut ties with everyone she knows," she continued, cutting off his response, her mind racing. "She disappeared with the help of the government, but while running on her own would be difficult, she's now had time to plan."

"Except it's hard to stay missing," Jonas said. "Especially with today's technology and cameras. Even the WITSEC perimeters keeping her safe didn't work. She has to know how dangerous it would be to try to disappear on her own."

"More dangerous than trusting a program that let her down? She has to be questioning that."

"I don't know." Jonas sat down on a large fallen log, then leaned forward, resting his forearms against his thighs. "I can understand why she might have trust issues with Wyse now. Why she might even be leery of law enforcement or wonder if there's a leak in the WITSEC program, but she's not a criminal with survival skills. She's got to know deep down that, despite what happened, the program is her best chance of surviving."

"Maybe."

"She was a wife and mom who got mixed up in a very bad situation. She might have had a plan for emergencies, but disappearing for good takes time, a lot of planning, and money. Not to mention that she has a baby with her who is also in danger. She needs WITSEC."

Madison sat down next to him, her mind continuing to wrestle with the situation. While each person they hunted down was different, there were some things that remained the same. People on the run tended to go to familiar places, like old stomping grounds, cities they knew their way around, or to friends and family for help. To break from that—like Ava had done through the WITSEC program—wasn't easy. It meant everything she dealt with on a day-to-day basis was new and often intimidating. Was she really willing to take the risk of running on her own? And what about Easton?

A gull cried out as it circled above them, momentarily shifting her attention. Waves continued to rhythmically pound against the shoreline, steady and constant. There was one thing that was undeniably true. DeMarco's men weren't going to stop looking for her. They had to find her first.

Deputy Fields ran down from the trail and onto the beach, stopping in front of them. "Sorry to interrupt, but I might have something."

"What is it?" Madison asked, standing up.

"There was a receipt on the floor from a convenience store up the road, and from the time stamp, I think it has to be her."

Fifteen minutes later, Madison walked into the small convenience store that sold everything from pepperettes to salmon, candy to local souvenirs. Jonas had gone with Fields to get a loaner car that the sheriff had offered them, while Madison talked to employees who might have seen Ava.

The woman from behind the counter looked up from where she was refilling a display of gum. "Evening."

"Hi, Zara," Madison said, reading the woman's name tag.

"Can I help you?"

She held up her badge. "I'm Deputy US Marshal Madison James. I need to ask you a few questions about a customer you had in your shop earlier today."

Zara rested her hands against the counter. "Okay."

Madison held up the photo of Ava on her phone. "We're looking for this woman. Have you seen her?"

Zara pulled down her glasses from the top of her head. "I have, actually. She was here this morning. She put ten dollars of fuel in her car, bought a couple snacks, and paid cash."

"Did she say anything?"

"She chatted a bit, actually," Zara said, reaching up and redoing the loose bun on the top of her head. "Told me how much she'd enjoyed her time visiting the area. Said she was just traveling through on her way back to Canada but had stopped long enough to see some of the sights like Ruby Beach and the Hoh Rain Forest."

"Did you see a baby with her?" Madison asked.

"No." Zara dropped her hands to her sides, seemingly surprised at the question. "No baby. Sweet girl though. Didn't like the idea of her driving alone, but she insisted she'd be fine. Said she'd taken this route a number of times."

"Do you remember which way she headed from here?" Madison asked.

"North, back onto the highway, I believe."

"Okay." Madison slipped her badge back into her pocket, frustrated she hadn't learned more. "Thank you for your help. I appreciate it."

"Of course. I just hope she's okay. You're not the first officer who stopped in looking for her."

"Someone from the local sheriff's office?" Madison asked, surprised at the statement.

"No, there were two of them, and they weren't in uniform. Said they were from out of town. FBI or maybe DEA . . . I'm not sure." She let out a low laugh. "Some three-letter acronym."

"What time were they here?" Madison asked.

The woman glanced at her watch. "An hour . . . maybe an hour and a half ago, I'd guess."

Madison glanced up and spotted a camera hanging on the wall. "Are your cameras working?"

"Yes, they are. You wouldn't believe how many people try to walk out without paying for stuff."

"I'm going to need to look at your footage."

"Of course. Just give me a sec to get things set up for you in the back office. Hey, Billy," she called out to the other employee who'd been stocking chips. "I need you to keep an eye on the cash register for a while."

Madison followed Zara into the small office at the back of the store, then stood behind her while Zara brought up the security footage and started fast-forwarding through it. Two men walked through the front door and straight to the cashier.

Zara paused the video, then stood up. "That's them."

"Thank you. I'm going to send still shots back to my office."

"Of course. Anything you want."

Jonas walked up to the office door as Zara was leaving.

"This is my partner," Madison said, motioning him to come inside. "We've got something, Jonas. Two men were in here a little over an hour ago, looking for Ava."

"How in the world did they manage to track her down so quickly?" Jonas asked.

"I'm not sure, but I was just getting ready to send Wyse a photo and see if he recognized them." She pulled out her phone and placed the call.

Wyse answered on the third ring. "Hey," he said. "What's up?"

Madison put the call on speaker. "I'm sending you a photo that was pulled off security footage at a local gas station. I need to know if you recognize either man."

"Sure. Give me a second while I look."

Madison stared at the grayscale screen while they waited for Wyse to download the photos. Neither man looked familiar, but there was no doubt in her mind who they were working for.

"I've got the photos," Wyse said, coming back on the line. "I don't know the one on the left, but the taller one works for DeMarco."

Madison leaned back in the chair. "So, these are two of DeMarco's hit men."

"That's a good way of putting it."

"Okay. Thank you." Madison hung up the call, then turned the chair around to face Jonas. "I just can't seem to get into Ava's head and figure out what she's doing, but I have this feeling she wanted Zara to remember her. Why?"

"To confirm that she was going to Canada if anyone asked. In a small town, people remember strangers. Not a bad idea if her plan was to misdirect anyone looking for her."

Jonas continued, "One of the deputies checked out the vehicle she was in. They'll have a mechanic look at it, but it definitely doesn't look as if it was forced off the road. It looks like there was an issue with the engine because it hadn't been driven for a while."

"So maybe her plan really was to head to Canada," Madison said. Her phone rang and she grabbed it out of her pocket. "Piper, please tell me you've got something."

"I do. I just got a trace on Ava's phone. She finally turned it on."

"Where is she?"

"It looks like about ten miles from your location in a wooded area off the highway. The phone isn't moving. There's a house on the property."

Madison glanced at Jonas. "She couldn't have walked that far on foot. Not with Easton."

"She could have gotten a ride," Jonas said.

Madison glanced back at the screen. There had to be a reason for her turning it back on, knowing it could be tracked. Which meant she'd probably taken a risk because she was in trouble.

"Keep us updated if her location moves," Madison said, pushing her chair back. "We're on our way."

TWENTY-FOUR

Ava had recognized Gino and Rocky the moment she saw them, but by then it was too late. Gino had used a rock to shatter the window, then unlocked the door and pulled her out. From what she knew about the men, their loyalty to DeMarco ran deep. They were willing to do anything, and had records to prove it.

Gino shoved the gun toward her, then motioned for her to sit down in the chair in the dimly lit dining room. Easton whimpered on a blanket on the floor beside her. She had no idea where he'd taken them. They'd driven for twenty, maybe thirty, minutes, then turned onto a dirt road. The small cabin they were in was off the road and more than likely isolated, like the one she'd escaped from.

Fatigue washed over her, seeping through the very core of her being. She'd fought them for so long, trying to stay safe in the shadows. Maybe she should have called 911 instead of running on her own, but DeMarco had connections, even within law enforcement.

"Make him shut up." Gino's voice pierced her thoughts.

"He's hungry," she said.

"Then feed him." He ran his hand through his spiky blond hair, clearly irritated. "I need him to be quiet."

"He's a baby," Ava said, reaching for the diaper bag. "Babies cry."

"I don't care. Make him stop."

"Forget the baby," Rocky said to Gino. "We need to talk."

She glanced at Rocky, which wasn't his real name, but instead a moniker he'd adopted since he was built like a body builder. Neither man seemed to have even a hint of sympathy for her situation.

Rocky glanced at his smartwatch. "I just got a message that he'll meet us at the marina first thing in the morning."

"Who?" Ava asked.

"None of your business." Gino spit out the words.

Gino motioned Rocky into the kitchen while she finished mixing up another bottle for Easton. She might not know their plan, but she knew the goal. They would dispose of her and Easton, and in the vast wilderness surrounding the cabin, that wasn't going to be difficult. Ava picked up snippets of the conversation as Easton latched on to the bottle, thankful he'd finally stopped crying, then tried to slow her own breathing as she looked around the room.

She could try to head out the back of the house with Easton, but it was dark now, and once again she had no idea where they were. Running would be hard enough—she'd learned that. With Easton it wasn't even an option. But then what? She knew she'd never be able to physically fight her way out of this situation.

She knew what she had to do. "There is something that the two of you need to know."

"Shut up," Gino said from the other side of the room where he and Rocky were still talking. "I didn't ask for your opinion, and there's nothing you can do to make us change our minds—"

"What if there was?" Ava caught his gaze. She would have to choose her words carefully.

Rocky held his hand up. "What are you talking about?"

"What if I told you that I have information that would ensure DeMarco and his associates are released with all charges against them dropped?"

"How is that possible?" Gino asked. "You recant everything you told the DA in your testimony? They wouldn't believe you."

"Why not? They're banking on my testimony. I could go to the DA and tell him I lied."

Gino pulled his gun out of his holster, then bridged the gap between them. "That's easy enough to say when you're standing here in front of us with a gun to your head, but we both know that they will never believe you."

Her jaw tensed as she forced herself to look Gino in the eye. "What if it was true?"

"Wait a minute," Rocky said. "You lied to the DA?"

Ava nodded.

"I don't believe you," Gino said.

"I have proof."

"Enough." Gino waved his gun into the air. "We don't have time for this. You're stalling. We have our orders, and we're going to follow through with them."

"And if she's not stalling?" Rocky asked, turning to Gino. "What if she's telling the truth? Don't you think it's worth hearing what she has to say? DeMarco would pay us top dollar if we could get him out of prison."

"She's stalling *and* lying," Gino said.

"But what if she's not?"

Ava closed her eyes, wishing she could block out the memories that had gotten her to this moment, but there was no going back. "Rocky's right," she said, sitting down to try to steady her legs. "Are you really willing to take that risk? Can you imagine what DeMarco would say if you were handed the opportunity to clear his name?"

Gino folded his arms across his chest, still holding on to his weapon. "What kind of proof do you have?"

"Emails. Documents. Bank account numbers," she said, thankful Easton was quiet and still eating. "Documents I never showed the authorities."

"Documents that would exonerate DeMarco?"

"Yes," she said.

"I don't understand."

"When I testified, I wasn't trying to take down DeMarco." She closed her eyes for a moment before continuing. "I was trying to take down my husband."

"Wait a minute." Gino pulled a chair out from the table and sat down across from her. "You were trying to incriminate your husband?"

She nodded, her heart in her throat.

"Why?" Gino asked.

"About a year ago, I found out that my husband had a second bank account." She shifted Easton to her shoulder and started patting his back, praying they didn't notice the tremble in her voice and suspsect she was lying. "There was over two and a half million dollars in it that he'd funneled offshore."

"Where did he get the money?" Rocky asked.

She let out a sharp breath, hesitating again before she answered. "He stole it from DeMarco."

"Whoa," Gino said, leaning forward.

"But that's not all my husband was involved in."

"You're telling me you set everything up to . . . to have your husband killed?"

Ava chose her words carefully, knowing she was only going to get one chance to convince them she was telling the truth, even though she was lying through her teeth. "When my husband and I first got married, everything seemed perfect, but things began to change as he moved up at work. He worked as a corporate controller for sixty, seventy hours a week, and then I found out he was having affairs with a number of women. I couldn't stay with him, and yet if I left him, I knew I'd lose everything. He'd make sure he got everything, including our daughter."

Gino leaned forward while Easton finished his bottle. "You'll excuse me if I find this all hard to believe. Your daughter is dead because of what *you* did. Even I couldn't justify making that choice."

Ava pressed her lips together, blinking back the tears. "That was never supposed to happen."

"And how did your husband get involved with DeMarco?" Gino asked.

"DeMarco knew he was an accountant and asked me if I would connect the two of them. He needed someone to help with some . . . financial issues."

She drew Easton closer as the rush of pain swept through her. She hadn't been able to hold Chloe since the fire, and yet sometimes . . . sometimes she felt as if she was in the room with her. She could still smell the scent of her vanilla shampoo and see the exact color of her favorite nail polish. And then, like right now, she was hit with the reality that those memories were a lifetime away.

She shoved back the pain. "Living with a monster can make you do things you never thought you'd do. Sometimes the consequences are far worse than you imagine, but when there is only one way out, it doesn't matter. My daughter's death wasn't a part of the plan, which is why sacrificing her is a burden I will live with the rest of my life."

Gino leaned forward. "You had to change identities, lost everything you had, and went into witness protection. How can you even begin to think that you won?"

"Like I said, I found the only way out I could. My husband had been going through my laptop from work and managed to gain access to DeMarco's accounts. He had everything he needed to set up an offshore account, and I was stupid enough to never notice. For a while, anyway. I knew if DeMarco found out what I had allowed to happen that he'd kill me. I knew his reputation . . ."

"So you took him down too?"

"It was the only way to save myself in the process. I managed to get rid of my husband by someone else's hand and never went to prison. How many people get the chance to start over in life? And I was able to do it with the government's blessing."

"I don't know." Gino rubbed the back of his neck, clearly still not convinced.

"We all have to do what we have to do, even when things don't turn out the way we thought they would." She looked at each of the men in turn. "You take orders from a man who has no value for life, which makes you a paid assassin. You have to deal with the guilt of that. I have to live with the death of my daughter for the rest of my life. That wasn't what I'd planned, but it's a win-win situation for both of us. I can disappear for good, DeMarco will go free, and you and Rocky here will get the credit."

Gino tapped his Glock against his leg. "The DA isn't going to believe any of this. They'll think you're being coerced into changing your testimony because you were being threatened." His expression got colder. "Just like I do."

"All they had was circumstantial evidence and my testimony. Without my testimony, the entire case falls apart and they can't keep him any longer." Ava's voice cracked as she tried unsucessfuly to press down the fear enveloping her. "So I'll make a video testimony and say everything that happened. But trust me when I say I have enough physical evidence hidden away as well that the DA won't be able to ignore it."

"So what you are saying," Gino said, "is that you lied. The entire time you sat on that stand and testified. If that's true, then you deserve an Academy Award."

"I took advantage of a situation to get what I wanted," she said.

"And what do you get out of this . . . confession?"

"Five million dollars."

"Five million—"

"I know how much money your organization really brings in," Ava cut him off. "That's nothing for you. I'll hand over all the files I have that will exonerate DeMarco and put the blame solely on my husband, and then I'll disappear."

"Do you really think we're stupid enough to trust what you're saying?" Gino stood up and pointed the gun at her, his face red with frustration. "You'd say anything to stop us from killing you, but it's too late for that. The DA will never believe this story. I know I don't."

"Then you're making a foolish mistake." Ava forced herself to hold his gaze. "Because what if I'm not lying? Is that really a risk you can take? We both know you need me. Think of the position this would place you in with your boss. You'd go from errand boy to—I don't know—second in command?"

"Prove it to me right now, and I might consider your request."

Ava hesitated. She shifted Easton, who had fallen asleep, to her lap, then took off the necklace around her neck. The steampunk heart she'd bought on Etsy made the perfect place to hide the flash drive. "Part of the proof you need for what I'm saying is in here." She undid a clasp and handed him the tiny drive. "I'll give you the rest once I have my money."

Gino held up the drive. "What kind of evidence is in there?"

"Evidence that my husband was behind everything. That he was actually funneling the company's funds into his own account."

"So you leaked the information and set up the hit?"

"I made sure DeMarco received an anonymous tip, along with a few photos. He ordered the hit the next day. Unfortunately for DeMarco, he left behind evidence in the hit, and the DA decided to go after him. And because I had to cover my own back, I had to give them what they wanted."

"Testimony against DeMarco."

Ava nodded.

"This will prove you got away with murder," Gino said. "How does that help you?"

"One"—she held up a finger—"there's no proof that I was the one who leaked the information on my husband. The DA doesn't need to know that. But the photos and documents—part of them, anyway—are in there. They will give me insurance that you don't kill me right now and allow me the financial security to leave WITSEC."

"There are no guarantees that this plan of yours will even work. If the DA doesn't believe you—"

"Two," she continued, ignoring his argument, "if I get what I want, you'll also get what you want. You'd be a fool not to agree to the deal."

Gino stepped up to the window, clearly trying to figure out what to do with the lynchpin she'd just thrown at him. "I need to make a couple phone calls."

"I wouldn't take too much time." She rocked Easton gently, praying he stayed asleep. "I have a feeling the marshals are still after me, and if they show up, you'll never see the rest of the evidence I have. Because the reality is, if you win, I win, and if they rescue me, I still win. You, on the other hand, are out of options."

Gino kept his gaze out the window. "You'll be running the rest of your life."

"I've learned from my mistakes and won't let that happen again."

Gino turned back and stared at her. "I'll have to look at this, but if what you're saying is true—"

"It is."

Gino dropped his hands to his sides. "What's going to stop DeMarco or Púca, if he gets involved, from ordering another hit out on you?"

"They won't. If you remember at the trial, I can be very, very convincing. That is, if anyone can even find me after I disappear."

Gino slipped the flash drive into his pocket, then grabbed the keys off the table. "I'm going out for a bit. Make sure she stays out of trouble, Rocky."

Ava's pulse raced as she watched him leave. If her plan didn't work, she knew they'd kill her.

TWENTY-FIVE

Darkness had settled across the peninsula by the time Jonas turned off the highway onto the gravel road. The forested area was thick, blocking out any moonlight. The sheriff and his deputies had been called out on a three-car wreck on the north side of town, but the marshals decided that waiting for backup wasn't an option. Their window of time for finding Ava could close any minute.

"We just lost cell signal," Madison said, "but the map is still up. Should be ahead on this road about a mile or so, on the left."

The car's headlights pierced through the darkness, guiding their way down the narrow road and attracting a steady stream of moths.

"A message came through from Edward while we were back at the gas station," she said. "I just had a chance to read it."

"What did he say?" Jonas asked.

"He's been working with the authorities on the evidence he put together on Sabrina, but he also received a call back from Thomas Knight's grandfather, Harold, today."

"That sounds promising."

"I think it is. Edward has been trying to get ahold of him,

but the man has never returned his calls. Knowing Harold's refused to talk to reporters in the past, Edward assumed that he still struggles with the death of his grandson, which makes sense."

"So why did he call?"

"He said that a little over five years ago, just a couple days before Luke was killed, Sabrina called him. She told him that he didn't have to worry. That she was going to take care of everything and make things right."

"Sounds pretty cryptic," Jonas said, avoiding a fallen tree limb that lay partway on the narrow road. "Does he have any idea what she meant?"

"At the time, he said it didn't make sense, so he just forgot about it. He was grieving the death of his grandson, and that in itself was more than he knew how to handle. But when he heard about Sabrina's arrest and started looking at the timeline of Luke's death and her call, he realized he should have spoken up years ago."

"It almost sounds like a confession."

"That's what I'm thinking," Madison said.

He couldn't help but wonder if that wasn't all she was thinking. She must be asking herself the same question he was: What if Harold Knight had spoken up and stopped Luke's murder? But there was no way to change the past and what had happened to Luke. No going back and stopping the sequence of events that had followed Thomas Knight's arrest.

"Harold agreed to give his statement to the DA," Madison added, "but Edward wants to talk with him in person. He's planning to drive out to the man's ranch, but I told him to wait until I was back. I'd like to go with him."

"I think you should, but it's starting to look like the evidence they need to add first-degree murder charges against her in Luke's case might actually come through." He glanced at Madison, unable to read her expression in the darkness. He knew her well enough to know that she still needed the closure, not just from the arrest of Sabrina but from her sentencing as well. Which would more than likely force her to live through the events surrounding Luke's death yet again, but it was almost over. She had to remember that.

Jonas slowed down as they came to the end of the gravel road, not sure what they were about to find. While Ava's phone should still be on, she hadn't answered Piper's numerous calls. On top of that, it seemed impossible for her to have walked here, in the dark, with the baby, which left the unanswered question, How had she gotten here?

"The curtains are drawn, but it looks like there's a light on inside," Jonas said, climbing out of the car.

There were no other vehicles in the circular drive in front of the one-story cabin.

Jonas knocked on the front door. "US Marshals. I need you to open the door."

Someone shouted from inside. A baby cried and a door slammed. Jonas was about to kick open the front door when he heard Madison's surprised voice from behind him.

"Jonas! It's Ava."

Jonas turned around and immediately recognized the young woman standing in the shadows of the trees with a baby in her arms and a look of terror on her face.

"We're with the US Marshals and we're here to help you."

She nodded.

Glass shattered from a window, followed by a shot that struck the porch post next to him.

"Get her into the car," he shouted. "Now."

He flew off the porch and ran toward the car, then jumped into the driver's seat to start the engine. Madison had just gotten in behind Ava and the baby when another shot hit the car, shattering the back window. He pressed on the accelerator and floored it back onto the gravel road that led toward the highway.

"Are you both okay?" he asked.

"I think so," Ava said.

"How many are inside?" Jonas asked.

"One right now, but a second man, Gino, left to go do something. He said he'd be right back."

"Are they armed?"

"Both of them are. Rocky heard your knock on the door and went to grab his gun, and I . . . I didn't even take time to think. I just ran out the back."

"You did the right thing," Madison said.

The car shook. Jonas pressed on the accelerator, but the engine cut out and rolled to a stop in the middle of the gravel road.

"He must have hit more than the window," Jonas said, turning off the headlights and pulling out his phone. "I don't have a signal."

Madison held up hers in the back seat. "I don't either."

He jumped out of the car, worried about the unraveling situation. Darkness meant it would be easier for them to hide, but it also meant they needed to find shelter and safety as quick as possible. They couldn't go after the men without first ensuring the safety of Ava and the baby.

"I know there are cabins scattered around here, but we're going to need to walk." Jonas stuck his head back into the car. "Do you have enough blankets for Easton?"

Ava looked down at the baby in her arms. "Yes. I think he'll be fine."

Madison grabbed the diaper bag off the back seat, then turned to Jonas as she hopped out of the car. "If Gino drives back to the house and sees the car on his way, he's going to figure out quickly that we went on foot."

"Good point." He motioned for her to get in the driver's seat, then went behind and pushed it off the side of the gravel road into the bushes while she steered. It might not completely solve their problem, but at least it would buy them some time.

"There's a light a couple hundred feet to the south that looks like it might be coming from a neighboring house," Madison said, adjusting the bag on her shoulder.

Jonas let Madison lead, then took his position behind Ava as they walked away from the road by the light of their cell phones, and down a narrow trail lined by towering evergreen trees. He'd seen the fatigue in Ava's eyes, but more than that, he'd seen the terror. Whatever her plans had been, she clearly knew now that she couldn't do this on her own.

"I'm sorry," Ava said, struggling to keep up.

"Sorry for what?" Madison asked.

"They're not after the baby. They're after me. This . . . this is all my fault."

"It's not your fault—"

"You don't understand. I always knew they'd find me, and now not only is my life at stake, and yours, but Easton's as well. Becca trusted me with him. What if I can't keep him safe?"

"We're going to make sure both of you stay safe," Jonas said. "I promise."

It was a promise he intended on keeping, but he also knew

the reputations of the men tracking them. They had an agenda and wouldn't stop looking until they found her.

Ava stumbled in front of him on a fallen branch.

Jonas grabbed her arm to ensure she kept her balance. "Are you okay?"

Ava nodded as Easton reared back in her arms then gave Jonas a toothless grin.

"Well, little man." He couldn't help but chuckle. "You certainly know how to lighten the mood."

Another fifty feet and the path opened up to where a cabin had been built on a small section of land surrounded by tall pines. Away from the lights of the city, the sky had cleared and above them was an amazing display of the Milky Way. Jonas wished he had time to enjoy it. But not tonight. Even Easton's smile couldn't erase the seriousness of the situation. Or the urgency pressing against him to get them to safety.

Except for the porch light, the house was dark with its curtains drawn.

"It looks empty," Jonas said, unsurprised. Because the weather was unpredictable, most people visited the area during late summer, when the weather was the warmest and roads were open.

He knocked on the door while Madison checked the front windows.

No answer.

He knocked again with no answer, then reached for his wallet and pulled out his lock pick. "Give me a minute and I'll get us inside."

Thirty seconds later, the door was open.

Jonas flipped on the light above the stove, casting a yellow glow across the room, then used his flashlight to quickly search the cabin for a landline.

"Did you find anything?" Madison asked, emerging from the bedroom.

"I've got some candles, matches, a few canned goods, and a flashlight, but no landlines, no radio. Nothing that we can communicate with."

"Me neither. There's one bedroom and a small bath. I did find extra blankets and a kerosene heater."

He held up his phone again, searching for a signal. Still nothing.

"What are we supposed to do?" Ava bounced the fussy baby in her arms as she paced the floor, trying to get him to settle down.

Jonas glanced at Madison, not knowing how to tell Ava the truth. DeMarco's men were probably out looking for them, but they currently had no way to communicate their situation to the authorities. And no one coming to their rescue. The men would find their abandoned car, then know there were only a handful of shelters if they weren't able to call for help and had to walk.

"Do you have enough formula for Easton?" Madison asked.

Ava nodded.

"Why don't you see if he'll settle down and sleep. You look as if you need some rest as well."

"Yeah, I didn't sleep much last night."

Jonas glanced again at the window. A crying baby would be a giveaway, and a vulnerability. The walls on this cabin wouldn't be enough to stop the noise from filtering outside.

He pulled Madison aside as Ava sat down on a rocking chair in the corner of the room and started rocking the baby.

"I have a lot of questions I'd like to ask her," he whispered, "but right now, we don't have many, if any, options. She can't go out there again. It's too cold."

Madison nodded. "I know."

The two of them could have easily hiked to the highway to get help, but having Ava and Easton completely changed the situation.

"There is one solution," Jonas said.

"What is that?"

"You stay here with Ava and the baby while I go for help."

"Jonas—"

"It's better than just waiting here for them to find us. Besides, I can move a lot faster on my own. Once I get to the highway, I should have cell service again, and I'll be able to call for backup."

Madison hesitated, but she knew he was right. His going for help was their best option.

"I don't like splitting up, but I agree it makes sense," she said. "I'll give you my weapon—"

"No, you can't go out there without a way to protect yourself. I have mine."

His frown deepened. "And if they show up?"

Madison glanced around the small cabin. "We'll be okay. I'll set up a perimeter alarm and be ready. Just hurry."

He hesitated, wanting to say something else, but just nodded instead before hurrying back outside, praying he was doing the right thing.

The stunning setting was eerily quiet at night. Gravel crunched under his feet, and the wind sent a chill through him, while the trees swayed above. He pulled out his phone and checked it again, frustrated at the sketchy cell service.

He looked back at the cabin one last time. Even though he knew Madison was still reeling inside from all that had happened the past couple days, her focus was back. She was going to have to stop at some point and take the time to deal with Sabrina's arrest and the memories it had brought. But something told him that when she did, she'd be ready to face whatever came next.

TWENTY-SIX

Madison locked the door behind Jonas and turned off the porch light, then did a second sweep around the room while formulating a plan. If Gino and his partner found the car, which she was sure they would, they'd start searching the area. And if they did that, it wouldn't take long for them to track them down. The men would know they needed shelter and a way to communicate for help. They were coming, and she had to be prepared.

Her gun was easily accessible in its holster, but she had only enough rounds to keep them at bay for a short period of time. In a normal situation when looking at security measures for a home, the perimeter was the logical place to start with a goal of making an intruder believe it wasn't worth trying to enter. Solid core doors, good hardware, protective window film, and a security system all helped with that, but she couldn't change any of those things now. What she could do was be prepared to defend the cabin if—no, when—they came.

"Easton's asleep." Ava had laid the baby down on a thick quilt on the floor and now stood in the middle of the room, her arms wrapped around her.

"Are you cold?" Madison asked.

"A little."

They could start a fire in the fireplace, but then it would look like someone was here, and that was a risk she wasn't willing to take.

"You could check the front closet for an extra coat," she suggested.

Ava nodded, then headed for the door. "I wonder who lives here?"

"I'm not sure, but it doesn't look like anyone has been here for a while."

There was a layer of dust on everything, and when she'd checked the fridge, all she'd found were a couple shriveled-up apples.

"I found one," Ava said, pulling a coat off the hanger and sliding it on.

"Good. Why don't you go lay down for a while? We don't know what might happen, and it would be good if you were rested."

"I don't think I could sleep. What are you doing?"

"Making sure we're prepared."

Ava shoved her hands into the coat pockets. "They're coming, aren't they?"

Madison hesitated. "It shouldn't take Jonas too long to track down help and bring in the authorities. We'll be okay."

"But they *are* coming."

Madison nodded, wishing they weren't in the situation they were in. But there was no use sugarcoating things. "We just need to be prepared."

"Can I do something? Please?"

"Okay," she said. Maybe keeping Ava busy was just as important as keeping her safe. "I need five or six of the canned goods emptied out so we have something that makes noise. Then go through the rest of the kitchen and find anything that could be used as a weapon. Flashlights, hornet spray . . ."

Ava nodded, then started pulling cans down onto the counter.

"And Ava"—Madison turned to her, needing her full attention—"if I tell you to run, I need you to grab the baby and leave through the back door. Don't wait for me. I'll find you."

Ava caught her gaze, not even trying to hide her fear. "I don't know—"

"Do you trust me?"

Ava nodded. "Yes, but you don't know these men or what they are capable of doing."

"I might not know them, but I've brought down others who are just as evil."

"What are you planning?"

"It's going to be a bit rudimentary," Madison said, digging through a drawer, "but my father used to build these low-tech perimeter alarms to let him know if an animal got close to his camp. It won't stop them, but at least we'll know if someone approaches the cabin."

"So, a zombie security system," Ava said.

Madison found a spool of fishing line in a bottom cupboard and pulled it out. "A what?"

"You know. String . . . rocks . . . tin cans . . . Something to scare away the zombies."

"I suppose that's a good description." Madison laughed. "But I'm hoping they don't ever discover where we are."

"Me too." Ava dug through a drawer in the kitchen, then pulled out a can opener. "And I wish I wasn't so terrified."

"Hey . . . it's okay. I don't blame you at all. But scared or not, your actions today have been extremely brave and selfless. You risked your life to save Easton, and it's because of you that he's here. And that he's safe."

"I don't feel very brave." Ava drew in a deep breath. "I lost my husband and daughter because of all of this, and now I'm not sure any of it was worth it. If I would have simply walked away—or looked the other way—my family would still be here with me."

Madison paused, searching for what to say. "I'm sorry. I truly am. I know what it's like to lose someone you love, but a child . . . I can't even imagine how horrible that has been for you."

Ava pressed her lips together and blinked, clearly fighting back tears. She took a deep breath before starting to open up the cans. "I'm not used to talking with anyone about what happened. Even Becca doesn't know the truth, and she's my best friend here."

"You work together, right?" Madison asked, prompting her to continue talking.

Ava nodded. "We both work at the diner and live in the same apartment building. I watch Easton while she's working, to help out, but in reality, it probably helps me more. I think I've needed someone to love during this time. Someone who loves me. Easton never fails to make me smile."

"Do you have other family?"

"Not really. A few extended relatives. No one close, and now . . . they think I'm dead. That I died in the same fire." Ava shrugged. "Who did you lose?"

"My husband." Madison swallowed hard, wondering if, like Ava, she'd ever be able to completely accept what had happened. "He was murdered five years ago."

"I'm so sorry. And the killer?"

"They . . . they've arrested someone, very recently actually, and the DA is working to put together the case against her."

"I know who killed my family." Ava stared at the counter. "They broke into our house and set it on fire. All to ensure their secrets were kept. I should have died that day too, but instead I somehow survived."

"It's hard to let go of the guilt," Madison said, reading between the lines. "Especially when you feel their death is your fault."

"Does it get any better?" Ava asked, looking up at her.

"Some days."

And then the grief hits again, like it did yesterday.

Madison forced back her own pain. "Can I ask you a question?"

"Of course," Ava said, opening up another can.

"There's something I don't understand. Why did you let Callum Burks into your apartment? We didn't see any sign of a struggle."

"I got a message from Robert, the man Becca was seeing." She poured the contents of the canned fruit into a bowl. "He said that Becca had been in an accident. That she was okay, but pretty banged up. Her phone had been smashed in the accident, which was why he was messaging me, but she wanted me to bring Easton to the hospital. Robert said he was sending a driver. I now know that the message wasn't from Robert."

"No," Madison said, as things started to make sense. "It was probably from his wife, Myra, on Robert's burner phone." Madison took a few minutes to explain the situation with the Saylors and Becca, detailing the real reason Ava had been abducted with Easton.

"I thought I'd been prepared for anything, but instead, all it took was letting down my guard for one moment." Ava shook her head, then finished pouring out the last can. "I'm still not sure how Gino tracked me down so fast."

"I'm not going to let them get you again."

"I know I should have contacted Wyse," Ava said. "I just didn't know who to trust."

"He's pretty shook up over what happened to you." Madison reached into her pocket and pulled out the strip of photos of Ava and her daughter. "I almost forgot, but I have something for you." She handed the strip to Ava.

She pressed it against her chest. "Thank you."

"I knew it was special to you."

"When I first went into witness protection, I had to leave everything behind. After the fire there were only a few things that survived, but this was the only printed photo. It was Chloe's last birthday. She'd just turned seven." She was silent a moment, then said, "Can I ask you a question?"

"Of course."

Ava dropped her arms to her sides, the photo still clutched in her right hand. "You understand what it's like to lose someone you love."

Madison nodded, then waited for her to continue.

"How did you move through grief? I've tried to convince myself that justice was coming . . . like that somehow would make it better. But even if DeMarco spends the rest of his life in prison and we take down everyone he works for, that doesn't change what I've lost. It will never take me back to the day before the attack. Sometimes"—her chest heaved—"sometimes I'm not sure I'll ever be okay again."

"I understand. People say that time heals all wounds, but

when the pain is so close to you, it doesn't take much to trigger a new wave of sadness." Madison leaned against the counter, needing to finish preparing the cabin but sensing the deep loss in Ava's eyes. "I've learned that pain and tragedy become a part of who we are. What happened to you changed everything, and you will never be who you were before that day. The scars and hurt become a part of the fabric of who you are. But that doesn't mean that you can't move forward despite the pain."

"But what do you say when people promise you everything will be okay? How do I find a way to move forward?"

Madison searched for words. So many people's attempts at encouragement after Luke's death had really been advice that had only made her feel worse. What had helped the most were those who simply were there for her and had loved her no matter how badly she hurt.

"For me, it's a journey I still haven't finished. But I've had to hold tight to my family and my faith. Knowing that no matter how bad it gets, the level of grief I feel won't be forever. But you know as well as I do that there's not a pat answer that will fix things. I know that while I might continue to heal, the pain I have will never be completely erased and that has to be okay. That God understands, even when I can't find the words to pray."

"And when I can't see God?" Ava gripped the edges of the counter. "Some days I can't find a way to hold on to my faith, no matter how hard I try. I feel like it was ripped away when I lost everything. Then I feel guilty."

"I've read through the psalms. Listened to worship music when I couldn't even sing a note." Madison met the woman's eyes. "Keep holding on. Tell God how you feel. Sometimes there are no words. Sometimes all you have is tears. Accepting that loss isn't easy, just like dealing with that pain isn't easy. And not only have you been forced to deal with the loss of your family, everything you knew and loved is gone too."

Ava shook her head. "I was just starting to find a life again. I agreed to witness protection, but now . . . they know where I am. They know my new name. I don't know if I can start over again. I've already lost everything once. I don't think I can do it again."

"I can't imagine how hard this is, Ava, but we're just going to take one thing at a time. And that's getting you and Easton out of here safely. And then we'll figure out the rest."

Ava wiped the tears off her cheeks and nodded. "Thank you."

"Of course." Madison smiled and grabbed the cans Ava had stacked on the counter. "I'm going outside to set up a couple perimeter alarms. Stay inside and keep the door locked until I return."

Madison glanced at her watch as soon as she finished setting up the primitive alarm, then headed back to the cabin. She calculated that by now Jonas would have made it to the highway and found service. Help couldn't be that far away.

Ava was waiting for her when Madison knocked on the cabin door. Once inside again, she quickly locked the door and put a chair beneath the handle. Buying time was all she could do at this point.

"I was looking for things we could use as weapons, like you asked me, and I found something," Ava said.

She hurried to the center of the room, then pulled back the edge of the carpet. There was a trapdoor with a handle in the middle of it.

Madison grabbed the metal handle, then pulled it open. "It looks as if they converted the crawl space into a cellar."

She shined a flashlight down the wooden ladder that went to the bottom of a small room with thick cedar log walls and a cement floor. There were a few old, wooden barrels inside and a stack of boxes, but other than that, it was empty. She worked through a revised plan in her mind. She just had to keep Ava safe until Jonas returned. Maybe this was the solution they needed.

Something clanged from out front.

"It worked," Ava whispered, terror in her eyes.

Madison signaled for Ava to be quiet as she pulled out her gun from its holster. Something—or more than likely someone—was out there. The baby whimpered, and Ava quickly picked him up.

"You need to get down there. Now," she mouthed.

Madison gripped her gun as she waited for Ava to hurry down the ladder into the small cellar. The front door handle turned slightly. Madison quickly set the rug back on top of the trapdoor, then repositioned herself in the corner of the room.

She was ready.

Wood splintered as someone tried to break down the door. Madison held her ground, praying that the baby wouldn't cry. Praying that they wouldn't find him and Ava. Two more kicks and the door flew open, slamming against the wall. The first man tripped over the chair that had fallen over. Madison aimed her weapon and fired, hitting him in the shoulder as the second man rushed toward her. His fist cracked against her jaw, throwing her backward into the wall and knocking the wind out of her.

He slammed her to the ground and pressed his forearm against her neck. "Where is she?"

Madison pushed back against his arm with one hand, struggling to breathe. "You're too late. She's gone. I told her to run."

"Where?"

"Away from here. Away from you."

With her free hand she reached behind her for the gun she'd dropped. All she needed was another inch.

But it was too late. Stars exploded as he squeezed tighter against her neck and everything went black.

TWENTY-SEVEN

Ava bounced Easton in her arms as she paced the small cellar, trying to get him to hush in the darkness. Her heart pounded in her throat. She wanted to put her hands over her ears to block out the noise. If the baby cried any louder . . .

"Please, Easton," she whispered in the darkness, her frustration mounting. "Please be quiet."

She started singing quietly under her breath, a lullaby she used to sing to Chloe, in an attempt to both calm Easton and curb her own fear. This nightmare she'd been thrust into wasn't his fault. Just like it hadn't been Chloe's fault. Her breath caught at the reminder. How was she supposed to keep Easton safe when she hadn't even been able to keep her own baby safe? How was she supposed to deal with the guilt if anything happened to Easton?

She'd heard of the threats in the courtroom to hunt her down. It was no longer just about keeping her quiet. It was about revenge for what she'd done.

If only she'd kept her mouth shut, or walked away, or refused to talk with the authorities. But then she would have been just as guilty as DeMarco. But the cost had been high, and not just for her but for her family and friends.

Shouts from the cabin escalated, and the wooden beam beside her shook. Another shot fired above her and then silence. Ava kept rocking Easton, terrified that something had happened to Madison. She was trapped, knowing if Madison had been hurt, they'd find her next. Because if Madison was okay, she'd come and get her. Wouldn't she?

Men's voices echoed above her, and Ava's heart raced as she grasped for options. She had to do something, but what? She gripped the pepper spray she'd found in the kitchen and started praying. It had been so long since she'd prayed. So long since she'd felt any life in her dried-up soul. Her heart was too tired to tell God how angry she was at him for taking away everything. And yet now, at this moment, the only light in the dark cellar was her sliver of faith.

Because that was all she had left.

TWENTY-EIGHT

"That was Madison, but the call dropped," Jonas told the sherriff as he held up his phone, trying to get a better connection.

He tried calling back, but instead of going through, it went straight to voice mail. He blew out his frustration as Sheriff Daugherty sped down the gravel road toward the cabin where Jonas had left Madison and Ava. A second patrol car followed just behind them. He tried not to go to the worst-case scenario in his mind. Madison had at least some coverage on her phone, which implied she'd left the cabin, but there was no way to know where she was.

This was his worst nightmare. Losing her. His judgment had been wrong. He never should have left them alone.

"Did she say anything?" the sheriff asked.

"Not that I could understand. I think she's in trouble."

"We don't know that," Daugherty said, swerving to the left to miss a deer perched on the edge of the road. "You did the right thing."

"Did I?"

He wasn't sure. He'd already lost one partner in this line of duty. It had been a huge part of his hesitation in opening up his heart again, especially with someone he worked with. He'd fought against the vulnerability and fear but had never been able to free himself from it.

"You know as well as I do that in this job there is little you can control beyond being prepared and doing what you're trained to do," Daugherty said. "You did everything you could. Getting help was the right thing. And I have a feeling that your partner knows a thing or two about taking care of herself."

The man was right. Jonas could hear Madison telling him to stop worrying. That she could indeed take care of herself. There were just so many things he wanted to say. So many things he wanted for them. Together. But today had been yet another reminder of the danger of what they did, and of the reality of what could happen.

"How long have the two of you worked together?" the sheriff asked.

"Just over four months, though we met a few years ago during some training." He took a deep breath. "And you're right, she's good at what she does. Very good."

"She'll keep them safe. You have to believe that."

He knew it was true, and wanted to believe it, but leaving her behind had gone against everything he'd been taught.

"We choose this life because of the desire to make a difference in the world," the sheriff continued. "And that's exactly what she's doing right now."

The cabin was dark as they slowed down and parked behind a four-door sedan that hadn't been there when Jonas had left. He jumped out of the sheriff's car and opened up the driver's door of the other vehicle. The keys were still in the ignition, but no one was in it.

"I'll have dispatch run the plates. See if we can get an ID on them."

After grabbing the keys from the ignition, Jonas headed toward the cabin, alert to the night sounds around him. The breeze rustling through the trees. The call of an owl. Insects chirping in the distance. But no baby crying. No voices. Instead, the house seemed quiet. Too quiet.

When he took another step, the rattling of a tin can broke through the quiet, and he was forced to untangle his foot from fishing wire. Madison had set up a perimeter trap so she'd know if anyone was coming.

Smart move. But a perimeter alarm wouldn't stop DeMarco's men. He knew the kind of people who'd come after them. Hired killers by a man who would do anything to stop Ava from testifying.

The front door had been kicked open and was splintered at the frame. Jonas held his gun steady in front of him, his breathing heavy as he stepped inside, followed by the sheriff and two deputies.

As they cleared the house, his flashlight lit the edge of a rug that was pushed back, revealing a closed trapdoor and a wooden ladder laying on top of it. He lifted the handle and pulled up the door and was immediately assaulted by the smell of pepper spray. Below him was a small cellar. And a body lying in the shadows.

"The rest of the cabin is clear," Daugherty said, coming up behind Jonas. "What have you got?"

"A cellar with a body. I need a stronger flashlight."

"Give me a second." The sheriff hurried outside, gun still at the ready.

Tension mounted in Jonas's gut as he waited for the sheriff. All he could see were a few boxes and the body. He'd read about DeMarco's scare tactics and the men and women he'd allegedly killed. But Madison and Ava . . . he couldn't let them get on that list.

Daugherty came back in and handed him a flashlight.

Jonas shined it down into the dark cellar. "It's a man. His shoulder looks like it's stained with blood from a bullet."

"Is he alive?" the sheriff asked, peering down into the cellar.

"I'm not sure."

"Hang on, and I'll get my team to get him up here," the sheriff said. He signaled for his deputies, then called for an ambulance on his radio.

Jonas watched while they set the ladder back up and brought the injured man up, but his mind was on Madison. There had obviously been a struggle. A wooden chair had toppled over. There was a pile of magazines strewn across the floor, and a broken end table lay in pieces.

What had happened in here?

The two deputies managed to pull their suspect out of the cellar and lay him on the rug.

"He's alive," one of them said, "but he's pretty out of it."

Jonas crouched down next to the man. Early thirties . . . pasty skin . . .

The man grabbed his shoulder, rolled over, and groaned.

"Where are they?" Jonas asked.

The man just groaned again.

Jonas got closer to his face. "Answer the question. Where are they?"

"I . . . I don't know. She shot me."

"And then what? Where are they?"

The man coughed, still holding his shoulder. "Gino took out that woman cop. Or . . . or at least he thought he had."

Jonas shook him when he started closing his eyes. "You're not done talking."

"Gino turned around and that cop—she got up and went after him again."

"Where are they now?"

"I don't know."

"Not good enough. Where's your partner?"

The man groaned, then looked away.

Jonas's frustration grew. "Answer me!"

"She ran out the back of the cabin."

"Did he go after her?"

He nodded.

"I . . . I found the celler, but then Ava . . . she pepper sprayed me and left me down there."

Jonas stood back up, realizing he wasn't going to get anything more out of the man. He didn't have time to waste. He had to go find them.

"There's a trail of blood across the back patio and down the steps," one of the deputies called from the back door. "We also found two slugs in the wall and at least four shell casings on the ground."

Jonas joined Daugherty, searching the shadows for movement. But his eyes caught the crimson stains on the steps. There was no way to tell whose blood it was. Gino . . . Madison . . . Ava. . . . And while they could still find more slugs in the wall or even more shell casings, the suspect found in the cellar had been shot, and more than likely, so had at least one other person.

"One of them has to be hurt," Jonas said. "Probably shot."

"Looks like Madison was as prepared as she could be," the sheriff said. "Knives, pepper spray . . . every self-defense item ready in case they showed up."

Jonas walked inside and turned back toward the middle of the room. The deputies headed out to start a search while the sheriff radioed for additional backup. The temperature was supposed to drop to freezing tonight, and with a baby, Madison wouldn't have wanted to risk them being outside. But they might not have had a choice.

Where would they have gone?

Heading toward the highway would have made more sense, but would Madison have given Ava instructions on what to do if they were separated?

He fought to keep his mind focused on finding them, not giving in to the dread bubbling in his gut. Instead, he tried to think the way she would. Logical. Precise. Not leaving anything to chance. She would have done everything in her power to save Ava and the baby and ensured she'd taken every precaution possible. Deterring the men from breaking in wasn't likely, but she had set things up so at least she'd know when they arrived. The door had a wooden frame and had been easily breached, and she would have known that. Which was why she would have put everything into defending and keeping Ava separate from herself. Like in the cellar. That's what he would have done.

She'd probably gathered tactical items to defend herself. She also would have made a plan of what she was going to do if they had to leave. But clearly her options were limited. Thinking one man was down, and Ava hidden in the cellar, she would have tried to get Gino as far away from the cabin as possible—even if she were injured—buying time until Jonas returned with the sheriff.

What she wouldn't have counted on was the suspect discovering the trapdoor to the cellar. Just like Rocky hadn't expected Ava to be prepared with pepper spray.

"I've called in some more deputies to help with the search," the sheriff said.

"Good." Jonas slowly turned around in the middle of the room. "I want to join them."

"Of course." The sheriff clasped his arm. "We're going to find them."

Three more cars pulled into the circular drive. The sheriff barked out directions, quickly dividing them into teams with directions on where to search.

"Keep in mind that our second suspect is armed," Sheriff Daugherty told them. "And while we think there is only one suspect out there, we can't be sure."

Jonas frowned. They couldn't be sure of anything at this point.

He compartmentalized his emotions as he followed the local officers outside. How he felt about Madison couldn't color his judgment or, even worse, distract him from the job they needed to do. He headed east along the tree line, following the grid directions Daugherty had given him. He could see deputies sweeping their lights through the darkness to his right and left. It made them targets, but their options were limited if they were going to find the women and Easton. He wasn't sure how far Gino would go, if it meant risking his own life, especially knowing his own partner was already down. If he was smart, he'd be long gone. Because even as vast as this wilderness area was, the chances of him not getting caught at this point were slim.

TWENTY-NINE

It was too dark to know exactly where she was or how close she was to the highway, but Madison could hear the snap of branches and crunch of dried leaves behind her. Gino wasn't even attempting to be quiet. He was simply trying to hunt her down. But as long as Ava and Easton stayed safe in the cellar, they were going to be fine. She'd lead him as far away from the cabin as she could, giving Jonas time to return with help. She'd feared that Gino would return to the cabin as well, but right now, she had him exactly where she wanted him.

But soon she would need to turn the situation around so she wasn't on the defensive. And she needed to get back to Ava. Until the two men were in custody and Ava and Easton safe, Madison wasn't going to be able to rest.

She moved as fast as she could, with the only illumination coming from moonlight scattered through the tree limbs above and the occasional lightning strikes from the coming storm. Turning on her flashlight would be too risky, which put her at a disadvantage, along with the fact that she didn't know the terrain. But she was pretty sure they were on an equal playing field in that regard. More than likely, Gino wasn't from around here, and had only been sent here to find Ava.

Madison stumbled over a hole, hidden by ferns, then quickly regained her balance. She kept moving, thankful she didn't sprain anything. From trips to the peninsula with her family, she knew there were things to avoid like stinging nettle and devil's club, but those were nothing compared to getting lost or injured in some of the more isolated terrain, where there were deep gorges, steep slopes, and dangerous waterways.

The sounds from Gino moving through the brush behind her stopped abruptly. Madison froze, needing to know where he was. She searched the shadows for movement.

Nothing.

Her heart raced as she squinted in the darkness. Where was he?

Something rustled to her left and she turned, but she couldn't tell what was out there. She'd seen deer and elk on the peninsula in the past, and as unlikely as an encounter would be, there were also bears. Still, she resisted the urge to turn on her flashlight. That would be like a homing beacon to her position. Even though she wished it were nothing but a deer rustling in the brush beside her, she knew it had to be Gino. Because while a deer wouldn't shoot her, Gino would.

She pressed her back against the rough bark of a tree and listened. He must have stopped to listen for her as well, which meant he wasn't sure where she was. The only sound was the wind moving through the trees above her.

She took the respite to catch her breath as she went through her limited options. She couldn't risk him giving up and returning to the cabin and finding Ava. She bit the edge of her lip, needing a different strategy. If she wanted to stop him, she had to quit playing defense. She had to go after him. She bent down, fumbling in the darkness until she found what she was looking for. She held the large stone in her hand, then heaved it into the forest to her right. It had the reaction she'd hoped for. The rustling of Gino's movements pegged his location, followed by a shot fired that slammed into a tree. She ducked down. Clearly, he had no intention of taking her alive.

"I know you're out here," he shouted. "Where is she?"

Madison stayed crouched down. She needed to keep him talking and moving farther away from the cabin. She needed to keep the upper hand. She tossed another rock to her right, throwing it low through the trees so it continued moving through the brush a few more feet after it hit the ground.

"How long do you think you can avoid me out here?" He appeared to be turning to the right, following the sound. "All I have to do is find her before you, and then how do you plan to protect her?"

Madison reached for another rock, then stopped as the ground crumbled beneath her foot. She jumped back as lightning flashed in the sky, illuminating the side of the large gully where she'd almost stepped off. She couldn't see the bottom of the ravine, but when she strained her ears, she could hear water rushing. Heart pounding from the close call, she moved closer to the tree line.

But this was what she needed.

"You'll never find her," Madison said, standing behind a tree for cover.

For a moment, the moonlight caught his movements as he switched his trajectory and headed toward her. She watched him walk past her tree, then stop a couple feet from the drop-off, listening again.

"Gino."

He spun around.

"Step back and you'll fall into the edge of the gully. Step forward and I will shoot."

She moved out in the open and shined her flashlight directly at his face. "Drop your weapon now."

He took a step backward to avoid the light, but it was too late—the brightness of her tactical light was enough to disorient him. He threw his hands against his face, confused, giving her the time she needed to gain the upper hand. She came at him quickly, striking him hard on his carotid artery, then noticed the blood staining the side of his shirt. He'd been hit back at the cabin. His weapon fell out of his hands, and he dropped forward in pain.

She kicked his gun off the side of the gully, then moved back.

He rolled over and groaned, trying to get up.

"I wouldn't do that if I were you. There's quite a drop at your back."

He pressed his hands against his head.

"On your knees. Hands behind your head."

She pulled out a zip tie from her pocket, then quickly secured his hands behind him.

"It's over," she said, taking a step back.

"That's where you're wrong." He spat. "If it's not me, it will be someone else."

She shook her head. "Where has your blind faith in your leader gotten you? Because you're not the only one going down. When this is all over, there's going to be nothing left of Púca's organization."

Voices sounded in the distance. Lights were sweeping through the forest. She recognized the signs of a police rescue party. They were searching for her. Madison blew out a sharp breath of relief and started running toward the shouts, this time leaving her flashlight on to help her maneuver across the mossy trail.

"Wait," Gino called out. "Please . . . Please. You can't leave me here."

"Over here," she called out to the rescue party.

Someone was moving toward her, and the light of her flashlight caught him. Jonas called in that he found her, then pulled her into his arms.

A wave of exhaustion swept through her. She'd been going on adrenaline for hours, and now that this was over, she just wanted to sleep.

"Please tell me you're okay," he said, pressing his hands against her back.

"I am." She saw the concern etched on his face as he looked down at her in the moonlight. "I've been so worried about you—"

"I know, but what about Ava and the baby? Did you find them? I left them in the cellar, praying Gino and Rocky wouldn't find the door."

"We found her, and she has quite a story to tell as well, but she's fine."

"You're sure?"

"Yes. I'll take you to her, but first I want to make sure you're okay." He reached up and touched the side of her mouth. "Your lip is cut."

She reached up to feel it but brushed her hand against his instead. She lowered her hand, pressing it against his chest for a moment, unable to look away from his gaze. "It's nothing," she said, trying to ignore the effect of his touch. "You should see the other guy."

"Oh yeah." He laughed. "Where is he?"

She pointed back the way she came. "A hundred yards that direction. And he's injured."

His eyes widened. "So it was his blood we found and not yours."

She nodded.

His shoulders dropped and he frowned. "I shouldn't have left."

"No. You did the right thing. And we're all okay. That's all that matters."

She caught the relief in his voice as he spoke. He shot her a smile. "I guess I never should have doubted your abilities."

"You doubted me?"

"Not really. I was just . . . just worried."

"You tend to do that."

"Just with people I'm in love with."

"So this is a common tendency?" she asked, not trying to hide her grin.

"Hardly. I know this isn't the place or the time, but you have to know that I've never felt this way about anyone." He cupped her face with his hands for a moment, as if he were afraid she was going to disappear if he let go, then took a step back. "I'm sorry. I told you I wouldn't push."

She could hear the other deputies heading their way. "We need to go back to the cabin. Get Ava and the baby looked at to make sure they're okay."

"And you need to see someone as well."

"Jonas, I—"

"Shh." He touched her lips with his finger. "No arguing allowed."

***

Ava and Easton were waiting inside the house with a few deputies when they got back. One of the officers was holding Easton while a paramedic finished checking Ava over.

"I'm so glad you're okay." Ava ran up and hugged her. "He would have killed me."

"You were brave. Don't sell yourself short. You saved Easton's life."

"With pepper spray," Jonas said.

Madison looked at him. "Wait a minute. What?"

"I used what I could find," Ava said. "But what happens now, with my identity blown? I . . . I don't know if I can start over again. Especially when I know it can all be stripped away in an instant."

"We'll see what the DA says," Madison said, "but I'm hoping you don't have to do that. I have a feeling that Gino will flip and maybe several more of his men. There should be enough evidence now to put them away and keep you safe."

"We still need to ID the person running the organization," Jonas said.

Ava pressed her lips together. "I know who Púca is, and I think I know how to find him."

THIRTY

Jonas led Ava to the couch and had her sit down while a paramedic checked out Easton, then he sat down on the edge of the coffee table in front of her.

"You know who he is? The man DeMarco works for?" Madison asked, sitting down on the other couch cushion.

Ava clasped her shaking hands in her lap. "I got Rocky to tell me."

"How did you do that?" Jonas asked.

"When I was down in the cellar, hiding, all I could do was pray. I had no idea what was happening above me. I was so scared they would kill Madison, and there were a couple gunshots and shouting . . ." Ava started hyperventilating.

Madison placed her hand on the woman's shoulder. "Deep breaths."

Ava closed her eyes, then breathed in and out slowly for a few seconds before continuing. "The man you just found in the cellar—Rocky—he'd been shot in the shoulder, but Easton started crying, and he found the trapdoor."

"He was out cold when I left," Madison said.

"He was still pretty out of it," Ava said. "He pulled the door open and started down the ladder. I only had two things with me besides the baby. The phone I turned on, hoping you could trace it. And the pepper spray I'd found in the kitchen."

Ava took a deep breath, her face still void of color.

"Take your time," Madison said.

"When he came down the ladder, I made sure Easton was covered up and out of the way. I waited in the shadows, then sprayed Rocky. I then somehow managed to get Easton up the ladder and pulled it up with me."

"Looks like Madison isn't the only tough woman in the room," Jonas said.

Ava ignored the compliment. "He collapsed and begged me for help. He told me he was bleeding out and didn't want to die, and I told him to give me the name of his boss."

"And he did?"

She nodded. "George Bennett."

"Wait . . ." Jonas leaned forward. "Who's that?"

She looked up, her eyes filled with tears. "The crime boss who ordered the death of my family."

"And you know where we can find him?" Madison asked.

Ava cleared her throat. "When we were in the cabin, after Gino and Rocky took me, I overheard some of their conversation. I guess they were trying to figure out what to do with me, but Rocky said they were supposed to meet someone in the morning at the marina."

"Who?" Madison asked.

"They called him Púca."

"Wow," Jonas said, sitting up straight. "Do you know how long the authorities have been trying to find him? Did you catch the name of the marina?"

Ava shook her head. "I don't remember. I only heard snippets of their conversation."

Jonas called over to the sheriff, "What marinas are close by?"

Daugherty scratched his chin. "Quileute Harbor Marina is the closest port and the only marina between Neah Bay and Westport, but then there are more around the top of the peninsula. Port Angeles."

"Wait. That's it," Ava said. "Port Angeles."

"Are you sure?" Madison asked.

Ava nodded.

"How far are we?" Jonas asked the sheriff.

"An hour and a half by car. I can get you there, no problem."

Jonas stood up. "We'll head into Port Angeles early in the morning, then, and see if anyone recognizes him, and have the coast guard on standby."

"I'll have my team finish going through the house and contact the owners, but for now, one of my deputies can take you to the B & B so you can get some sleep. I can guarantee that Brenda makes the best salmon and homemade rolls you've ever had."

"Thank you. We appreciate that."

"What about me?" Ava asked.

Jonas glanced at his watch. "I know it's late, but we can arrange an escort for you and Easton back to Seattle tonight. I'll also make sure Becca knows her baby is safe. You'll have to stay in protective custody for the next few days, but this will all be over soon."

"Is there anything else you need?" Madison asked Ava.

"I don't think so, I just . . . "—she let out a deep sigh—"I need this to be over."

***

It was a quarter to seven when they drove into Port Angeles, a small port city located on the northern edge of the Olympic Peninsula. Ediz Hook was a long, narrow moraine that projected out into the water and created a harbor. It was also where the US Coast Guard Air Station was located.

A good night's sleep had been what Madison and Jonas both needed, along with a breakfast of bacon and eggs and coffee. Madison had been talkative on the drive over, though Jonas noticed she never let the conversation veer toward anything personal.

And that was okay as far as he was concerned. At least for now. At some point, they would have a chance to sit down and talk about their future, but as much as he wanted to have that conversation, now wasn't the time.

He glanced up at the darkening sky as he pulled into the marina and parked, noting that another storm was heading through. They headed straight to the harbormaster, who'd been expecting them. Jonas made quick introductions, then held up the photo of Bennett. "We need to know if this man has been here today."

"I don't recognize him. Sorry. He's definitely not an owner."

Jonas glanced at Madison, worried they were wasting their time on another wild-goose chase. They knew George Bennett had access to vast financial resources and that it wouldn't be that difficult for him to disappear, once and for all. If they didn't find him soon, they might miss their window of opportunity.

"Could he have rented a boat?" Madison asked.

"We do have a handful of boats we rent out by the day," the

harbormaster replied. He typed something into his computer. "Here we go. I didn't check them in, but yes. Looks like a couple guys rented one of our boats last night for a couple days. Paid cash. There's a chance they haven't headed out yet."

"We need you to take us to the boat."

"No problem," the harbormaster said, motioning for them to follow him toward the docks.

Jonas looked out at the rows of boats bobbing on the edge of the scenic bay that gave access to the Olympic Peninsula, Puget Sound, and Vancouver Island.

The harbormaster stopped at the end of one dock, then turned back to them. "The boat's gone, and I can't tell you when she's heading back."

A man in his midfifties approached them from the adjoining slip. "Are you looking for *The Annabella*?"

Jonas held out his badge. "Have you seen her?"

"They took her out not more than five minutes ago."

"Do you know where they might have gone?" he asked.

"Couldn't tell you that. They seemed more focused on getting out of here, though it did seem like they were waiting for someone and then decided to leave."

"How many people were onboard?" Madison asked.

"Three. Not the greatest weather to be out on the water if you ask me, but they seemed to know what they're doing."

"Was this one of them?" Jonas asked, holding up the photo they had of Bennett on his phone.

"Yeah, actually, I believe it was."

"We've got the coast guard standing by," Jonas said, turning back to the harbormaster. "Do you have a way to track your rentals?"

"We have live tracking on all our rental boats."

"And since the coast guard can board any vessel—" Madison began.

"We don't have to have permission to inspect, search, or make an arrest," Jonas said as he put in a call to the chief petty officer he'd already been in contact with.

The harbormaster nodded, then turned to Madison. "I can give you the website information so you'll be able to track them yourself."

As soon as they had the information they needed to track the boat, Jonas and Madison rushed to the end of the pier to intercept the coast guard patrol boat that had just moved in from the edge of the marina.

"Chief Petty Officer Hannah Nash," the young officer said as they boarded the vessel. "My partner's below deck."

"Thank you for meeting us here." Jonas shook the uniformed woman's hand, then tugged on the bottom of his US Marshals vest.

"Of course. I spoke with your boss, and he gave me a brief update on what was going on."

"Good, then you should be up to speed."

"We have the tracking information from the harbormaster," Madison said. "They are currently about five nautical miles up the coast."

The pilot at the helm quickly turned the coast guard vessel around, and they headed out to sea with the patrol boat tracking Bennett's boat while they coordinated the plan with Officer Nash. It didn't take long to find *The Annabella* moving west, parallel to the coastline. One of the coast guard crew turned on the flashing blue lights, then maneuvered the patrol vessel alongside the other boat.

Two men from *The Annabella* met them on the side of their boat.

"Morning, officers," one of them said. "Is there a problem?"

"We're just doing a routine safety check," Nash said as the boats bobbed in the water next to each other. "We need to see the boat's registration."

"Of course. We're just renting it for a couple days from Port Angeles."

Jonas and Madison waited behind them while Nash spoke with the men, neither of which was George Bennett.

"Ben Horn and Thomas Copeland?" Nash said, setting the paperwork they'd handed over onto her clipboard.

"Yes."

"And the purpose of your voyage?"

"Just taking a few days off for a guys' trip. We normally go to the Cape but always wanted to visit the Northwest and compare the fishing."

"What about weapons onboard?" Nash asked.

"Two handguns near the helm, but we have open carry permits."

"Is there anyone else onboard?" Nash asked.

"No, ma'am, it's just the two of us."

Nash jotted down a few notes, then glanced back up. "We're going to need to board the vessel and do a safety search."

Jonas didn't miss the subtle look that passed between the two men. He and Madison boarded *The Annabella* with Nash following close behind.

"I don't understand what the problem is," the older of the two men said as they started searching the boat. "We have all of our paperwork in order—licenses and our catch record card."

"This is just routine, sir. We check safety equipment like life jackets and fire extinguishers as well as check for any violations."

Jonas stepped in front of the older man. "We were told back at the marina that there were three of you onboard today."

He shoved his hands into his pockets and shrugged. "Whoever told you that was mistaken."

Jonas took a step forward while Madison and Nash continued searching the boat. He held up the photo of George Bennett on his phone again. "They told us that this man boarded this boat."

"Sorry." The man's eyes shifted. "I told you, it's just Ben and me. Don't even know who that is."

"Appreciate your cooperation, gentlemen," Nash said, stepping up to them. "I'll get you a receipt, and then you'll be free to go."

"Anything?" Jonas whispered before following the women back onto the coast guard vessel.

"Nothing," Nash said.

"So if three men got on this boat when they left the marina, where's the third one?" Jonas asked.

"I don't know," Madison said, "but someone's lying. If he's hiding on this boat, we would have found him."

Jonas glanced out at the water as his mind worked through possible scenerios. "What if he's here, but not on the boat."

"What do you mean?" Madison asked.

"There was built-in storage for tanks and gear," Jonas said.

"I looked in it," Madison said. "There were also a couple dry suits."

"You think he jumped overboard?" Nash asked.

"It would be the perfect place to hide until we left," Jonas said. "And I've been itching to dive again."

Nash nodded, then turned back to the other boat. "I'm sorry, gentlemen, but we're not quite done here, after all. You might both want to have a seat for a few minutes."

"Listen—" Thomas started to argue, then stopped as all three of them stepped back onto the deck.

Jonas grabbed a dry suit that was hanging up, then put it on with the diving gear before gently lowering himself into the water, feet first. The waves churned around him as he searched beneath the boat. He knew it would be cold, but even with the dry suit, the cooler temperature seemed to shoot straight through him. Kelp swayed beneath him, but he didn't notice much else about his surroundings, because he'd been right. George Bennett was waiting beneath the boat for them to leave.

The man had one hand against the hull and was turned away from him, giving Jonas the advantage. He swam under the boat and came up behind him and closed the man's tank valve.

It didn't take long for Bennett to realize he'd just lost his air source. The man pushed away from the boat, turned, and caught sight of Jonas. Bennett swung a knife at him, slicing against Jonas's forearm, ripping through the fabric of his suit. But he barely felt anything.

Seconds later, Jonas surfaced, with Bennett popping up behind him, gasping for air. Madison and Nash were there, ready to pull him up out of the water.

"George Bennett," Madison said. "It's nice to finally put a name with your face."

"This is harassment—" he started.

"Hardly." Madison stepped in front of him and smiled. "We have a string of warrants out for your arrest—fraud, tax evasion, extortion, money laundering, murder, and more recently kidnapping."

"You forgot to include evading the authorities," Jonas said as he climbed back onto the deck.

"You'll never be able to prove any of this—"

"Forget it, Bennett," Jonas said as Nash made the arrest. "It's over."

THIRTY-ONE

Madison stepped into the squad room of the marshals' office the next morning, happy to be back in Seattle but even happier to have the last couple days behind her. As soon as she was done here, she was going to take some of her personal leave, giving her time to spend with her father and her sister's family.

And Jonas.

Despite her tiredness, the thought brought a smile to her face.

"Welcome back," Piper said, far too perky in Madison's opinion for seven thirty in the morning. "I hope you were able to get a good night's sleep. You've got to be exhausted."

"I was definitely happy to be back in my own bed, though I could have used a couple more hours of sleep."

"I brought you both something," Jonas said, walking in behind her with a drink tray and a paper sack. "Coffee and croissants."

"How do both of you manage to wake up so perky?" Madison asked, as she took the offered coffee.

"It's just a part of our charm, I guess." He handed the second coffee to Piper. "That's for all the help you gave us on the case."

"Thank you."

"You can put all the paperwork and croissants on hold for the moment," Michaels said, stepping out of his office. "I've got a couple things you need to know."

Madison set her coffee down on the desk and gave him her full attention.

"US Marshals arrested Cervantes and the remaining two suspects in connection to the courthouse attack in a raid last night."

"That's good news," Jonas said.

"It is." Michaels rested his fists on his hips. "The second thing is that the DA is moving ahead with murder charges against Becca, but she has asked to speak to you both before she goes in front of the judge this morning."

"Why? What's going on?" Madison said.

"I'm not sure, but she's already been brought over from holding and is waiting for you in the interview room right now. Apparently, it was approved by the DA."

Jonas shook his head as they left the squad room. "I'm glad we found Easton, but unfortunately, he'll probably end up in the foster care system if Becca's convicted of murder."

Madison stopped in front of the interview room. "Unless Judge Saylor takes him."

"That is possible."

Inside the interview room, Becca sat at the table, hands folded in front of her, bags under her eyes from the lack of sleep. "Thanks for agreeing to see me," she said, drawing in a deep breath. "I wanted to thank you for finding Easton. I don't care what happens to me at this point, but Easton . . . I couldn't handle it if anything happened to him."

"You're welcome, but you don't have to thank us," Jonas said. "It's our job."

"We're glad he was found," Madison said, "and that he's safe."

"There is one other thing," Becca said as Madison turned toward the door. "Just five minutes. Please."

Madison glanced at Jonas, then sat down across from Becca. "Okay."

"I told them I wanted to thank you in person, which I honestly did, but I need someone I can trust to listen to me. Unfortunately, that isn't my lawyer. I'm sure he's a good person, but he's too busy to really look at my case."

"Okay," Jonas said, sitting back in his chair. "We're listening."

"I should have told you this at the beginning of this nightmare, but I don't know . . . I was so scared." Becca cleared her throat and looked away. "A couple weeks ago, Robert came over to my apartment, and he seemed . . . I don't know, distant and agitated. I tried to ask him what was going on, but he kept ignoring my questions. When he fell asleep, I checked his phone. I knew I shouldn't have, but I wanted to know if maybe he was seeing someone else. If he'd cheat on his wife, it was more than plausible that he'd do the same with me."

"Did you find evidence there was someone else?" Jonas asked.

"No. But I did find something disturbing." She hesitated. "He always used a burner phone to communicate with me."

"You mentioned that in your statement," Madison said. "The problem is, the judge denies having a second phone, and we haven't found it."

"I know it's my word against his, but I saw conversations he hadn't deleted that implied he was involved in accepting bribes. I tried saying something to my lawyer and even to the DA, but neither of them would listen to me. They assumed I was making up things to make Robert look bad."

"Did you ever talk to him about what you saw?" Jonas asked.

"I confronted him the next morning."

"What was his reaction?"

"He was clearly shaken and angry. I told him I wouldn't tell anyone, but he wouldn't listen to me. He yelled at me, then stormed out, and for the first time . . ." She gnawed on the edge of her lip. "For the first time, I was afraid of him."

"What happened after that?" Madison asked.

"I told him we needed to talk, but that's when he started making excuses not to see me. He was always busy."

"Why didn't you tell us this before?"

"Like I said, I was scared, and besides, it didn't seem important or connected at the time. But I should have told you. Everything." Becca bit the edge of her lip and looked down. "All I could think about was the fact that Easton was missing. You have to understand that. And besides . . . despite everything that has happened, I can't help it. I still love Robert."

Madison frowned. Apparently love really was blind.

"We were told that the DA has filed murder charges against you," she said, "and I am going to be straight with you, from where I'm sitting, Judge Saylor really doesn't seem to care what happens to you."

"No." She was crying again. "You're wrong. He loves me. And now that Myra's dead—"

"You still think he's going to marry you?" Madison's patience was waning. "That the three of you are somehow going to be a happy family?"

"I don't know. But I didn't go to his house to kill Myra. I shot her in self-defense. She had a gun, and she shot at me." Becca's hands clenched together on the table in front of her. "You have to believe me, because no one else does."

"Becca, it doesn't matter what we believe. This isn't our jurisdiction," Jonas said. "In the end, it's up to the courts to decide."

Madison followed Jonas back out into the hallway. "What if she is telling the truth?" she said after they'd closed the door behind them. "She has a public defender who's spread thin and just sees her as another case."

"So what do you want to do?"

"I want to talk to Detective Victoria one more time and make sure we didn't miss anything."

They arrived at the southwest precinct and were quickly ushered to the detective's desk in the back corner of the busy bullpen.

"Thanks for taking the time to talk with us," Madison said, as Detective Victoria motioned them into the empty chairs across from her.

"Of course. I was actually getting ready to call you but go ahead. What can I do for you?"

"We have a few questions about Myra Saylor's murder. Specifically, we need to know what happened when the judge showed up at his home."

The detective tapped a pen against her desk. "I'm not exactly sure what you're looking for, but we found Myra's body, and had started photographing the scene before we cleared the judge to come inside."

"He went in to see her?"

Detective Victoria nodded. "I didn't think it was a good idea for him to see his dead wife at the crime scene, but he insisted."

"And once inside," Madison continued, "was he ever alone with the body?"

"No. We gave him a moment with his wife before the coroner came in—seemed like the least we could do—but we were always in the room with him."

"What about a burner phone?" Madison asked. "Did you find one in the house?"

"That's one of the things I wanted to talk to you about, actually," the detective said, lifting a file off her desk. "We found it hidden in Myra's things."

"Did you find anything on it?" Jonas asked.

The detective nodded. "From the messages, the phone clearly belonged to Judge Saylor. And while he was good at deleting the majority of his . . . indiscretions, including his relationship with Becca Lambert, our tech guru was able to recover most of the text messages."

"We'd like to see them," Jonas said.

"Of course, but I can tell you what we found. Not only was he having an affair, we have evidence that he was also accepting bribes to manipulate the outcome of certain cases."

Madison glanced at Jonas. "So she was telling us the truth."

"Who?" Detective Victoria asked.

"We just got done meeting with Becca Lambert," Madison told her. "She told us that she saw conversations on the judge's burner phone implying that he was involved in accepting bribes."

"She was right," the detective said. "We're looking into the connection now, but we've also found evidence that he was being blackmailed by Cervantes to guarantee he would be granted bail."

"So Cervantes found dirt on him—probably the fact that he was taking bribes—and then decided to threaten him?" Jonas asked.

"That's exactly what it looks like."

"Then why the attack on the courthouse, if they thought Judge Saylor was going to let Cervantes out on bail?" Madison asked.

"I think they were prepared for the judge to deny Cervantes bail—which he did—but the judge was up against a tough decision. If he were to let someone with multiple felony charges out on bail, there would be staunch pushback against his decision."

"And since he couldn't afford the scrutiny," Madison said, "the judge tried to call their bluff."

Detective Victoria nodded. "It looks like Cervantes's backup plan was to change tactics and have his men take the judge hostage so they could use him as leverage to force Cervantes's release. Thankfully the two of you were able to stop that."

"We're glad it turned out that way," Madison said, "but we have reason to believe that taking bribes wasn't the only corrupt thing the judge has tried to do. We think he tried to frame Becca for murder."

"To be honest, at this point, I wouldn't be surprised at anything he did." The detective leaned back in her chair and frowned. "Explain."

"First we need to see the photos of the crime scene again," Madison said.

"Sure." Detective Victoria turned to her computer, then pulled up the photos. "Anything in particular?"

"Just in sequential order," Madison said, still not sure exactly what she was looking for.

The officer who had taken the photos had started with wide-angled shots of the scene, before continuing on to close-up photos of the room, and then ones of the victim.

"What was the timeline here?" Jonas asked. "When did the judge come in?"

"After the majority of the photos were shot."

"Go back about four or five photos." Madison waited for the detective to scroll back. "Okay, stop. There. Look at that one." She pointed at the screen. "There's something under the couch, just barely showing, and now later, after the last photos were taken . . . it's not in this photo." Madison leaned forward. "Where was the judge standing when he went to see his wife?"

"He came into the room and knelt down on the left side of her."

"Next to the couch?" Jonas asked.

The detective nodded. "Yes. I just remembered that he dropped his keys as he stood up, then reached down to grab them. It seemed insignificant at the time, but now . . ."

"Can you blow up that section of the photo?" Madison asked, pointing to the couch.

The detective did so, zooming in on the place Madison indicated.

"That's definitely a gun," Jonas said.

"Why would he take the gun?" the detective asked.

"Becca told us that Myra shot at her, but missed, and she shot back in self-defense," Madison said. "If she was telling the truth—which I think now she could have been—then that means there has to be a second gun."

"And a good possibility that Becca Lambert is being framed for murder," Jonas said.

"I think we're going to need to pay a visit to the judge," Madison said, "but there's one other thing we're going to need from you before we go."

***

Judge Saylor met them at the door of his house with half a sandwich in his hand. "I was just finishing my lunch. Can I help you?"

"I'm sorry to bother you," Madison said. "I know this all has to be very difficult. We just need to ask a few more questions in order to wrap up the case, and Detective Victoria and Officer Rogers need to be let back into the living room again."

The judge dropped his hands to his sides. "This really isn't a good time. All I want to do is put all of this behind me. I have a funeral to plan and a child I have to think about—"

"Are you planning to take custody of Easton?" Jonas asked.

"Of course I am. He is my son. And while I'm sure not everyone will understand, the more I think about it, the more I'm convinced it is the right thing to do." He took a step back and motioned them inside. "But come in. I'm sorry. I'm not thinking straight right now. What are you looking for?"

"There are some discrepancies regarding what happened that morning," Jonas said while Victoria and Rogers headed to the living room. "You arrived at the house right after the ambulance and police."

The judge nodded. "At first, they told me I couldn't go in, but I insisted and told them this was my house. That's when they told me my wife was dead. That she'd been shot."

"Did you go near Myra's body?" Jonas asked, stepping into the living room where they'd found the body.

"They told me not to touch anything and I didn't. In fact, at first, I just stood in the threshold of the living room, completely frozen. I managed to compose myself, then went and knelt down next to her."

"You dropped something on the carpet at one point?" Madison asked.

"My phone rang, and I reached into my pocket to silence it. My keys fell out so I picked them up. But what does any of this matter?" He combed his hands through his hair, clearly agitated. "My wife's killer is in custody. We know who did it. Myra's blood was on Becca's clothes, and there's even video evidence that she was in my house when my wife was killed."

"We're not questioning the fact that Becca was here when Myra was killed," Jonas said, "but we have reason to believe she acted in self-defense. You told the authorities that Myra had some issues with her grip and had taken her gun in to have it upgraded."

The judge dumped what was left of his sandwich into a small trash can against the wall, then turned back to him. "You both need to stop, right now. We know what happened. What has Becca been telling you?" The judge's voice rose. "I know now that she's a con artist, and clearly she's conned you. I don't even know how you can question what happened."

Detective Victoria stepped back into the foyer and nodded at Madison. "We found what you asked us to look for. Both of them."

Madison nodded, then aimed her next question back at the judge. "You have more than one phone, don't you?"

"Why would I need more than one phone?"

Madison caught the judge's gaze. "Because you needed a burner phone for your . . . indiscretions."

"Excuse me?"

"When you were at your wife's side, you were actually looking for something," Madison continued. "The burner phone you realized Myra had to have found. It was the same phone she had used to send a message to Becca and make her think it was from you. That's why Becca showed up at the house. You knew when you arrived at the scene that Becca wouldn't have come to see your wife, and you realized Myra must have found it—and you couldn't let the police find it. But while you didn't find the phone, you did find your wife's gun."

"One small slipup of leaving out your burner phone for your wife to discover that you were actually living a double life." Jonas shook his head. "But besides you having a mistress, we also learned you were taking bribes in exchange for ensuring bail."

"No." The veins on the judge's neck bulged. "None of this is true."

"We have the phone and a witness," Madison said. "See, you were smart, but not smart enough. Because Becca saw some messages on your phone that implied that you were taking bribes, and she confronted you. And on top of that, your wife found that burner phone, and she saw messages to Becca, clearly someone you were romantically involved with. We have evidence that Myra hired a private detective, and it didn't take long for her to discover that not only did you have a mistress but you also had a child."

Madison folded her arms across her chest and continued, "So we believe you both removed evidence in the room where your wife was murdered and planted evidence at Becca's."

Jonas held up a photo in front of the judge, who looked away.

"I've seen the crime scene."

"Look there. Under the couch. When we said you were trying to find the phone, we realized that you actually found something else. Your wife's gun. In the next photos taken, after you were next to her body, it's gone."

"Now you've really crossed the line. Both of you. My wife

was lying on blood-soaked carpet, and you think I had the frame of mind to mess with evidence. Your *theory* isn't possible." The judge shook his finger at her. "I let you search my house, and there were officers here."

"Which is why your wife's gun never left the house." Madison glanced at Jonas. "The whole time you were talking with the police and talking with us, you had to have been carrying that gun. Inside your coat pocket, I'm guessing. But then you needed to hide it somewhere. We do have a warrant, which is why Detective Victoria now has your wife's gun that has been in your office all this time, hidden in plain sight in your gun collection."

"You can't prove any of this."

"You should know that it's not hard to check if a gun has been recently fired," Madison said. "Plus, while we've been talking, the detective has been searching for a second bullet, and she just confirmed that they found one. Isn't that true, Detective Victoria?"

"It was embedded in the leg of the dining room table," the detective said.

"It won't take much to tie everything together and prove that your wife shot at Becca and you tried to cover it up."

The judge folded his arms across his chest in clear defiance. "I'm done talking. You can't prove any of this. I want my lawyer."

"Not a problem," Madison said. "It was a clever plan, actually, especially considering you had to come up with it on the fly. But it allowed you to do two things you'd been wanting to do for a long time. Get rid of your wife, who you'd grown tired of and who also couldn't give you a child, and also get rid of your mistress who had discovered you were taking bribes. You needed to silence her, so you framed her for murder. Leaving you unattached and with sole custody of your son."

"No one will believe such a ridiculous story. I'm a respected judge with a good reputation in the community—"

"I will." The district attorney walked into the room from behind Victoria, his hands in his suit pant pockets. "I should have listened sooner. The missing gun, the burner phone, the bribes . . . we have everything we need."

The judge held up his hands and took a step back, the panic clear on his face. "You don't understand. I was trapped with one woman who didn't love me, and another one who I couldn't love enough. I just wanted to be free from it all."

Madison motioned for Detective Victoria to do the honors of arresting the judge. "Unfortunately, your decisions aren't going to get you that freedom. I have a feeling a judge and jury are going to guarantee that happens."

"I guess there are three sides to every story," Madison said as she watched the detective and the DA lead the judge out of his house.

"And you weren't naive, after all," Jonas said. "Deception and lies never lead to happily ever after. Especially when they end in murder."

Madison's phone rang as they started out of the house behind the judge.

"What's the update?" Michaels asked.

Madison switched her phone to speaker. "Local PD are taking him in now."

"Good."

"And I don't know about Jonas," she said, "but I'm planning to finish up my paperwork as quickly as possible so I can head home."

"There's one other thing I need you to do before you head out."

Madison glanced at Jonas and frowned. "What's that?"

"I'll tell you when you get here, but trust me," Michaels said, "it's a whole lot better than paperwork."

THIRTY-TWO

Madison sat down at her desk with her reheated coffee and a slice of cold pizza and logged in to her computer. After a person had been arrested by the marshals service, the paperwork for each case had to be completed and the database on each fugitive updated.

"Michaels is ready for us in the conference room," Jonas said, drumming his hands on her desk.

She took a sip from her mug, then groaned. "I haven't even gotten through one cup of coffee yet."

"I'll get you a fresh double shot when we're done here."

"Promise?" she asked, shooting him a grin.

"Scout's honor." He crossed his heart.

The conference room had a long table with chairs, photos of Seattle lining the walls, and tech equipment set up for meetings. Inspector Peyton Wyse and Ava looked up when Madison walked in ahead of Jonas. They were sitting at the end of the table talking when they stepped in.

Madison's brow rose. "Wyse? Ava?"

Ava pushed her chair back and ran up and hugged Madison,

then took a quick step back. "I'm sorry . . . That probably wasn't appropriate."

"It's fine." Madison's smile broadened. "I'm really glad to see you, actually. I've been worried about you. You've gone through so much these last few days."

"So have you." Ava reached out and squeezed Madison's hands. "I wanted to thank you for everything you did. For risking your lives for me and Easton. For helping me find my courage. I know Becca would agree, and I wish she was here, but if it wasn't for the two of you, I'm not sure I'd be alive."

"And I have to add my thanks for finding me in that parking lot," Wyse said. "I just received word that the woman who knocked me out has been ID'd and arrested."

"That's fantastic," Madison said, slipping her arm around Ava.

"We really are grateful you're both okay as well," Jonas said, leaning against the side of the table as Ava sat back down. "Though I do have a question for you, Ava, if you don't mind." He turned to her. "How did you convince Rocky and Gino not to kill you?"

"I told you she had a plan," Wyse said, motioning for them to sit down as well.

Madison took a seat across from them and waited for Ava to talk.

"I always knew they would find me," she said, blinking back the tears. "And I knew I had to be prepared. To me, it was not *if* but *when* they found me. And I knew that when they came after me, I was going to have only one chance to convince them that they needed me if I wanted to stay alive. So that's what I did. Peyton gave me advice, and we discussed options. I figured I'd face one of two scenarios. One, they'd come after me, and

I'd have to be ready to run. Or two, they'd catch up with me, and I'd have to convince them they needed me."

"Which is exactly what happened," Madison said.

Ava nodded. "At first I thought Callum worked for Robert, but then I realized that he knew nothing, which confused me. So not knowing who to trust, I decided that I first needed to ensure Easton's safety, then I needed to disappear."

"Having Easton changed things," Jonas said.

Ava grabbed a tissue from the box next to her and blew her nose. "I'd hoped and prayed that if they did find me, I wouldn't have Easton with me, but I tried to prepare for any scenario. I put a false bottom in the diaper bag that I kept at my apartment. Becca found the burner phone I kept in there, but I also rented a couple small storage units in north and south Seattle and filled them with emergency supplies I might need."

"Wow," Jonas said. "I'm impressed."

"I did what I had to do," Ava said. "When I wasn't working, I was researching and trying to track down the identity of DeMarco's boss in the organization. But in the meantime, I had fake files made up, all pointing to the fact that I'd actually framed my husband who had been funneling the company's funds into his own account. I even created documents that would prove the evidence I gave the authorities was actually false. I told Gino that I'd lied when I said I'd testify against DeMarco and had the documents to prove it. My goal was simply to make them doubt the truth."

"And it worked," Madison said.

"I knew I'd have to totally immerse myself in the role. I'd have to be able to look them in the eye and not hesitate at anything, and have something on me that would prove my story to them. To prove that they needed me to get DeMarco out of prison by changing my testimony."

"This organization—they took a lot from you," Madison said, feeling the woman's pain mirrored in her own losses. "Your husband, your daughter . . ."

"There's something else I wanted to tell you." Ava glanced at Wyse, who nodded. "My daughter's alive."

"Wait a minute." Madison sat back. "She's alive?"

"I wanted so much to tell you that day in the cabin, but I couldn't."

"It's okay, but wow . . ." Madison shook her head. "That's fantastic."

"On the night of the fire, I managed to get Chloe out the back of the house. I thought Jason was behind me, but he . . . he never made it out. The news ran the story of the tragic fire that killed an entire family, so we decided to go with it."

"Where has she been?" Jonas asked.

"She's been living in Montana on a ranch with a sweet couple who have been taking care of her. Until Púca—George Bennett—was behind bars, we didn't feel like it was safe for us to be together. It's been the hardest thing I've ever done, but if I wanted us to be free, truly free, I had to work with Peyton until they could find a way to take down the entire crime ring. And to do that, we had to prove who was behind the organization. I knew my boss was simply a pawn in the game, but I didn't have a way to prove who he worked for. And now, thanks to you guys . . . we do."

"More news," Michaels said, stepping into the room. "I've just been told that the DA is dropping the charges against Becca."

"That's wonderful," Ava said. "She deserves to be with her son."

"And Ava . . ." Michaels said, motioning to someone behind the doorframe. "We have a surprise for you, though you can thank Wyse when we're done here. He's the one behind it."

The little girl Madison had seen in the photo strip stepped into the room and ran to her mother. "Mommy!"

"Chloe!" Ava shoved her chair back and gathered her daughter into her arms. "I thought you weren't coming until tomorrow."

"Wyse managed to get her an escort a day early," Michaels said.

Madison blinked back her own tears as she watched the reunion.

"I'm not sure I can stop crying," Ava said, pulling gently on one of Chloe's ponytails. She turned to the marshals. "I'd like you to meet my daughter, Chloe May."

"I hear you've been living on a ranch," Madison said. "That sounds like so much fun."

"It is," Chloe said, clutching her mom's hand. "I get to ride horses and feed the chickens . . . but I'd rather be with my mom."

"I know she'd rather be with you as well," Madison said to Chloe, then directed a question at Ava. "Do you know your plans?"

"This is all moving so fast," Ava said, grabbing another tissue, "but I've agreed to take a job at the ranch as an assistant chef. We'll stay in the WITSEC program for as long as there's any kind of threat, but that way, Chloe will be able to ride as much as she wants, and we can hike and fish. It's what Jason would want. For me to go on with my life and find something meaningful. And now I can finally do that."

"What do you think about going back to the ranch, Chloe?" Wyse asked.

Chloe's smile broadened, and she nodded her head. "Yes!"

"There is one other piece of news," Michaels said. "With the DA dropping charges against Becca, the Turners—the owners of the ranch—would like to offer her a position as well."

Ava's eyes widened. "I don't even know what to say but giving her a chance to start over as well . . . thank you."

"Sounds like the two of you will be working together again," Madison said.

"And we'll be safe." She pulled her daughter against her chest. "That's all that matters."

Madison glanced at Jonas. That, and having someone to share life with.

THIRTY-THREE

Madison turned on the bathwater, adjusted the temperature, then poured in some Epsom salts. She couldn't remember the last time she'd soaked in the tub, but after finishing things up at the office that afternoon, it was exactly what she needed.

She was still working to shake off the shards of pain from the past five years, but with Luke's killer behind bars, and a conviction she was sure was on the horizon, she finally felt free enough to take the first steps forward.

She walked down the hall and into the office and stood in front of the board where she'd tacked one of the black roses that had been left at Luke's grave. She pulled it off and the dried petals crumbled in her hand. She shook them into the trash, then started pulling off the photos one at a time and dropping them into the trash as well. There was no longer a fear of someone coming after her. Of anyone coming after her family or Jonas. And while losing Luke still made her heart ache, she couldn't ignore the peace knowing Sabrina couldn't taunt her anymore. She would never hurt her again.

She picked up a photo of Luke laughing on one of the short

trips they'd taken out of Seattle. They'd boarded a ferry and spent a weekend hiking while enjoying the incredible views of the Cascade mountain range, Puget Sound, and Mount Rainier. She closed her eyes. For a moment she was there again with him. Wind blew across the deck as the ferry moved through the water. It had been the perfect getaway. A perfect moment.

He'd held her hand as they stood at the railing of the ferry looking out over the water. "Why don't we do this more often," he said. "You and me. Alone with no schedule or plan."

She smiled up at him. "You're right. We should take more trips like this."

"Good. I'll make a reservation once we're back, and we can clear our schedules again." He wrapped his arm around her waist and pulled her against his chest. "Do you know how much I love you, Madison James? Marrying you was the best thing I ever did."

She cocked her head and looked up at him. "So you'll still love me when I'm old and wrinkled?"

He laughed at the question. "Nothing will change. Nothing could ever change how I feel about you."

"Promise?"

"I promise."

"Good, because I feel the same way about you, Luke James."

He leaned down and kissed her slowly on the lips, stirring that deep part of her that made her feel safe and loved and cherished.

Madison opened her eyes and pressed the back of her hand across her mouth.

A week later she'd had to plan his funeral.

And she never imagined that she'd feel that way again.

The lump in her throat swelled as she stared at the photo.

"You know I'll always love you, Luke. I still miss you every single day. Your smile. The way you used to make me laugh over the silliest of things. The feel of your arms around me at night. But I . . . I met someone else."

She didn't try to hold back the tears as she stared at the photo. "I never thought I'd say that. Never thought I'd feel for anyone like I do . . . like I did for you. His name is Jonas, and he's good to me. Good for me. He's funny. Handsome. He challenges my faith." She drew in a shaky breath. "He knows what it's like to lose someone he loves. Gives me space to deal with my grief while pushing me to move forward. This is so much harder than I thought, and yet it's what you would want me to do. I just felt so much guilt after you died. I don't know why you're gone and I'm not. I don't know why, but I know I can't change what happened. I can't bring you back. I know you would want me to live life to the fullest. Just like we talked about. Family, faith, service—it's why we chose to do what we do. To make a difference in the world. And while I always thought I'd do it by your side, I have to let you go, Luke. It's time to let you go. It's taken me a long time, but I know it's what you'd want for me."

It was time to move on.

Her phone rang in the bathroom.

Madison took one last look at the board, then hurried back down the hall to answer it. She grabbed it off the vanity and checked the caller ID before answering. "Edward?"

"Madison. How are you doing?"

She sat down on the edge of the tub. "It's been a long week, but I'm good."

"I know you're busy, but I'm calling because I finally heard back from Thomas's grandfather. I need to update him, but I'd like to do it in person."

"Of course." She shut off the water. "When?"

"That's the problem. I know it's last minute but is there any way that you could meet me at his place in a little while? He doesn't like driving in the city, but he, like you, needs closure. I was hoping we could help provide some of that for him."

"Of course." She glanced up at the clock in the hallway. She should still have time before she was supposed to meet Jonas for dinner. "I'll make it work."

She hung up the call, then drained the tub. So much for the long soak in the bath and the mud mask she had planned. Instead, she quickly got dressed, grabbed her leather bag, then headed out the door to the rental car she'd picked up while hers was in the shop. She dialed Jonas's number.

"Jonas, this is Madison," she said, leaving a voice message when he didn't answer. "Call me when you can. Thomas Knight's grandfather wants to meet with Edward and me. I'm heading out to his property right now." She spouted off the address. "I might be late for dinner, depending on traffic. I'll let you know when I'm on my way back to the city."

The scenic drive through the mountains with its miles and miles of evergreens slowly began to melt the stress away. The older Madison got, the more appealing the thought of moving out of the city became. She'd buy a little cabin up in the mountains near water and live off the grid.

And probably be bored out of her mind.

The thought made her chuckle as she checked her GPS, then took the next right. The property was picturesque and surrounded by national forest. Quiet. Remote. There was an old barn to the left that had seen better days and a tractor and ATV sitting next to it. No sign of Edward's car. No sign anyone was even here.

She shoved away the nudge of concern as she parked on the side of the house, then pulled out her phone and gave Edward a call. No answer. That wasn't unexpected. Phone service was often spotty the closer you got to the mountains. A coyote howled in the distance as she stepped out of the car, sending a chill through her. Which was ridiculous. She felt for her Glock sitting in its holster and shook off the uneasy feelings. Sabrina had managed to get under her skin these past few years, but it was over now. And there was no reason to allow those uneasy feelings to take control.

The house itself had to have been built at least fifty years ago. It was a one-story log home with large windows. She knocked on the door, then took a step back. A woman opened the door. She had long brown hair and was wearing boots, jeans, and a button-down shirt. As Madison took in her appearance, a memory sparked, then faded.

Where had she seen her before?

"I'm sorry. I must be at the wrong house," Madison said. "I'm looking for Harold Knight."

"You have the right place." The woman smiled. "I'm Kate Knight. Harold's my father."

"Oh," Madison said, surprised at the confession. "Then you must be Thomas's mother. I didn't know you lived here."

"I don't. I'm just here for a visit."

Why did she seem so familiar? Madison shook her head, trying to clear her mind. She'd seen photos of the woman, but it was more than just recognizing her photo. It was something more. Like remembering the smile that didn't quite reach her eyes. And the voice. There was something about her voice.

"You disappoint me, Madison James."

Cold seeped into her at the tone the woman used. "I don't understand."

Kate pulled out a Glock and pointed it at her. "Put your weapon on the ground, then kick it out of the way."

Madison blinked, her mind scrambling to figure out what was going on. Sabrina, not Kate, had killed Luke and shot her, unless . . . unless she'd remembered everything wrong. But how was that even possible?

She reached for her weapon, knowing if she could get in the first shot and take Kate down—

"I know what you're thinking," Kate said, "but I really wouldn't do that if I were you. You should know by now that I'm an excellent shot. I shot your husband from across the parking garage. And I shot you at point blank in your house. I won't hesitate to do it again. My only regret is that somehow you managed to survive that last bullet. I won't make that mistake this time."

Madison leaned down slowly, placed her weapon on the porch, then shoved it aside with her foot.

"Now toss me your phone."

Madison pulled it out of her pocket, hesitated, then complied. "Where's Edward?"

"Unfortunately, he won't be joining us," Kate said, dropping the phone and stomping on it with her boot. "I just received a message. He had an accident on the way. Someone ran him off the road, I believe."

Madison's heart raced. "What did you do?"

"Just something to make certain he didn't make it here."

"And your father wanting to meet with us? Was that all a ruse as well?"

"He's not far. He's always been as predictable as a clock. He heads into town every day at this time for coffee and a piece of Claire's pie. He always had such a sweet tooth, and apparently, nothing has changed."

Memories flashed to the surface like a slow-motion movie reel as they came into focus, but instead of bringing clarity, they left her confused. Her memories had already returned and Sabrina . . . Sabrina had been the one who'd shot her. Hadn't she? She could still see her standing in front of her in her kitchen. That memory was real. Wasn't it?

"I heard you lost your memory of that day. The day I shot you in your own house."

"What do you want, Kate?" Madison asked.

"I knew you'd want to talk with my father, so it wasn't too hard to figure out when you'd set up this reunion. Though to be honest, I didn't think you'd come alone. And I guess your boyfriend will live to see another day, after all. I'll just have one more mess to clean up."

Madison glanced behind her, realizing the mistake she'd made. It could be hours before anyone realized she was gone, and by then . . . by then it could be too late.

"They all think I'm crazy," Kate continued. "My daughter. My sister. My ex-husband. I'm not."

Madison gritted her teeth. "I just want to know why you shot Luke if I was the one you were after."

"That's what I had planned. But then I followed your car to the hospital, and realized it was your husband driving. It seemed like the perfect plan. An eye for an eye. A tooth for a tooth. You were responsible for the death of my boy. I wanted you to know what it was like to lose someone who meant everything to you."

"Killing Luke could never bring Thomas back."

"No, but it could assure me that you were suffering as much as I was."

Madison frowned at the woman's logic. "Did it actually help?"

"I'll never get over losing Thomas, but yes. It helped ease the pain on those sleepless nights, knowing you were suffering as well."

It was clear there was no reasoning with her. Nothing Madison could say or do was going to change the woman's perspective. "So, what happens now?" she asked, taking a step backward.

"I will kill you this time."

"All those times you had a chance. The black roses on Luke's grave, and the one in my bedroom?"

"They were just reminders. Like the reminders I get every time another birthday passes for Thomas. Or another Christmas I missed spending with him."

"I'm sorry about your son, I truly am, but he didn't die at my hands. He died because of the choices he made."

"That's where you're wrong." Kate shook her head. "If you hadn't arrested him and testified against him, he might still be alive. He was eighteen years old and a good kid overall."

"He killed a man."

"In self-defense."

"I can help you get the help you need," Madison said, changing tactics. "Help to deal with the pain you're going through. There are answers. People who care."

"You sound just like everyone else, except we both know your so-called sympathy has nothing to do with any concern over my life. It's nothing more than a ploy to save your own."

Madison started to argue, then stopped. Engaging Kate wasn't going to help, and neither could she deny the truth in the woman's words.

"Besides, I don't need help," Kate said. "All I need is my son. Something no one can help me with. Because no one can bring him back."

Because there was no going back to that day.

Madison took another step backward. "I know. I'll never see my husband again either."

"So you understand what it feels like. Thomas's father told lies about me. One day, child services came and took my children away, but it was all because he fell in love with someone else and wanted out. I've never gotten over that."

"I'm sorry. I truly am."

"When Thomas turned eighteen, I wrote to him again. He told me he wanted to see me. I couldn't believe it. After all those years of not being allowed to see him and his sister.

"We met for coffee. I remember every detail of that day. But mostly, I remember Thomas. He was grown-up and so handsome. He told me how much he loved video games and showed me his gaming ring. Told me about this girl he'd fallen in love with."

"The ring," Madison said. "We found it where you murdered my husband."

Kate sneered. "I left it there as a clue."

"And Sabrina?" Madison asked. "How did she fit into all of this?"

"She was the perfect scapegoat, wasn't she? And so easy to set up. If she loved him, she wouldn't be with someone else now. She hurt Thomas like his father hurt me. I had to protect my son."

"So it was really you all along?" Madison asked. "You shot at us at the apartment building, you were at King Street Station and sent me those messages, and you broke in and bugged my house."

"And don't forget sending you after Sabrina. It was so easy it almost wasn't fun." Kate tossed her a pair of handcuffs. "Put them on."

"Where are we going?"

"Somewhere no one will find you."

Madison hesitated, but the look in the woman's eyes told her this was no game. The final outcome was going to be the same no matter what Madison did. Anger coursed through her. She'd let a personal situation cloud her judgment and, apparently, her memory. And those mistakes might end up costing her life. The thought was sobering, but this woman had tried to kill her once before. She had no doubt she'd do it again. And out here—Kate was right—no one would ever find her. But even more than for herself, Madison felt sorry for the woman who'd spent years seeking revenge. And in the end, gaining nothing.

"Any final words?" Kate asked.

"However this ends for me, I wish you hadn't spent so much time feeling rejected."

"You don't know how I've felt."

"Rejected, insecure, guilty . . . we might not have gone through the same situations, but I know those same feelings. And I'm sorry I was a part of that hurt."

"Enough," Kate said, motioning her down the porch steps and toward the side-by-side, four-seater ATV that was parked near the barn. "I told you I didn't need help. And sweet-talking me, or bringing up religion, won't change anything."

Dark clouds had gathered in the sky. It was starting to get cold, and she had no idea where they were going.

"Get in." Kate waited for her to comply, then zip-tied her handcuffed hands to one of the bars.

Clearly Kate was taking no chances on Madison getting the upper hand. She drove along a gravel trail that followed the edge of the property, then turned away from the main road and headed uphill, making several turns along the way through the wooded landscape.

"What are we doing, Kate?" Madison asked, trying to keep herself upright as they sped down the bumpy, narrow path.

"I want you to see something before you die."

Kate stopped in the middle of the trail a few minutes later and got out. Behind them were acres of forest, while in front of them, the terrain opened up and led to a steep drop-off with a flowing stream below. It was beautiful, but Madison barely noticed.

Kate came around to the other side of the ATV and popped off the zip tie with a knife, leaving the handcuffs on. "I want you to see Thomas's favorite place. He loved tracking and hunting and came here with his grandfather. They even built a blind just ahead." Kate stopped in front of Madison. "I shouldn't have lost him."

"I'm sorry, Kate. I really am."

"Sorry won't bring back my Thomas."

"No, it won't."

Kate held up her gun. "And I'm sorry too, but I know that eventually you would have figured out the truth. I have to make sure that doesn't happen. And that they never find you."

Madison's jaw tensed, but she was running out of time.

She lunged forward and knocked the gun out of Kate's hands, then pushed her backward as hard as she could with her shoulder. Kate stumbled from the impact but regained her balance and quickly dove for the gun. Still handcuffed, Madison knew she'd never get to it first. Instead, she scrambled to the other side of the ATV for protection, almost twisting her ankle in a pothole in the process. Madison crouched on the other side of the ATV.

"I always knew it would end this way for you," Kate shouted, coming around the front of the vehicle. "I just wanted to be a mother. Was that asking too much? To watch my kids grow up? You took that away from me."

Madison kept moving, keeping the ATV between them. Kate fired a shot in Madison's direction, but it went wild, and hit the ground to her left. Madison squatted down again, trying to come up with a way out, but she was out of options.

Kate rushed at Madison from behind, attempting to push her toward the ledge, but she managed to duck out of the way. With too much forward momentum, Kate tried to stop herself from sliding in the gravel, but she lost her footing and fell over the edge of the ravine. Madison felt as if her heart stopped as she watched Kate's fall in what seemed to be slow motion, ending in her body lying twisted on the rocks below.

Madison closed her eyes as bile rose from her stomach to her throat. No matter what Kate had done, this wasn't how she wanted things to end. But that wasn't the only thing she had to worry about. She glanced around her. She was at least a mile from the house, handcuffed, and was only wearing a light jacket. Her hands shook as she climbed into the ATV and looked for the key, but Kate must have had it with her. And even if she could get it started, she wasn't sure she could find her way back with darkness falling soon. All she could do now was pray that Jonas heard her message and would somehow find her.

THIRTY-FOUR

Jonas checked his messages as he left the gym with Tucker, surprised that he'd missed a call from Madison and two from Michaels. He'd spent the last couple hours at the gym. Partly working out with Tucker. Partly sitting in the steam room trying to clear his head. He'd returned to Seattle tired from the month of training, and the past few days had intensified his fatigue, both physically and emotionally.

"Ready for your big date with Madison?" Tucker asked as they headed to the gym parking lot.

"Hopefully it's still on," Jonas said. "Just give me a second, there's a message from her."

Jonas must have looked concerned because when he took his phone from his ear, Tucker asked, "Is everything okay?"

"I don't know." He stopped next to his car.

His return call went straight to voice mail.

He tapped his phone against his leg. "Apparently, Madison headed out with Edward to meet with Harold Knight, the grandfather of Thomas Knight."

"I thought you told me that case was pretty much wrapped up."

"She didn't say why, but I thought it was too. I know Edward contacted Harold in the past. The man probably needs closure like Madison."

"Makes sense. I don't think you should worry," Tucker said, pulling his keys out of his pocket. "For one, Madison isn't alone, and two, Luke's killer is in custody. She's finally safe."

"I know. I've got a missed call from Michaels as well." Jonas dialed Michaels's number. "Sorry, I just saw you tried to call me."

"I've been trying to get ahold of you and Madison. Is she with you?"

"No." Jonas's frown deepened. "What's going on?"

"We've got a problem. Sabrina just got out on bail."

"Wait a minute . . . What?" His mind struggled to take in the news. "How did that happen? What about the gunpowder residue test and—"

"It was taken after she arrived at the station, which meant there could have been traces from the police car or handcuffs."

"A technicality, but what about the fact that Madison can identify her as the person who shot her? They can't dismiss that."

"I'm not in on the decision, and I know you're frustrated. So am I. What I can do is get Madison into protective custody."

Jonas leaned back against the car. "She left the city."

"Where is she?"

"She got a phone call from Edward, asking her to meet him at Harold Knight's ranch. He wanted to talk to them. But"—Jonas blew out a sharp breath—"I haven't been able to reach her."

"I'll get a trace going on her cell, though service can be spotty out in the country, or her phone could have died. I'll have the local sheriff stop by his property just in case."

Anxiety pressed against Jonas's chest. What Michaels really meant was that he was worried this was a trap and Sabrina Rae was planning to pull the curtain on the final act. The timing of Sabrina's release and Madison being called out to see Harold Knight was too close to not consider the possibility.

"What's going on?" Tucker asked as Jonas ended his call.

"I think Madison could be in trouble," he said, unlocking his car. "Sorry, but I've got to go."

"Hold on," Tucker said, running around to the passenger side of Jonas's car. "I'm coming with you."

Jonas's phone rang before he could respond. He slid into the driver's seat and started the engine. "Madison?"

"Sorry, no. This is Ruth, Edward's wife."

"Ruth . . . I was just about to call Edward."

"Listen, I'm sorry to bother you, but he was driving out of town to meet Madison, and he was in an accident."

"What?"

"Someone ran him off the road, and he hit a tree."

Panic welled inside Jonas. He never should have let Madison out of his sight.

"Is he okay?" Jonas asked.

"Thankfully, we think it's just a sprained wrist. He's waiting to get X-rays taken right now, but the airbags probably saved his life. I'm really calling, though, because I can't get ahold of Madison. She was supposed to meet Edward at Harold Knight's property. The accident happened while he was on the way."

"I know," Jonas said, pulling out of the parking lot and heading toward the freeway. "I can't get ahold of her either, but I'm headed to Harold's now."

"Good. Just keep Edward updated."

Jonas stayed on I-5 until they hit I-90, then headed east.

The highway crossed the entire state and managed to go from the bustling city to thick forests and mountains to more arid grasslands and drier terrain. But he barely noticed the scenery or Tucker's attempts at distracting him with small talk.

"We'll find her," Tucker said. "She's very good at what she does."

"I know," Jonas said, tapping the brake as the road veered to the left. "She's gorgeous, smart, and can shoot better than you and me."

Tucker chuckled. "You're in love with her, aren't you?"

Jonas's hands gripped the steering wheel. "She's honest, wise, courageous, and yet not afraid to be vulnerable in front of me. She challenges my faith and pushes me the way I need to be pushed. Bottom line is that she makes me a better person when I'm with her."

"Sounds like she's perfect for you."

"She is." Memories of the moment he walked into her house after she'd been shot flooded through him. The truth was, the career they'd chosen was dangerous, and there were no guarantees that they would both come home at night. But whether he had one day left or a lifetime, he knew he wanted to spend it with Madison. "I can't lose her, Tucker."

"Then stop waiting to make things official between the two of you."

Jonas's brow furrowed. "I promised to give her time."

"If you wait until the timing is perfect, it will never happen. Trust me."

"You sound as if you know what you're talking about."

"Let's just say I let someone get away, and I've always regretted it. It was a combination of a scarred past and doubting myself, but in the end, I let her walk away."

"I don't know."

"I do. As soon as we find her—and we will—talk to her. Because the girl's obviously head over heels in love with you. And besides, you didn't get to where you are today by playing it safe and making excuses."

Jonas slowed down as they approached the turnoff to Harold Knight's property, praying he would get the opportunity to actually tell Madison everything he was feeling. He turned onto the long drive and drove another hundred yards or so until he could see the house and barn.

"Is that her car?" Tucker asked.

"I'm not sure," Jonas said. "She rented one while hers is getting fixed."

"I'll call the sheriff again," Tucker said. "See if they were able to find Harold."

Jonas parked, then jumped out of his car and hurried up to the house. He knocked on the front door, then glanced through the window. Nothing looked out of place, but neither was there any movement.

Where is she?

He knocked again, then turned around as Tucker walked up the porch stairs.

"Did you get ahold of the sheriff?" Jonas asked.

"He said he sent out one of his deputies, but no one was here."

Jonas knocked a third time as an old, beat-up truck pulled up behind them. An older man climbed out of the vehicle. "Can I help you?"

"Harold Knight?" Jonas asked, stepping off the porch and walking to the truck.

"Yes."

"We're with the US Marshals. We need to talk," Jonas said, holding up his badge. "I'm looking for my partner, Madison James. She left me a message and said she was coming out to talk with you."

"I just got back in from town. Had some errands to run, but I have no idea who that is, I'm sorry." He slammed the truck door shut and shoved his hands into his back pockets. "You must have the wrong person."

"Do you know Edward Langston?"

"Langston . . . Yes. I spoke to him on the phone a while back. He said he was some kind of detective?"

"He's retired from the police department and runs down cold cases."

"He asked me about Thomas's high school girlfriend. Said he was trying to find her, but I told him I haven't seen her for years." The older man's face paled. "What's going on?"

"I'm not sure, but Edward received a message from you, saying that you needed to meet with him."

"I didn't send him a message."

Jonas felt a wave of panic hit him. "We think someone lured my partner out here."

Harold rubbed his day-old beard and frowned. "I'm sorry . . . I've been in town all afternoon, but my ATV is gone." He started for the barn, then stopped. "It was here when I left."

"Did you leave the key in it?"

"No." Harold walked over to a tree and looked inside a handmade birdhouse. "The key's gone."

"Meaning?" Tucker asked.

"Sabrina's never been here. But my daughter Kate has."

Kate?

Madison had told him she had her memories back. That

Sabrina had been in her kitchen. That *Sabrina* had been the one who shot her. What if her memories had somehow been wrong?

"Jonas?" Tucker laid his hand on Jonas's arm. "Are you okay?"

He shook his head. "If Kate is here, where would she go?"

"I don't know." Harold shrugged. "One of her favorite things to do on the property was ride the trails on the ATV. She's the one that always insisted on keeping the key in the birdhouse."

Jonas frowned. "When's the last time you saw her?"

Harold shoved his hands into his back pockets. "A few months after my grandson died in prison, and that's been years. I know she had been in and out of rehab and shelters, but his death . . . his death seemed to push her over the edge. I did everything I could to get her the help she needed, but in the end she made her choices, and I couldn't do anything."

"If your daughter is here, where would she go?"

"I don't know." Harold combed his hands through his hair. "I'm not sure why she would even come here."

"Think. Please. I think that could be Madison's rental car. She's not answering her phone, and there's no sign of her."

"Kate had a favorite place where she liked to go as a kid. Thomas loved it as well. It overlooks a ravine and is the prettiest spot on the property."

"Will you take me there?" Jonas asked.

Tucker walked up to Jonas and handed him a smashed phone. "I found this on the porch."

"This is Madison's," he said.

It made no sense. How had someone gotten the upper hand on her? Unless she'd been distracted. Or ambushed.

"I've got horses. That would be the fastest way to get up

there. It's a couple miles, but the trail is too narrow for a car. It's why I have the ATV," Harold said, heading into the barn to start saddling up the horses. "My daughter wasn't always like this. There was a time when she seemed happy. She always loved it out here."

"Was it just what happened with Thomas that changed her?"

Harold tightened the last strap on a speckled mare, then turned to the next horse. "She never talks about it, but her firstborn, Molly, drowned when she was three. She eventually had Thomas and Stephanie, but she never could get past Molly's death. Her marriage ended. She'd started drinking, just trying to find peace. Nothing seemed to get through to her. She just . . . spiraled out of control."

"Wow . . . I'm sorry."

"Me too. But this place . . ." He absentmindedly rubbed a hand over the haunch of the second horse. "I think I always thought if I held on to this property, maybe she'd come back. I know I sound like a foolish old man. My wife wanted to move to Seattle before she passed away, but something held me here. I just couldn't walk away from this home."

Harold finished prepping a third horse and held the reins while the men mounted. "There's a hunting blind not too far up the road that I built with Thomas," he told them, getting onto his own horse. "Kate used to come here and watch the sunrise or spend the day reading. And then everything changed, and I lost her."

Jonas glanced up at the sky as they rode in silence on the trail. Clouds were moving in, and the temperature was dropping for an unseasonal cold snap. He looked out across the valley edged with thick forest that spread in front of them. This was the perfect place to dump a body. The chance of someone simply running across it was slim.

"There's my ATV," Harold said, pulling on the reins of his mare before sliding off.

Jonas followed suit with Tucker right behind them. He scanned the area. There were fresh boot prints on the ground and scuff marks like there had been a fight.

Madison had to have been here.

"Madison?" He called her name, but the only response was the howling of the wind through the trees.

His gut clenched. If she was out here, why wasn't she answering?

"Where's the blind?" he asked Harold.

"Just up the road, to the right. There's a small clearing."

If Madison had been looking for shelter, it would be the perfect place. His feet pounded against the gravel trail as he ran up the road, then climbed up the ladder of the wooden structure. He shined his flashlight inside, terrified of what he might find.

She was asleep, curled up in a ball in the corner of the blind, her hands cuffed together in front of her.

"Madison?" he said, pulling out his wallet and grabbing the handcuff key he kept there. "Can you hear me?" He quickly undid the cuffs, then pulled her against him. "Hey. Everything's okay now."

She didn't say anything, but instead leaned into him and nestled her head against his shoulder.

Tucker climbed up the ladder.

"She's here," Jonas said, "but we've got to get her back to the house and get her warm."

"You need to find Kate."

"Where is she, Madison?" Jonas asked.

"She fell down the ravine." She looked down. "I don't think she made it."

Jonas swallowed hard, wanting to just hold her and forget about everything going on around them. "Can you show us where?"

"Yes . . . It's not far."

"It's okay," Jonas said. "I'm going to take care of everything."

"I'll call the sheriff, and talk to Harold about his daughter," Tucker said from the entrance, "but you need to get Madison back to the house and warmed up."

Jonas nodded, then wrapped her up in his coat before he helped her down the ladder and onto the horse. Harold handed him the keys to his house, then stepped back.

"I'm so sorry," Madison said. "I wanted to save her, but I couldn't."

Harold rubbed his hand across his face. "Young lady, I lost Kate a long time ago."

Madison leaned forward against Jonas's back once he was settled in, arms tight around him. He'd never seen her so vulnerable. Never seen her look as if the fire in her eyes had been extinguished.

THIRTY-FIVE

Madison walked into Danielle's kitchen and breathed in the smell of blueberry muffins and bacon. "I can't believe you didn't wake me up. It's half past nine, and the only reason I'm up is because I smelled bacon."

"I was just following doctor's orders."

"You mean Jonas's orders?"

"I was told to let you sleep as long as you could," Danielle said.

"Well, I did. I don't remember the last time I slept in so long."

Her sister smiled at her. "Good. You needed it."

"And I'm hungry too," she said, grabbing the dirty mixing bowl and spoons off the counter and carrying them to the sink.

"Whoa." Danielle turned around. "What are you doing?"

"Cleaning up. It's the least I can do— "

"That's Lilly's job."

"Stop babying me, Danielle." Madison set her hands on her hips. "I've been through far worse."

"Like the plane crash?" Danielle wasn't smiling. "Or the time you were shot in your house?"

"Danielle—"

Her sister held up her hand. "You don't know what it's like for me to know you're out there risking your life. But it's more than that. I'm worried about the emotional toll. You were face-to-face with the woman who shot you—the woman who murdered Luke—and your reaction is like it was nothing more than another day on the job. You can't just brush this off."

"I'm not brushing it off. Really." Madison grabbed a coffee mug and poured herself a cup. "I'm taking a few days off and talking to a counselor."

"That's a start." The timer went off, and Danielle pulled out the muffins, then put two on a plate along with a couple pieces of bacon for Madison. "I just . . . I want you to know that I'm here. You can talk to me about anything, anytime. You don't have to do this by yourself."

"I know. And I appreciate everything you've done for me, Danielle. More than you know. I just . . ." Madison sat down at the kitchen table, searching for the right words as she munched on a piece of bacon. "It's like I'm still frozen. I can't convince myself it's really over. It's been so long. And on top of that, I can't believe that my memories were wrong."

"It's not that surprising, really." Danielle slid into an empty seat next to her. "You've been forced to deal with not only Luke's death, but a woman who wanted to make sure that your grief was compounded."

Madison took a sip of her coffee, knowing that having her sister to process things with her would help. "I'm still a bit in shock over everything that's happened, and I'm not quite sure where to take my next step. I'm used to living in this perpetual state of needing to find out the truth, and now that I have . . ."

"That makes total sense, actually. You've needed closure for so long, but sometimes when it comes, your body finds it hard to process that next step."

Madison nodded. "That's exactly how I feel."

"I know how hard it is to feel out of control, but there was nothing you could have done to change what happened to Luke. God knew the number of his days before he was even born, and nothing that happened that day in the hospital parking garage took God by surprise."

"I know. At least deep down I know that."

She filed away his words, knowing she was going to need to revisit that truth. Sometimes over the past few years, she'd felt as if her whole life was spiraling out of control, and yet at the same time, she knew the reality was that God was still on the throne. Holding on to that truth, though, wasn't always easy. She saw so much evil and hurt around her on a daily basis. Sometimes it was easy to lose her focus and forget that just because they lived in a fallen world didn't mean God's purpose had changed or that he was no longer sovereign and mighty.

"I'm just . . . I'm still trying to take in everything that happened," she said, breaking the comfortable silence between them. "Luke's death. The threats on me and our family. My fear of losing Jonas like I lost Luke." Madison looked over at her sister, the memories still so clear. "I remember her standing in front of me in the kitchen. Her telling me she was going to shoot me. And she did. But when I close my eyes, I see Sabrina. How did I get that so wrong?"

"My studies in psychology taught me that memories are interesting, because they are rarely a hundred percent accurate. And what you're seeing in your mind—even though it isn't the reality—is very normal," Danielle said. "It's just like at a crime scene when you have several witnesses who all see something completely different. Car makes and colors . . . suspect descriptions . . . the caliber of a weapon. Your mind did the same thing. It compensated for fear and trauma going on around you at the moment and gave you what's called a false memory."

"Okay, but Kate couldn't have calculated what I would or wouldn't remember into her plan."

"No, but from what you've told me, I'm not sure she ever really had a plan. She just took advantage of the amnesia. And if you think about your memories in the context of the past few days, it makes sense. Edward talked to you about Sabrina's possible guilt, sparking the seed in your mind. And then while you were looking at a photo of Sabrina you received an anonymous text message, and you naturally believed it was her."

"And my mind, fighting to put it all together, came up with the wrong person . . ." Madison hesitated. "Because that was what I wanted to believe."

"You wanted closure. And yes, maybe enough to convince yourself that the answer was right in front of you."

Guilt welled inside her. "I just thought I was . . . better than that."

Danielle reached out and squeezed her hand. "This isn't something you need to feel guilty about. Our minds are incredible, but we all know that our memories aren't perfect, as much as we want to trust them. Time can alter them, and in your case, you have the added twist of the amnesia. It caused you not just to forget something that happened, but to vividly remember something that didn't."

She picked at her muffin. "And feeling sorry for her? How does that fit into all of this?"

"Everyone's journey through grief is different. Allow yourself to move forward through it without bringing with that grief a load of guilt."

It was the guilt she'd fought with for so long.

"According to Kate's teachers growing up, she was brilliant," Madison said. "But she had a nervous breakdown when she lost her firstborn. She's been in and out of a mental hospital ever since. Her reality shifted to the point that, after a while, she could no longer see the truth."

"So she blamed you," Danielle said. "When Thomas was arrested and then later died, it triggered those same pathways in her mind again. But having said all of that, this wasn't your fault. You do realize that."

"I'm trying to." Madison wrapped her fingers around her coffee mug. "But despite everything, it's hard not to feel sorry for her after all she lost."

"She had a choice to follow the path of resentment and fear or the path of forgiveness, and she chose to let the former control her."

Madison weighed her sister's words. "I'm afraid of letting that resentment control me as well. I know it sounds so cliché, to be afraid of losing someone, but I also know it's caused me to push Jonas away. And that's my wrong choice as well."

"It's okay to grieve and feel anger. It's also okay to move on and live life to the fullest again. I know that's what Luke would want. And I think that's what you want as well. You've been given a fresh start."

Danielle's eyes darkened.

"What is it?" Madison asked.

"There is something else you need to know."

"Okay . . ."

"I didn't want to bring it up because of everything you're going through, but it's Daddy."

Madison leaned back in her chair.

"I heard from his doctor yesterday," Danielle said. "He's recommending that we place him in a skilled nursing facility. Ethan and I talked, and I can't take care of him alone anymore."

Madison nodded. "I know."

"You do?"

"I've struggled watching him decline, but you've cared for him for so long, and Daddy knows that. It's time."

"I thought you'd be upset. Like I was giving up."

Madison leaned over and pulled Danielle into a hug. "Of course not. It's okay. He knows we both love him, and he'll get the extra care he needs."

"Thank you. I guess I knew that's what you'd say, but it's still such a hard decision." Danielle grabbed a tissue and blew her nose. "I don't want him to think we've abandoned him."

"He would never think that, and we'll still be there for him."

"I know."

Their father shuffled into the kitchen wearing his favorite T-shirt, sweats, and ball cap, and Madison felt the ache of loss. Life was full of seasons. Nothing stayed the same. Watching him move into his last season of life was challenging, but they would make sure he didn't feel as if he were alone. They'd walk this road together, just like they always had.

"Daddy." Madison wiped her cheeks, then stood up to give her father a hug. "I've missed you."

"Your sister told me you went on a trip."

"I did, but I'm back. And I thought we could go for a drive tomorrow. See some of the fall leaves. Would you like that?"

Her father smiled. "Yes. What about Luke? Is he coming too?"

Madison pressed her lips together. "Luke's not here, Daddy. But I thought I might invite someone else. His name's Jonas. He's actually picking me up in a few minutes."

"Are you going somewhere?"

"We are."

"A date?" Her father smiled, and that familiar twinkle was in his eye as he joined them at the table. He'd always loved to tease her and Danielle when they'd started dating back in high school, but more than that, he'd always been their greatest supporter.

"We're actually going to pick up a young woman at the airport and take her to meet her grandfather," Madison said, handing her dad a piece of bacon.

"They've never met?" he asked.

"They haven't seen each other since she was small. And then," Madison added, "Jonas is going to take me out for lunch."

"So it is a date." Her father glanced at her sweats and T-shirt. "I hope you're planning on changing."

"Don't worry, Daddy," she said. "I will."

Lilly, Danielle's oldest daughter, skipped into the kitchen. "Do you have a boyfriend, Aunt Maddie?"

"Lilly—" her mother started.

Madison laughed. "It's okay. Right now, he's just a good friend."

"Do you like him like a boyfriend?"

"I do, actually," she said. "I like him a lot."

Jonas stepped into the room, and Madison felt her cheeks flush as he caught her gaze and smiled.

"I know I'm a few minutes early. Ethan was coming in at the same time and let me in."

Danielle's phone alarm went off. "Daddy, why don't you

come with me. It's time for your medicine, and Lilly, I need you to load the dishwasher."

A moment later, the kitchen was quiet again except for the sound of Lilly rinsing the dishes and humming to the music coming through her earphones.

"How did you sleep?" he asked.

"Pretty good."

"Good. I just got a message from Stephanie," he said. "Her flight is on time."

"How did she sound?"

"Nervous but excited."

"I know nothing can make up for losing his daughter, but I hope this will bring some closure for Harold."

"What about you?"

Madison pressed her lips together. "I'm taking baby steps forward. Trying to process everything."

"It will come. At least that's what I'm counting on. Because I kind of overheard that you like me. At least, I hope you weren't talking about another guy you'd fallen for." He flashed her a smile that somehow managed to melt away any remaining icy shards still trying to protect her heart. Blue eyes stared back at her, and her breath caught.

"I might have been talking about you," she said, "but don't let it go to your head. I have to like you. You're my partner."

"I don't remember that being a part of the job description." He grabbed her hand, making her stomach flip. "Tolerate me, maybe, but like . . ."

"Very funny."

"I kind of like it when you're embarrassed. Your cheeks get flushed, and your palms get sweaty."

She pulled her hand away and stuck out her tongue at him.

"I'll stop teasing. I just . . . it's good to see you smile."

"And I'll admit, it's good to smile again."

"You still want to go? You were told to take it easy."

"I'm fine. Really. And the drive will be a nice distraction from everything that's happened."

Or maybe I need a distraction from the way you look at me. The way I react to being around you.

"Have you spoken to Edward?" she asked, changing the subject.

"I did. He has a fractured wrist, but he's okay. And they arrested the man Kate hired to run him off the road."

"So this is really over?" she said.

He pulled her against him and nodded. "Yeah. It's finally over."

***

Two hours later, they'd picked up Stephanie and were almost at the ranch where they'd arranged to meet Harold.

Madison turned to the back seat as Jonas pulled onto the familiar gravel driveway. "Are you ready for this?"

Stephanie nodded and pressed her hand against her heart. "I don't know why I'm so nervous. It's just been so long since I saw him."

"I'd be surprised if you weren't nervous," Jonas said. "It's going to be okay."

Harold Knight was waiting on the porch when they drove up.

Stephanie slid out of the car ahead of them and ran up to him.

"Stephanie." Tears ran down the old man's rugged face. "I've prayed for so long that I'd get to see you again."

"I'm here now," she said, letting him pull her into a hug. "I'm sorry I didn't come sooner."

Harold took a step back. "You're so beautiful. Just like your grandmother."

"I'd like you to tell me all about her," Stephanie said.

"I'd love to." He turned to Madison and Jonas, his arm still around his granddaughter. "Thank you. Thank you for bringing my granddaughter."

"Of course, though there is one other thing you both need to know before we leave you," Madison said. "I received a call from a friend of mine on the way here. I asked him to look into something for me. It's about Thomas."

Stephanie pressed her hand against her chest, then nodded.

"I wish you knew this a long time ago, but we just found out that Thomas died saving another inmate. He was getting his life together in prison. I know it doesn't soften the hurt of his death, but you should be proud of him. He wasn't the same person who went into that prison."

"Wow . . ." New tears ran down Harold's face as he pulled his granddaughter against him. "After losing so much, I feel as if you've given me back both of my grandchildren. Thank you." He turned back to Stephanie. "I wanted to be a part of your life, and even your mother's life, but she wanted nothing to do with me. I'm sorry I didn't try harder to contact you."

Stephanie smiled up at him. "I was where I needed to be, but I'm here now. There was nothing any of us could do. I learned—and am still learning—to accept that. And since I'm here, I have some ideas about the ranch. Have you thought about offering riding lessons, or boarding horses in the barn—"

"Whoa, slow down. You haven't been here five minutes and you're already talking about changing things." Harold let out a deep belly laugh. "And I couldn't be happier. You can do anything you want with the place as far as I'm concerned."

He picked up Stephanie's suitcase. "Would the two of you like to stay for lunch?"

"Thanks," Madison said, "but I think you and Stephanie have a lot of catching up to do."

Stephanie stepped forward and hugged Madison. "Thank you for calling me and for helping me get here so quickly. Thanks. For everything."

"Of course. I know how important family is."

"And please know how sorry I am," Harold said, "for everything you've had to go through because of my daughter."

"You have nothing to be sorry about. Go enjoy this time with your granddaughter," Madison said. "God's just given you a new lease on life. A new season."

"I know, and I'm not going to forget it."

"Are you up for a surprise before lunch?" Jonas asked as they headed to the car.

"A surprise?" she said, stopping by the passenger door. "What is it?"

"It wouldn't be a surprise if I told you." He smiled back at her. "Get in."

THIRTY-SIX

Jonas took the Snoqualmie Parkway exit, then headed north. Tucker had been right. If he and Madison kept waiting for perfect timing—the moment that everything aligned—there would always be an excuse, always something pulling them in different directions.

He followed the signs to Snoqualmie Falls, then found a parking space in the upper lot.

"I thought we could walk around a bit, if you're up for it," he said as they got out. "It's not far."

"How did you know I've always wanted to come here?"

He just smiled and took her hand, quiet as they made their way toward the observation deck and the two-hundred-and-seventy-foot waterfall. "There's a bench."

Instead, she went ahead of him to the railing where visitors could look out over the falls. "It's mesmerizing, isn't it?"

"That's not the only mesmerizing thing," he said.

She turned to him, lips pressed together as she looked up at him.

"I know I promised to give you time," he said, then rushed on before she could say anything, "but what if that time is now?

Madison, you make me a better person, and while I know you're still working through grief, I also know that I want to spend the rest of my life with you. And as someone recently told me, I don't want to play it safe anymore."

I want you.

He watched as she turned away, his heart sinking. He'd rehearsed what he'd wanted to say, and he'd just spewed everything out in one awkward monologue.

"I'm sorry—" he started to say.

"No. I wanted to thank you for being patient with me. I might seem unflappable on the outside most of the time, but these last few days really threw me. These past few months, really."

"I get it, and that's okay."

She locked her hands in front of her. "I also owe you an apology."

"An apology?" He studied her face. "For what?"

"I never meant to push you away. I just . . . you—us—it took me by surprise, and I've needed time to sort everything out."

He ran his hand down her arm, not missing the current he felt pass between them. "It's me, Madison. You don't have to be sorry for how you feel."

"I know. Thank you for saying that." She shot him a smile. "I have been trying to figure out how I feel. Doing a lot of thinking about us and what that might look like."

"Have you now?" He felt his heart rate kick up a notch.

"I have." She smiled up at him. "And I think I've been making all of this more complicated than it needs to be."

"In what way?"

She smiled up at him, giving him hope that all of his doubts had been in vain. "You're not going to make this easy for me, are you?"

Jonas laughed, realizing that no matter what she said, he'd already completely lost his heart. "Where would be the fun in that?"

She rested her hand against his chest for a moment. "I'm trying to be serious. I've been rehearsing what I wanted to say all day and now . . ."

Now, all I see is you.

He struggled to focus on her words instead of the emotions swirling through him. He'd have time to deal with those later. For the moment, all he wanted was to hear her say that she felt the same way he did, and that she was ready to move forward.

She dropped her hands back against her sides and smiled up at him. "I didn't think it would be quite so hard, saying what was on my heart."

"Take your time. I'm not going anywhere."

"Good. Because I don't want you to."

Her confession made him want to pull her into his arms and show her exactly how he felt, but instead he waited for her to continue. He owed it to her to let her finish.

"You told me once you'd finally had to stop trying to fix Felicia," she said. "It made me think how I've tried for so long to find out the truth about what happened to Luke, to the point that it stopped me from moving on. In the end, while I believe it will give me some closure, it can't change anything. It's kept me wrapped up in this world of regrets." She drew in a deep breath. "I've come to realize that I will never be able to change what happened that day. Then Edward came and made me realize something I didn't even know. I always knew what I wanted in life and worked to get it. From the academy to detective to becoming a marshal . . . But then things happened that weren't a part of my plan. Luke and

I were going to have a family and grow old together, which meant this . . . this isn't what I expected. But I'm learning that I need to be able to move on with my life and enjoy what's right in front of me."

"How do you feel about that?"

"Liberated and at the same time a bit terrified." She chuckled. "Apparently, I'm not as good at interpreting my emotions as I thought I was. Or letting myself feel again. Because allowing myself to feel makes me vulnerable, and that's something I don't like. But not feeling is also keeping me trapped."

He didn't respond, just listened as she processed her feelings. Grateful that she felt open enough with him to share.

"I'm learning there is a point where I have to simply let go and let God take over," she said. "That has never been easy for me. I like being in charge. I like figuring out solutions to problems, but sometimes . . . sometimes that desire isn't enough. I will never be able to change what happened, no matter how much I want to."

He smirked. "You've learned you're human?"

She chuckled again. "A human with more limitations than I wish I had." She pushed a strand of hair behind her ear. "I'm tired of living as if I died that day as well." She looked up and caught his gaze. Tears glistened on her lashes, but he didn't miss the peace in her expression. "This is the other part I've been rehearsing. If I'm being completely honest with myself, there are . . . other feelings I'm interested in exploring."

"What kind of feelings are those?"

Her fingers intertwined with his. "When I met you at the training house, I was still reeling over losing Luke. People kept telling me that I was young and it was time I moved on.

The thought of falling in love again had me frozen. But you impressed me from the first day we met. You were tough, focused, and cared about making each one of us the best."

"And you called me the Terminator behind my back, as I recall."

She let out a low laugh. "Yes, and while you frustrated me, you also pushed me until I was sure I couldn't be pushed any more. That was what I wanted."

"You know I fell for you back then." She'd been so closed off, he'd never acted on his feelings. He'd never known she was struggling with the death of her husband. He'd just thought she was focused only on the training.

"Looking back, I suppose I could see that," she said, "but while the timing was off back then, we're now faced with a second chance."

He rubbed his thumb across the back of her hand. "What does that mean for us?"

"I'm ready to take that step forward. Together. You and me."

His heart reeled at the revelation. "And you're sure?"

"Yes. I am."

"Then I guess it's about time we had an official first date."

She laughed. "There have been a few blockades in our relationship."

"Then how about dinner and dessert tonight . . . the whole works," Jonas said. "And then we just move forward from there. However fast or slow you want to take things."

"We'd been having dinner together every week for months until you left for your training."

He ran his thumb down her cheek, catching a glimpse of gold in her eyes. "Yes, but as just friends. Remember?"

Jonas's heart stirred at the implications of his words. Four months ago, she'd walked unexpectedly back into his life. Today, he'd managed to fall in love with her all over again.

"Have I told you how beautiful you are?"

"No, but flattery will get you everywhere."

"Good, because I would really, really like to kiss you right now."

She wrapped her arms around his neck and smiled. "I was afraid you'd never ask."

He pulled her tighter against him, smiling before he brushed his lips against hers, then deepened the kiss.

Whatever new roadblocks might appear down the road for them didn't matter, because he was willing to fight to hold on to her.

READ ON FOR AN EXCERPT FROM BOOK 1

of the Nikki Boyd Files series

from LISA HARRIS.

AVAILABLE NOW

Northeast Tennessee near the Obed River

The initial step off the sheer face of a three-hundred-plus-foot drop was always the most terrifying. Nikki Boyd leaned back into her harness as far as she could, locked her knees, then peered over the edge of the sandstone cliff that dropped into the ravine below. The terror faded, followed by a shot of pure adrenaline as she kicked off and plunged over the edge.

Legs horizontal to the rock face, Nikki shimmied down the side of the cliff, kicking loose a few rocks along the way. The stress of the past few weeks began to dissipate into the crisp morning air. A day climbing and rappelling with Tyler Grant had definitely been the right thing to do. They'd come not to dismiss memories of Katie's death but to celebrate her life. Which was exactly what they were doing.

Halfway down, Nikki glanced up, then slowed to a stop. The rope had shifted and now ran over a sharp edge of the cliff wall. She caught her toes against a narrow ledge and fought to catch her balance. While perhaps not common, it was possible to sever a weighted rope on a descent.

"You okay?" Tyler hollered down at her.

"The rope moved and it's running over a sharp edge."

She'd been told by more than one experienced climber that

they hated rappelling because it was the most dangerous part of the day. And this was why. No matter how much training and preparation, no matter how many times she checked her equipment, things could still go wrong. And it just took one mistake. But all she needed to do was unweight the rope and move it to a safer place.

"Can you move it?" Tyler asked.

"I'm trying."

"You're going to have to take some of your weight off the rope."

"Like I said, I'm trying."

Her gloved fingers held on to a crack in the rock face while she searched for another crack for her feet. Her fingers cramped. A trail of blood dripped down her arm. She didn't even remember scraping it. Her feet finally found a narrow crevice, alleviating her weight on the rope enough to give it some slack. All she needed to do now was redirect the rope's path.

Simple.

But she couldn't get enough leverage to unweight the rope.

"Nikki?"

"Just a minute . . ." Sweat beaded across her forehead as she stood on her tiptoes, her fingertips pressed back into the crack, heart pounding against her chest.

She'd heard plenty of stories about things like this happening. Freak accidents against the side of a sheer cliff. Climbers plunging to their deaths.

You know this isn't how I want to die, Jesus . . .

And certainly not today. Not on the anniversary of Katie's death. She glanced at the ground below, then felt her breath catch. If she couldn't move the rope to a safer spot, it could snap above her.

"Nikki?" Tyler shouted from the top of the cliff. "What's happening?"

She drew in another breath. "I'm okay, but I'm having trouble moving the rope."

She hung balanced on the ledge, trying to figure out what to do. Accidents like this weren't all that common, but as with any sport, there were always variables you couldn't count on. She shifted her gaze to the ground. Two months ago, a college student had plunged to his death near here. The steep, rocky terrain made it a popular spot for risk takers.

She pushed the thought aside. What she needed to do was focus on solving the problem. Theoretically she knew what to do, but she was going to need both hands. Which was a problem. Currently, with her right hand holding the rope behind her to keep her from sliding down, she'd need to run the end around her legs a few times in order to secure it. But that was a move even an experienced rappeller would hesitate performing. Unless—

"Stay put, Nikki, I'm coming to you."

"I can figure this out."

"Stay put," he ordered. "I'm coming down."

"Okay, just be careful."

A handful of small rocks bounced off her helmet as Tyler descended toward her on a separate rope.

"How was your date last night with Ryan?" he called down to her.

Her date? Was he serious?

She never should have told Tyler about Ryan. Now he was simply trying to distract her. Trying to get her to focus her thoughts away from the fear and panic. Panic because she was stuck on a narrow ledge a hundred-plus feet off the ground with the potential of a severed rope. And with it the reminder of how quickly life could spiral out of control.

"The date went fine," she finally answered.

She could hear him making his way down the sheer cliff above her. His feet scattered another volley of pebbles.

"Fine doesn't tell me anything," he countered. "Give me some details. Last night was your third date with Mr. Perfect. You've got to have something interesting to share."

Details? He really wanted details while she was hanging off the side of a cliff praying she wasn't about to plunge to her death?

A cramp gripped her calf as her fingers dug deeper into the rock crevice above her. She tried to wiggle her leg without losing her footing on the ledge. There honestly wasn't much to tell. Ryan was six foot three and looked like a model straight off a Banana Republic ad. On top of that, he made a great living, owned his own house, and was completely debt free.

None of those things, though, was the real reason she'd agreed to a second and third date. She'd half expected him to be a snob, but surprisingly, he wasn't. At all. Instead, he was down-to-earth, complimented her without making her feel he wanted something in return, and treated her like she was the only one in the room when they were together. She'd never met another guy quite like him—except perhaps Tyler.

Which was why Tyler had dubbed him "Mr. Perfect" the first time she'd told him she'd gone out with a guy set up by one of her mother's friends at church. Making it to the third date was something of a record for her—as of late anyway. But despite Ryan's "perfection," she still wasn't completely convinced he was perfect for *her*. Everyone—including her mother—had already made the decision she'd finally found Mr. Right in Mr. Perfect. But making that decision for herself felt a lot like taking that first step off the cliff. A shot of terror along with a huge rush of adrenaline.

A sharp pain jetted through her head, and Nikki realized she was clenching her jaw. She took in a deep breath and forced herself to relax. "He's not perfect, and there's nothing new I want to share with you."

Tyler laughed as he dropped next to where she hung and stopped. "The guy owns his own company, runs half marathons for fun, and supports orphans in Africa."

"So he's a good guy. That doesn't mean I'm planning on—I don't know—*marrying* him."

"Yet."

Nikki frowned. No, those were her mother's plans. Besides, talking with Tyler about her date was . . . well . . . awkward.

"One of us needs a bit of a boost in the romance department, and since I'm not going there, that leaves you," he said.

She caught a flicker of pain in his voice. How did you start dating again after losing the love of your life? She wasn't even going to ask that question.

"There's a slightly deeper ledge six inches to your right for your feet. It will give you some extra support, but I think the simplest solution at this point is to transfer you to my rope."

Nikki drew in a deep breath as she felt for the ledge, then managed to shove her toes into the crack.

"What did the two of you do?" he asked.

She watched while he locked off his belay device and ran the bottom of his rope through hers, grateful for his special ops training.

"We went to dinner and the symphony."

"And . . ."

"That was it. Dinner, good food, and interesting conversation."

"Do you like him?"

She hesitated. "He's nice. A gentleman."

"Like I said. Mr. Perfect, though I'm not sure that *nice* is what a guy wants to hear."

"Then what does he want to hear?" Nikki wiggled her toes while still trying to keep her balance. The cramp had spread from her calf to the arch of her foot.

"That he's intriguing . . . intelligent . . . funny . . . a bit romantic."

"He brought me flowers," she said. Somehow he'd found out she loved wildflowers and had brought her a bouquet.

"But no fireworks yet?" Tyler asked.

"I'm just getting to know him."

For Tyler and Katie, it had been love at first sight. She'd never believed in the notion until the day they'd met. But that wasn't exactly her own experience. Her longest relationship—two and a half years—had ended in a nasty breakup. Not exactly a scenario she wanted to repeat.

Like the scenario she was dealing with right now.

"You're good to go," Tyler said finally. "Ease down slowly."

Nikki tightened her fingers on the rope as she made her way down the rest of the cliff with Tyler following. She skidded down the slight incline at the bottom of the rock, then disconnected from the rope.

"Let's not try that again," she said, thankful her feet were finally once again on solid ground.

"You're telling me. You okay?"

She brushed the dust from her pants, then peeled off her

gloves. “I think my ego’s more bruised than I am. I anchored the rope in the wrong spot.”

“Sometimes you do everything right and it still isn’t enough.”

She caught the sadness in his eyes as they began collecting the equipment. Why was that statement always so hard to accept?

“You’re sure you’re okay?” he asked again.

She held out her hands, unable to stop them from shaking. “I’ll admit, that was a bit sobering.”

He pulled her against his chest while she tried to let go of the fear that had surrounded her only moments before. She snuggled into his shoulder. His heart was beating as fast as hers. She looked up at his familiar brown eyes and short, military cut hair and felt his day-old beard brush lightly against her cheek. His arms tightened around her shoulders, making her feel safe and protected.

He knew as well as she did that sometimes doing everything right simply wasn’t enough.

But thankfully, today hadn’t ended in tragedy.

“As long as you’re okay,” he said, “that’s all that matters.”

She let out a soft swoosh of air. She didn’t want today to hold another reminder of what could go wrong. How in one fragile moment life could suddenly slip away and be gone forever. But that fact wasn’t something either of them could ever forget.

“Thank you.” Her heart rate was beginning to slow to normal. “You saved my life, you know.”

He brushed away a strand of her shoulder-length blond hair that had fallen across her cheek, then took a step backward. “Being here with you today has made me realize—not for the first time—that I’m the one who needs to thank you.”

“For what?”

"For coming with me today." He squeezed her hand before pulling off his helmet. "For everything you've done for Liam and me. I'm honestly not sure I would have gotten through the last year without you."

"I miss her too. Maybe that's why I'm feeling so distracted today."

Nikki felt the tears well in her eyes and tried to blink them back. She'd promised herself she'd be strong for Tyler. Blubbering like a baby wasn't keeping that promise. But while the pain had dulled even a year later, sometimes the loss still felt like it had happened yesterday. Sometimes she still heard Katie's voice. Heard the phone ring and expected it to be her, until she remembered that Katie would never call again. But as much as she missed her best friend, her grief was nothing compared to what Tyler and Liam had gone through.

"You ready to call it quits for the day?" he asked.

"Are you kidding?" Nikki blinked back the rest of her tears and smiled. "We've barely started. I didn't wake up before dawn to give up and go back home again before breakfast."

They'd planned this day for months. A day out of the city, near the place where they'd sprinkled Katie's ashes. A day to celebrate Katie's life. She would have wanted them to be here today.

"How about a break then?" he asked. "Your hands are still shaking."

Nikki pressed her palms against her sides. "I could use some coffee. And if you're hungry, my mom packed breakfast to go along with the thermos she sent with us."

"I love your mom." Tyler smiled as he started for the trail leading away from the cliffs. "But the smell drove me crazy the entire trip here."

"Me too, and there's plenty."

There always was. Boyds' BBQ in downtown Nashville had been in the family for three generations, and Nikki's mom never missed an opportunity to ensure her daughter stayed well fed.

"How about we take care of that scrape on your arm first," Tyler said. "Then we can eat some of your mom's breakfast and get at this again."

Nikki nodded, then glanced at the gash where she'd noticed the blood earlier. "You know you don't have to baby me."

He smiled at her and shook his head. "You've always been there for me, Nikki. Just let me do the same thing for you."

Five minutes later, she sat on the tailgate of Tyler's pickup truck in the parking lot while he pulled out the first-aid kit and started cleaning her wound. He washed away the trail of blood caked with dirt from the mountainside, then covered it with an antibacterial spray.

Nikki winced.

"You're worse than Liam," he teased.

"Funny, but that stuff—whatever it is—stings. Remember you're going to school to be a psychologist, not a doctor, Mr. Grant."

"I think I can handle this assignment, Special Agent Boyd."

She laughed, thankful that most of the panic was finally wearing off, because she still had her eye on conquering a couple of climbing routes that had gotten the best of her the last time she was here. Today, she was determined to stay focused and make it to the top of at least one of them.

Her phone rang, and she pulled it out of her back pocket.

She glanced at the caller ID. Unknown. "I should ignore it, but it could be my sister-in-law trying to get ahold of me. She was supposed to go see her obstetrician this morning."

"Anything wrong?"

"Maybe. She's only got a couple weeks before her due date, but she started bleeding last night."

Which had Nikki worried. She'd watched Matt and Jamie navigate an emotional roller coaster through eight years of infertility and three miscarriages. This pregnancy finally promised the first grandbaby of the family, and just last week they'd finished the nursery. If anything went wrong now . . .

"Go ahead." Tyler pressed a butterfly Band-Aid over her cut. "I've got my phone on in case Liam needs me. You'd better answer."

Nikki nodded and took the call.

"Agent Boyd." The voice of her boss, Tom Carter, took Nikki by surprise. "How is the great outdoors treating you?"

She glanced at Tyler, who'd started putting the first-aid supplies back into the plastic case. "I'm fine, sir, thanks."

"Good. Listen, I hate to put a wrinkle in your day, but I have a favor to ask of you."

Nikki frowned. Saying no to her boss was somehow harder than saying no to her mother. "I'm here with Tyler Grant, sir, we're—"

"I remember you mentioned you were going climbing." He paused. "Today's the anniversary of his wife's death, right?"

"Yeah."

"How's he doing?"

Tyler had met her boss during a joint military training exercise designed to increase the military's ability to function in an urban setting. According to Carter, he'd been highly impressed with Tyler's skills and instincts.

"He's okay. We're having a good time. The weather's perfect." There was no use mentioning she'd been clinging to the side of a cliff a few minutes ago, afraid for her life. "What's the favor, sir?"

"I just got a call from a friend. Actually, I went to university with his father, and we stayed close until he died. The son's name is Kyle Ellison. He's not far from where you are with his sixteen-year-old sister, celebrating her birthday over the weekend. Problem is, she went out for a walk this morning and didn't return."

Nikki glanced at her watch. It was just past eight. "Has he called the local authorities?"

"Not yet. He's convinced she probably just wandered off the path to get a closer look at some wildlife and sprained her ankle, something like that. He called me for advice."

"How long has she been gone?"

"He's not sure. She was gone when he got up, around seven."

Which meant they were already looking at a minimum of two hours ago, and maybe longer.

There was another pause on the line before her boss spoke again. "Listen, all I'm asking is for you to look into it for me. I'll text you the address of the private cabin where they're staying. Interview the brother and the girl's friends, then pass it on to the local law enforcement if you need to. The boy's scared."

"Okay. I'll see what I can do."

Nikki hung up the phone and glanced down at her climbing clothes. With her tan, lightweight climbing pants, orange T-shirt, and hiking shoes, she wasn't exactly dressed for the job, but it would have to do for now.

She jumped down from the tailgate. "That was my boss."

"What did he want?" Tyler asked.

She hesitated. "A favor."

"He wants you to work a case."

Nikki nodded, trying to read Tyler's expression. "It shouldn't take long. A quick interview about a missing girl who's probably just lost out here somewhere."

"I don't mind." He shot her a smile. "As long as I get some of your mama's cooking as soon as we're done."

Nikki laughed, hoping he truly didn't mind. She'd already begun sorting through the limited information she had. Because with missing persons cases, time was never on their side. If the girl *had* been abducted, at a mile a minute she could easily be across the state border by now. But hopefully the girl's brother was right. She'd simply gone out walking and gotten lost or turned her ankle. Most kids who went missing were found.

Nikki tossed Tyler the truck keys that he'd laid on the tailgate. "They're staying in a private cabin not far from here. I'll pull up the directions on my phone while you drive."

The familiar feeling of guilt swirled through her as she slid into the truck and fastened her seat belt. Because not knowing what's happening to someone you love can be the hardest thing in the world to handle. And something she understood far too well.

ACKNOWLEDGMENTS

A huge thanks to the fabulous team at Revell, who work tirelessly to help make the stories in my head come to life, to Ellen Tarver for her eagles eyes in first-round edits, and to my family and readers for their encouraging support. I'm so grateful for each and every one of you!!

Lisa Harris is a *USA Today* bestselling author, a Christy Award winner, and the winner of the Best Inspirational Suspense Novel from *Romantic Times* for her novels *Blood Covenant* and *Vendetta*. The author of more than forty books, including *The Escape*, *The Traitor's Pawn*, *Vanishing Point*, *A Secret to Die For*, and *Deadly Intentions*, as well as The Nikki Boyd Files and the Southern Crimes series, Harris and her family have spent over seventeen years living as missionaries in southern Africa. She is currently stateside in Tulsa, Oklahoma. Learn more at www.lisaharriswrites.com.

Don't Miss the First Two Books in the

US MARSHALS SERIES

"The second book picks up right where the first left off with all the action, drama, suspense, and romance a book lover could ask for! . . . The US Marshals books are by far my favorites by Lisa Harris."

—*WRITE-READ-LIFE*

a division of Baker Publishing Group
www.RevellBooks.com

Available wherever books and ebooks are sold.

"The **HEART-POUNDING ACTION** doesn't stop until the very end."

—*Interviews & Reviews*

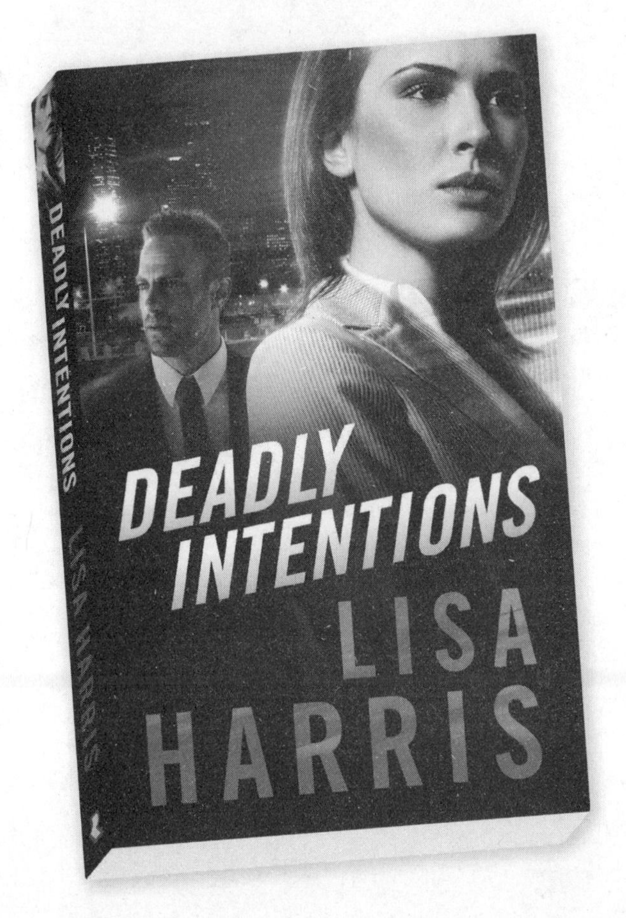

Detective Josh Solomon always believed his wife's death was the result of a home invasion. But when he is pulled into a case with striking similarities, it doesn't take long for him to realize the chilling truth—the attack that took his wife's life was far from random.

Revell
a division of Baker Publishing Group
www.RevellBooks.com

Available wherever books and ebooks are sold.

meet

LISA HARRIS

lisaharriswrites.com

@AuthorLisaHarris

@HeartOfAfrica